New York Times & *USA Today* Bestselling Author

CYNTHIA EDEN

This book is a work of fiction. Any similarities to real people, places, or events are not intentional and are purely the result of coincidence. The characters, places, and events in this story are fictional.

Published by Hocus Pocus Publishing, Inc.

Copy-editing by: J. R. T. Editing

PROLOGUE

Her hands grabbed desperately for the French doors, her broken nails scraped against the ornate knobs, and she left dark, dirty smears on the pristine surfaces. A fierce shove had the doors flying open, and Eliza stumbled into the ballroom. "H-help..." A gasped cry.

One that none of the dancing, laughing figures seemed to hear.

She staggered forward. Her bare feet left bloody footprints on the hardwood flooring. "*Help!*" Louder. But still, no one seemed to notice her.

More laughter filled the air.

Until...

She bumped into someone. The woman turned with a gasp, and horror quickly flashed on her face as she took in Eliza's form. Her torn, dirty, and blood-stained clothing. Her wild hair. Her bare feet.

"Eliza!" Her father's voice thundered across the ballroom as he charged for her. "What in the world is the meaning of this? I can't believe you'd pull off another of your stunts—"

Her knees gave way, and she hit the floor. “Help me,” she said again, as she felt the tears trail down her cheeks.

Her father staggered to a stop beside her. His eyes widened as he finally seemed to *see* her. She lifted her hands toward him. Knew he’d notice the bruises around her wrists. The handcuff that still encircled her right wrist.

“My God...” Her father blanched.

The band stopped playing. The crowd swarmed in.

And Eliza Robinson prayed that she was finally safe.

CHAPTER ONE

"Come on, Eliza," her friend Bethany Bancroft chided her, "don't you ever want to cut loose? Where is the wild girl who used to be the life of the party? The one who made *me* seem like a wallflower?" Bethany laughed and turned back to survey the busy crowd inside the bar. "Look at all those men. Gorgeous. Sexy. Just waiting to be selected as our lucky partners for the night. They are out there hoping we will make their dreams come true."

"I don't know that they're waiting for that." Eliza swiveled slightly on her barstool. The place was packed. Super loud. And way too dimly lit.

"They are. Trust me." Bethany tossed her red hair over her shoulder. "Why else would they be in this place? They're ready for a hookup, and so am I."

"Um..." *I am not ready. So not.*

Bethany glanced back at her. "You are, too, ready. Don't even try denying it. That's why you're here. You're going to stop being a nun, right?"

"I'm not a nun." Eliza's shoulders stiffened because the accusation hit a little too close to home. So she didn't date a lot. Her life was extremely busy. Hardly her fault that there just wasn't time for a relationship.

Lie. Lie. Lie.

A satisfied smile curved Bethany's lips. "Then prove it. Find a man. Dance with him. *Now.*"

"Is that a dare?" She tried to make her voice sound light. Casual. Like this was something *fun.*

It wasn't. Being at the bar was hell, and she'd really like to leave, ASAP.

"Yep, just like in our college days. Only then, you would have been the one already dancing on the bar top by now, and I'd be the one you were trying to talk into doing something crazy." Bethany caught Eliza's hand. Gave it a squeeze. "Come on. For the first time in ages, you don't have one of those annoying guards dodging your steps. You are *free* tonight. Time to live a little bit."

Those annoying guards. Yes, Eliza had thought that she'd managed to get out without a guard following her. Or, at least, that *was* what she'd believed until about five minutes ago.

Until she'd seen him. The man with the dark hair. Stony features. An attitude that promised trouble. And a laser-like gaze that he'd locked on her the minute he'd walked into the bar. The guy had muscles for days and days—muscles that bulged the short sleeves and the chest of his black t-shirt. An aura of danger surrounded him, and Eliza knew he was the kind of man with whom one just did not fuck.

He was also probably the best-looking man she'd ever seen in her life. If you went for that type. The whole bad boy, devil-may-care, I-give-screaming-orgasms-to-my-partners type.

She fanned herself a little because the place was hot. Too many people inside.

Her gaze darted to him, almost helplessly, as he sat in his booth.

He was still watching her. He didn't smile. Didn't incline his head. Didn't do anything but stare.

He hadn't approached her, though. The guards rarely did. They knew their orders, after all. They were to watch from a distance. To trail her. To make sure that she was never hurt. That she was always safe.

And always trapped in her prison.

Eliza forced a smile for her friend. "I don't really see any guys here who interest me."

Bethany rolled her eyes. "Wake up that libido, girl, and get moving." She turned to survey the crowd again, and as she did, a tall, sandy-haired man in a Polo and gray pants pulled away from a group of guys in the corner. His head tilted as his gaze swept toward the bar—toward Bethany and Eliza. His stare lingered on Eliza.

He smiled.

And started forward.

"Ooh, look at that," Bethany began, voice humming with excitement. "We have a live one. Closing in fast. Dance with him, and I won't ask for anything else the rest of the night."

Eliza's hands clamped around the edges of her barstool. He *was* closing in. A friendly grin curved his lips, and his eyes seemed to sparkle as—

Blocked.

A big, powerful figure stepped into the approaching man's path. The figure of the badass who'd been sitting in the booth just moments before. For someone so big, he'd sure moved fast.

He said something to guy in the Polo, and Eliza's would-be dance partner turned away. He headed back to his circle of friends.

"What just happened?" Bethany squeaked.

The badass glanced over his shoulder at Eliza. His head moved in a slow, negative motion.

"Oh." Bethany sucked in a breath. "Hello, hotness. Well, okay, Eliza, you can trade up for him—"

He went back to his booth. Sat down. Tapped his fingers on the tabletop.

Eliza felt heat stain her cheeks. "I don't think he's interested in dancing with me."

"Then *what* is he doing, other than cock-blocking—"

Eliza pushed off the stool. Lightly touched her friend's shoulder. "I don't think I escaped the guards tonight." Apologetic.

Sympathy flashed on Bethany's face as understanding dawned.

"I really enjoyed hanging out with you," Eliza continued gamely. "Thank you for inviting me. But I think I should go home." She mustered up a smile. "Want to ride with me?"

Bethany shook her head. "No, I'm gonna stay a while. Got some other people who were planning to meet up here later." Her stare swept over Eliza. She nodded with sudden intent. "I have a different dare for you."

"Excuse me?" Her stomach seemed to twist.

"Forget the dancing. I want you to walk over to that gorgeous guy in the booth—and I want you to tell him..." Bethany leaned toward Eliza's ear and whispered, "Fuck off."

Eliza's gaze instantly darted to the man in question.

Bethany hugged her. Tight. Then pulled back. "They can't send guards after you forever. It's been years, and you can't live your life by being afraid."

Bethany was one of the few people who knew all of Eliza's secrets.

"Go tell him," Bethany urged. "A big, proud 'Fuck off.' Say it like you mean it, and I guarantee you will feel so good that you'll think you just had an orgasm."

So, um, Eliza doubted that it would feel that good. But the idea of going over there...of standing up for herself...

Why not?

"Now, my darling, while you handle your dare, I'm off to find a dance partner. If you don't mind, I think I'll try my luck with your blond. I like the preppy ones." With that, she sashayed away, heading for the man in the Polo.

Eliza put some money down on top of the bar. She inclined her head to the bartender, squared her shoulders, and then strode for the door. As she made her way for the exit, she remained hyper-aware of the man in the booth.

When she was halfway to the door, he started to rise.

Because, of course, he will follow me. I'm sure his job is to make certain I get home without any incidents tonight. Nothing that could possibly embarrass the family.

She stopped.

He sat back down.

Eliza turned abruptly on her heel and advanced toward him. The music drummed and had her temples throbbing.

The man in the booth leaned back, tilted his head, and studied her approach with a wry grin on his face. On his ridiculously handsome face. Eliza figured he probably used that grin to get all sorts of things that he wanted in this world. He probably smiled like that and plenty of women dropped at his feet.

I'm not going to drop.

She stopped at the edge of his table. Noted that he had a beer bottle in front of him. Open, but it didn't appear that he'd actually had any of the beer to drink. That would go along with his cover. Her bodyguards didn't get to drink while on the clock, but he would want to blend in.

You're failing in that regard. You stick out far too brightly. A man like him would always stick out.

Up close, he was even more attractive. Sculpted cheekbones. Hard jaw. Straight blade of a nose. Lips that were pure sensuality.

"Hey, there, princess," he drawled. It was a low, deep voice, one that rumbled and held the faintest hint of the south.

"I'm not a princess." In contrast, her voice came out sounding too prim. Too stilted. Too controlled.

"No?" His dark brows rose. "My mistake." He smiled.

She didn't smile back. "I know who *you* are."

"Really?" He blinked. "That is impressive."

He was mocking her? If possible, her cheeks burned hotter.

"But, hey, good for you, and if knowing who I am speeds the process along for us..." He motioned between them. "Then good for me, too, am I right?"

What he *was*...It was an asshole. "Your services are not needed."

His eyes narrowed. "But you haven't even heard the full list of the services I offer." His pose remained casual. Almost careless. "Pretty damn extensive list, if I do say so myself."

"I am not impressed."

He smiled again. A slow, wicked, sexy-as-hell grin that made her heart lurch hard in her chest.

Do not let him see your reaction. He's playing you. He wouldn't be the first guard who'd thought that if he acted interested in her, he might be able to worm his way into her family. Or rather, into getting hold of her family's money.

"I can see that you're not," he told her. "And got to say, it hurts." His hand moved to his chest. Rested over his heart. "Right in here."

"You're laughing at me?"

"Nope. Though I will tell you, I am finding you pretty damn charming. Did not expect that." He winked.

Winked. Like this was all some big joke. Like her life was a joke and he got to watch her, mock her, and isolate her. The guards *always* isolated her. No one ever got close when they were near. She stayed locked away from the world. And it was—

"*Enough.*" Her hands slapped down on the table. His beer bottle rocked a little.

A faint furrow appeared between his brows, and he slowly leaned toward her.

"I saw what you did," she gritted out. "You stopped that man from approaching me."

He fired a glance to the right. Smirked. "Like you would have been happy with a boring asshat like him." His gaze returned to her. "Not you."

He could not be serious. "You know *nothing* about me."

"Of course, I do. I always believe in being thorough on a case. Insulting of you to suggest otherwise."

On a case. "So you read a file," Eliza snapped and heard the anger vibrating in her voice. "Big deal. That doesn't mean you know *me.*" She wasn't sure anyone knew who she really was. How could they? She had to pretend all the time, with everyone. *Sometimes, I don't even know who I am anymore.*

His gaze—a deep, bold green—never left her face. "I know you can have a lot more fun tonight if you don't waste your time with some former frat boy who is just looking for a fast hookup."

She sucked in a breath.

"Besides, he's already settled in with your redheaded friend. Anyone who moves on from you that quickly definitely belongs in the dumbass category." He arched a brow. "I assure you, I am not a dumbass."

This was unbelievable. "So...what? You're offering to hook up with me in his place?" Wait, no, she had not meant to say—

His gaze dipped over her. Lingered. Warmed. Rose back to trap hers. "That is a bonus I did not anticipate."

A bonus? Sex with her was a bonus? Like a perk that just came along with the guard job? Anger shook her body. She leaned even closer to him.

He inched forward a bit more, too, as if he expected she was going to eagerly accept his offer or—or kiss him.

Instead, she very softly, very sweetly, told him... "Fuck off." Then she took that bottle of beer, and she poured it on him.

His lips parted. His green eyes widened. "My God." Beer dripped down his shirtfront. The wet shirt clung lovingly to his muscles.

She shoved back from the table.

He laughed. "I think I might be in love," he added, seeming somewhat dazed.

"And I think you might be insane." Her chin jerked up. "Consider yourself *fired*." With that, she whirled and stormed for the door. This time, she didn't stop. This time, she sailed out of the bar with all the grace and dignity she could manage.

Under the circumstances, it wasn't a whole lot of grace...and she feared it was with even less dignity.

And, for the record, she would have to remember to tell Bethany that she'd been wrong. No way, no day had that felt even remotely like an orgasm.

CHAPTER TWO

"So, um, do you want another beer? Or maybe...a towel or something?"

Memphis Camden dragged his gaze off Eliza Robinson's ever-so-gorgeous ass and forced himself to respond to the waitress who hovered near his table. "Nah." He yanked some cash out of his wallet and ignored the trickle of beer that dripped from his hand. "But thanks." Memphis rose.

Eliza was storming out with all the elegance of a true queen, but he wasn't about to let her just make a dramatic exit and vanish on him. He had too many plans in place.

Plans that wouldn't, *couldn't* be altered. Not when he was this close.

Whistling, he headed out the door, too, and when he hit the busy Houston street, he immediately saw his prey. She stood near the edge of the sidewalk, and she clutched her phone tightly in her hand. He was rather pleased to see that she kept her head up, and she swept the area with her gaze. Good situational awareness but...

She was still too close to the road. She should move back a few feet.

Her searching gaze found him. Locked on him.

He smiled. Sauntered toward her even as she stiffened.

"What part of fired did you not understand?" Eliza demanded. Light from a streetlamp fell on her. Another point in her favor. She'd picked a well-lit spot. The light illuminated her dark, gleaming hair. Thick and long, she'd styled it to curl loosely around her face. Her eyes were dark, too—inside, they'd seemed to be almost black. She had warm honey skin, something he suspected she'd inherited from her Spanish mother. Her full, gorgeous, kiss-me lips were currently pressed into a stony, unhappy line. And her cheeks—already sharp—had hollowed even more with her anger.

He pulled at his wet shirt. Hell. He probably smelled like a freaking brewery. Their first meeting had not gone as planned. That was okay, though, because he'd always enjoyed the unexpected. He didn't have time to waste being bored. "To be honest with you," he finally responded as her glare just became even cuter to him, "I pretty much didn't understand any part of the firing." How could she fire him when he didn't work for her?

"Ohhh!" More a frustrated growl than anything else. "You can't be serious!"

He was.

She stalked closer to him. Her delicate nostrils flared.

He was pleased to note that she'd moved away from the busy road. "I was worried you might slip and get hit."

"What?" The bracelets on her wrist jingled. She frowned.

He pointed to her. Then to the street. "You were too close to the edge of the sidewalk. Don't worry, if you'd started to slip, I would have jumped in to save you."

"I just bet you would. All part of the job, am I right? Protecting me from any and every threat." She kept coming forward. Stopped only when she was right in front of him. Her heels gave her a few extra inches, but she was still way shorter than he was. He figured that without the heels, she'd probably clock in around five-foot-seven or eight.

He was an easy six-foot-three.

She was also far too delicate.

Memphis shifted his attention to her small, black bag. "Tell me you have a gun in there."

"*What?*"

"You've got a gun in your bag, don't you?"

"What I have in my bag is none of your business."

He took that answer as a no. "Crap. You don't have a gun. A knife? You got one of those?" He peered hopefully at her bag. Memphis noticed that the hand *near* her bag—the hand Eliza still had holding her phone—tightened around the device. If she wasn't careful, she just might shatter the phone.

Eliza made no response to his query.

"I'll take that as a no," Memphis murmured in disappointment. "What about pepper spray? A taser? Tell me that you've got *something—"*

Her other hand shoved into her purse and came back up with a rather gorgeous-looking taser. He knew the make and model instantly. *Nice choice.* "I approve."

"I don't care. If you don't get the hell away from me, I will be using this thing on you." But her grip shook just a bit around the weapon.

"Now why would you want to do that?" Once more, he pulled on his wet shirt. It just kept wanting to stick to his skin. "I'm not a threat to you."

Her gaze darted down to his chest. Then a little lower to his abs. She licked her lower lip.

Well, well. He knew interest when he saw it. "Aw, that is so flattering. Thank you."

Her stare snapped back up.

"You think I'm hot." A nod. "Fair enough. I think you might just be the sexiest woman I've ever seen. Did not expect that. You have this whole don't-touch-me vibe going on that I thought meant you were cold—"

She stiffened. "*Bastard."*

"But that vibe is so wrong. I get it. "

"You don't get *anything.*" Low and angry. "I have a taser in my hand. I just told you to back away."

He didn't back away. He *did* notice some bozo in an overpriced suit who decided to scuttle closer. A suit. In *this* humidity?

"Everything all right?" A Texas accent thickened the suit's voice. His dark hair had been carefully styled away from his high forehead. "This guy giving you trouble?"

Seriously? Memphis sighed. "This is so not your—"

The man moved his suit coat to the side in order to reveal the badge clipped to his hip. "I'm Detective Daniel Jones, and before you say anything else, yes, this is most definitely my business."

Fabulous. He was making friends with the local law enforcement team on day one. Memphis was just checking off all the boxes. Contact with Eliza. New police resource. This night was full of wins. As long as a person looked at things the right way...

It was all a matter of perspective.

The detective leaned toward Memphis and took a long inhale. "You been drinking?"

Well, he was standing outside of a bar, but... "No." The beer bottle had never had the chance to so much as touch his lips.

"No?" Doubt coated the detective's response. "You smell like you've been drinking for hours."

"That's because I'm wearing beer," Memphis returned easily.

"You're *what?*" The detective's voice rose about two octaves.

Eliza put the taser back in her bag. Glanced down at her phone. "My ride is here." She turned her head toward the detective. "Thank you for your assistance."

"No problem, Eliza."

Wait, he *knew* her?

"I see your driver is here," Daniel continued with a warm smile for her. "You have a good night. I'll take care of this guy."

Her driver. Yep, because a limo had just rolled to the corner. The driver had already gotten out and opened the back door for Eliza.

"Don't suppose I could get a ride?" Memphis asked hopefully.

Her mouth dropped open.

"Next time," he said. "Got it. We'll make that a date."

Daniel swore. "Who is this joker, Eliza?"

"Well, see, I never got to introduce myself to the lovely lady before she poured beer on me and then pulled out her taser." He considered the situation. "Honestly, maybe you should have asked me if I needed assistance. But no matter." He waved the issue away. For now. Obviously, the cop had a personal deal going on with Eliza. The guy looked like he might be a few years older than her, and his whole body posture was way too tuned to Eliza. He leaned toward her. Moved when she did. Kept his hand close to her.

Oh, you had better not be a problem.

"Who the hell are you?" Daniel blasted.

"He's a new bodyguard," Eliza blurted.

"I'm Memphis Camden." He looked expectantly at them both. Waited.

They stared back at him.

"The name means nothing? You've never heard it?" Surely the cop had.

Daniel scratched his jaw.

"A legend in my own mind," Memphis decided. "But that's okay. If you don't think you're awesome, who else will?"

Shaking her head, Eliza turned away. She marched for the limo.

"I'll see you tomorrow!" Memphis called after her.

His shout had her stilling. After a tense beat of time, her head swiveled toward him. "Fired. Look it up in the dictionary. See what it means."

He knew exactly what it meant. He also knew he wasn't working for her, so there was no way she *could* fire him. Obviously, the lovely Eliza had him confused with someone else.

She slipped into the limo. The driver shut the door, and moments later, she was being taken away from him. Unfortunate. But he *would* be seeing her again. She was a very necessary part of his plan.

"Are you going to be a problem?" the detective asked.

"I was wondering the same thing about you," he admitted with a smile. *Don't get in my way, Daniel.*

The detective's gaze raked over him.

Eliza was long gone, but, hey, who said the night had to be a total waste? The detective knew Eliza—why not see what he could spill?

"You were heading for the bar, detective," Memphis said. "Off-duty?"

"Yeah, dammit, I—"

"Then drinks are on me." He'd always found that when you wanted to get someone talking, booze helped. He very much wanted Daniel Jones to spill every secret he knew about Eliza Robinson.

Once more, Memphis pulled at his beer-soaked shirt. He certainly hoped that his second meeting with Eliza would go better than the first. He made a mental note to keep alcoholic beverages away from her, particularly if she seemed in a throwing mood.

***

"Why is he here?" Eliza almost snapped the stem of her champagne flute in half.

Her brother frowned at her. "Excuse me?"

"Him." She glared daggers at the man who'd just strolled into the country club and was striding around with a cocky grin on his face. Acting as if he owned the place. "Why is *he* here?"

"Perhaps because he's a new member?" Benedict snagged a pastry as the tray drifted past him. "Can't say that I've seen him before, so it stands to reason that the man you're currently singeing with your stare is either a new member, a guest, or—"

Her *singeing* stare whipped to him. "You don't know him?"

He made the pastry vanish. "Should I?" Now he frowned at the approaching male, too.

"Yes! You usually run the clearance checks on all the guards that Dad sends my way." Her heartrate doubled. *He has to be a guard...*

Benedict's shoulders tensed. "I don't...Eliza, what are you talking about? That guy is not one of your guards."

"Memphis Camden," she whispered. "That's his name."

"A name that means nothing to me." Benedict edged closer to her. "As far as I know, we haven't hired any new guards." A confused pause. "Why would you think he was employed by the family?"

"Because...because he was there last night..." Her words trailed away as Memphis closed in.

"Where?" Benedict demanded. A worried edge had entered his voice. He took her hand. Squeezed. "Eliza, what is happening?"

She didn't know. Fear beat through her. This man...

If he isn't a bodyguard, who is he?

Memphis halted in front of her. The grin that had been curving his lips instantly faded. "What's wrong?" His body tensed, and a hard, dangerous mask seemed to slide over his face. "Who in the hell has scared you?"

Her elbow hit her brother because she'd instinctively moved ever nearer to him. "*You* have." Husky. Breathless.

It was the middle of the day. A luncheon at her father's country club. A completely safe environment. *You are okay. You are okay.* But her breathing came too fast, and Eliza feared her heart might leap out of her chest.

"I would never hurt you." His voice was pitched low. Almost...soothing. Or as soothing as she suspected his voice could get. "You don't ever need to worry about that. I might not be one of the guards that your family seems so fond of hiring—by the way, most of their work is shit—"

"I beg your pardon," Benedict began in his most pompous tone. He could do pompous better than anyone else. She'd always believed that.

"Yeah, you should." Memphis's gaze finally swept to her brother. "If you have anything to do with the guards who are currently on staff to protect her. There was no sign of any security for her last night when she was at the bar—"

Benedict swung his head toward her. "You went out to a bar? But...but you never go out!"

Memphis made a faint humming sound. "And no one stopped me from strolling right in this fancy place. No one even glanced at me twice, and all I had to do in order to fit in was wear clothes that were too damn expensive. Oh, hey—" He broke off when the pastry tray darted around again. "I want one of those." But he actually snatched two petit fours and gobbled them right up. "That's a little slice of heaven." He licked the crumbs from his lips.

Eliza felt glued to the spot. *What is going on?*

A tender light seemed to fill Memphis's eyes. "Want to go somewhere and talk?"

"Who are you?" she demanded.

"Told you last night. I'm Memphis Camden." He inclined his head toward her. "It's a pleasure, Eliza. I have to say, I am a big fan."

Was she dreaming? Having a nightmare? Normally, her nightmares involved her running through the darkness. Screaming and falling and trying desperately to get home. "Why would you be a fan?" She made a point of *not* making any headlines these days. That was what her family wanted, after all. For her to keep a low profile. To work at Robinson Corporation. To be elegant and poised and say all the right things to all the right people. But she didn't know what to say in this instance.

"Why?" Memphis blinked, as if surprised.

Benedict motioned toward one of the security guards—staff at the country club—who'd been lounging near the door.

"Why would you be a fan?" she repeated.

"Because I admire survivors. I fucking love fighters. You're both."

Her breath caught.

"You escaped from the man who abducted you."

She could feel all the blood rushing from her head. Her body swayed. Eliza bumped into her brother.

"You got away," Memphis continued, and his green eyes were lit with what looked like admiration. "You made it back to your family."

"Get him out of here!" Benedict snapped as the guard joined their group. He pointed to Memphis, then threw his arm around Eliza's shoulders. "This man is trespassing. Get him *out!*"

The guard slapped a hand on Memphis's shoulder. "Mr. Robinson says you need to leave."

"Yes, I heard him. Would have been hard to miss it. But I don't particularly care what he says. I'm not here for him." His gaze—still oddly tender—remained on Eliza. "I'm here for you," he told her.

"He's some kind of stalker." Benedict pulled Eliza closer to him. "Haul him out! Don't ever let him back in again—"

The guard's hold tightened on Memphis as he began to haul—

Memphis's right hand flew up. He curled his fingers around the security guard's wrist in a seemingly light touch.

But the security guard *howled* and immediately dropped to his knees.

Memphis let the other man go even as everyone at the luncheon turned to gape at their little group.

"Feeling will come back soon." Memphis didn't even glance down at the security guard. "You shouldn't manhandle guests. I would think that sort of thing would be bad for business. But, hey, what do I know? It's my first time at a swanky country club like this one."

More security guards were closing in. So were her father's associates. People wearing tense and worried expressions.

"You're making a scene," Eliza heard herself whisper. Wait, he was there because of her. *I can't do this.* "I'm not supposed to make a scene."

His eyes narrowed. "Who the fuck told you that? Half the fun in life comes from making scenes." A beat of silence. "You didn't seem to mind making a scene when you poured that beer over me last night."

"I—"

Benedict stepped in front of her. "Get away from my sister."

When Eliza peeked over his shoulder, she saw that the useless security guard had scampered back. He flexed his wrist. Glared at Memphis.

"If your sister wants me to stay away from her, I will." Memphis seemed completely calm. Way too casual. "But before I take my exit, I thought she might like to know why I wanted to talk with her in the first place. And, no, it's not because I'm a stalker."

The other guards were almost on him.

"I'm a hunter," Memphis announced quietly. "I'm currently on one of the biggest hunts of my life."

"Good for you," Benedict fired back. "You are in the *wrong* place for a hunt."

"Benny..." She wanted to hear this. There was something about Memphis's tone...

"I'm hunting for a dangerous predator," Memphis continued as the security guards swarmed behind him. "A man who has abducted several women. The man I'm after...I suspect he also abducted you, Eliza. But you got away from him. The others didn't. They never made it home."

A dull ringing filled her ears.

The guards clamped their hands on him.

"I could have them all crying on the floor," Memphis said as he raised his brows. "But I won't. For you, Eliza, I'll be civilized. Though it's not something I often am. So I do hope you remember this one special time."

They pulled him back.

She stared after him with her mouth open in shock. Ice seemed to fill her blood, and chills skated down her spine.

He didn't fight the guards. In fact, he did a fast turn and just evaded their grip. "I know my way out." He strolled away as the crowd at the luncheon backed up and murmured.

"Pay him no attention, Eliza," Benedict said as he gave her arm a squeeze. "Just someone coming to stir up old trouble. He was just baiting you. Nothing he said was true. Probably some opportunist who is just looking to cash in on the Robinson—"

She jerked away from her brother. "Stop!" Eliza shouted.

And everyone looked at her.

So much for keeping a low profile. Her father would be so disappointed.

CHAPTER THREE

At Eliza's sudden cry, Memphis turned back to look at her. From the corner of his eye, he noticed that the guards froze. Memphis had thought he might need to teach them some manners. It should be a normal fact of life—don't put your hand on someone else. Not unless you want to lose feeling in that hand. Or, if he was feeling particularly annoyed...*not unless you want the hand broken.*

Eliza gazed back at him, and her beautiful, dark eyes appeared stark. Scared. He didn't like that. She didn't need to fear him. He had never hurt a woman in his life, and he never would. He was there to help, not to hurt, and he damn well needed to make that clear to her.

As he stared at her, Eliza pulled in a deep breath. The tension smoothed away from her lovely face as she straightened her shoulders—they'd already been plenty straight—and lifted her slightly pointed chin. "There has been a mistake," she announced, voice cool and clear.

Yeah, sure, there had been a mistake, she'd *mistaken* him for one of the dumbass bodyguards her family hired—

"This man was invited," she continued even as her brother blanched and threw her a look of utter surprise. A weak smile curled her lips before she added, "I apologize for any confusion that was created."

Anger beat through him. She didn't need to apologize to the roomful of gawkers who were excitedly whispering about her—and him. She should tell them all to go to hell. That would work better for him than an apology they didn't need.

The man next to her—Memphis knew it was her older brother, Benedict—leaned in closer to her. The brother was dressed in a starchy white shirt. Khakis. Gleaming leather loafers. He appeared tall and lean, and he shared his sister's dark hair and eyes.

Beside him, Eliza wore a pale blue dress. Delicate straps slid over her shoulders, and the flowing skirt ended a few inches above her knees. Her hand reached up to touch her brother's shoulder, and she murmured something to him.

Benedict looked none too pleased, but he nodded.

Ah. Bet she told him to handle the guards.

"Please," Eliza said, her voice strong and clear again. "Enjoy your lunch. I'm sorry for the interruption."

And just like that, everyone went back to business as usual. Sure, there were a few more murmurs. Some covert glances. But the shocked silence and gawking disappeared.

Because the queen had spoken.

With her chin up, she walked straight toward Memphis. He had to admire that walk of hers. In two-inch, strappy heels, she managed a rather runway-ready walk that was full of grace and the faintest sensuality. A sensuality that seemed bottled up. Hesitant.

He could help her *unbottle* it.

When she was right in front of him, Eliza extended her hand. Pale, pink polish adorned her fingernails. "How about we take a stroll in the garden and...talk?"

His fingers curled around hers. No, more like his fingers swallowed hers. She had to feel the rough edge of calluses along his fingertips and his palm. A side effect of his workout regime. But he made sure to keep only a light grip on her. He would never crush her fingers.

Fragile things were always handled with care in his book.

"Just so you know..." Memphis heard himself murmur even as a flood of awareness filled his body. Her skin was fucking *soft*. "We are going to do one hell of a lot more than just talk."

As he watched her, Memphis noticed the small shiver that slid over her body. But her chin didn't lower. Her stare never wavered. "Perhaps."

And he realized she wasn't as fragile as the world—and he—believed.

She turned and led him toward the already-open balcony doors.

Her brother stepped forward, and Memphis was sure that Benedict would try to stop them from leaving. *Yeah, go ahead and try.*

But Eliza just gave a faint shake of her head. Then kept going.

The brother didn't follow.

Interesting. Memphis didn't speak again until they'd eased down the stone steps that led to the garden. Lush flowers surrounded them almost immediately, and the rich scent filled his nostrils. The flowers smelled nice, but he liked Eliza's scent better. He'd first noticed it last night. A light, faint lavender scent had clung to her...as she'd emptied his beer on him.

But that woman—the woman who had told him to "fuck off" in such a beautifully savage tone—she seemed a far cry from the carefully poised lady beside him. The lady who looked entirely too serene and untouchable, even though he *was* touching her.

And I'd like to touch her a whole lot more.

A development he had not anticipated. When he'd planned for their meeting and eventual partnership, he hadn't thought there would be any sexual component involved. He'd looked at her pictures, yes, and he'd recognized that she was indeed lovely. But Memphis didn't typically let a physical attraction get in the way of his goals.

He already knew that things were going to be different, with her. There was nothing typical about Eliza.

She tugged her hand free of his grip.

His brows snapped together. "Why did you do that?"

"Excuse me?"

"You can hold my hand anytime. Don't have to do it just for show." Just so she'd know for the future.

Her head tilted. "Are you quite all right?"

Memphis considered the question. "Feeling a little annoyed, truth be told."

She blushed. Not the first time she'd done that. A rather amusing trait. It wasn't a deep blush. With her honey cream skin, it just looked like a cute little dusting of pink on the edge of her super sharp cheeks.

"You're annoyed because of the scene in the ballroom." Eliza released a faint sigh. "I'm sorry that the guards—"

"That's it." A quick nod. "That's exactly why I'm annoyed."

"Ah, yes, as I was saying, the guards—"

"Nah. Not annoyed with them. They were just doing their jobs. Poorly, but still trying." He edged closer to her. Caught the scent of lavender. Loved it. Greedily inhaled more. "I'm pissed because you didn't need to apologize to those assholes who were gaping at you. So what if their fancy lunch got interrupted? They'll live."

"It...was the polite thing to do."

His fingers rubbed along the stubble that coated his jaw. "Was it?" A shrug. "Can't say that I ever worry too much about doing the polite thing."

Her gaze swept over him. "I think I'm learning that." A delicate pause. "I think the guard you injured probably learned that, too."

Memphis had to laugh. "Not injured. He just has a temporary loss of feeling. I promise, no permanent damage was done. Well, maybe just to his pride. But the dude should really sharpen up his skills if he wants to play in the big leagues."

"And you, ah, are a big league? Is that what you're saying?"

Now he made sure to wipe away all amusement from his face and voice. "I'm whatever you need me to be."

She paced away from him. Went toward the overflowing, bright red roses. Reached out to touch one. Her fingers trailed over the petals and carefully avoided the thorns. "I thought you were hired by my family."

"Yes, I got that." He couldn't take his gaze off her. "Guessing they've hired quite a few bodyguards for you over the years?"

"You could say that." Her hand fell from the rose. "There might even be someone watching us right now. Half the time, I don't know when the guards are there. You could say that my father became somewhat hyper-vigilant where I was concerned." She seemed to brace herself as she turned back toward him. "Even though most of the cops and the media seemed to all decide that I just staged the whole event. The bored heiress who thought it would be hilarious to vanish for a few days, then to show up at her father's engagement party covered in blood and dirt. What a fun way to steal the spotlight from her soon-to-be-stepmother."

Yes, he knew that she'd been crucified in the media. "I think the cops did a shitty job of handling your case."

A hard shake of her head. "It wasn't their fault. I-I couldn't show them where I'd been held. Couldn't remember clearly what had happened in the days I was missing. Couldn't—"

He stalked toward her. "Do you always make excuses for other people? Make excuses, apologize when you don't need to…if we're working together, that shit has got to stop."

She wet her lower lip. "What do you mean?"

"I mean I want the woman back who told me to 'fuck off' last night. I liked her. She had some good fire in her. Bring her to the surface."

"I-I…" Her lashes swept down to conceal her gaze. Her chin dipped toward her chest. "That wasn't me."

"No? Sure as hell looked like you. Even down to the midnight eyes." He'd never seen eyes quite as dark as hers before. Even Benedict's hadn't been the exact shade. Close but…

"It was me, yes," she retorted, seemingly flustered, "but I meant I don't normally act that way."

His fingers slid under her chin. Tipped it up. *I like touching her too much.* "How do you act?"

"Careful," she breathed as her lashes lifted and she met his stare.

He leaned toward her. His thumb slid up to touch her lower lip. A light caress. "That sounds boring." He wanted her mouth. Badly.

"Wh-why are you looking at me that way?"

Because I want to kiss you until you forget about being careful. And that was the way wrong reaction. Memphis didn't normally deny his impulses, but this scene was different. She was different.

He'd rarely wanted to both fuck someone and protect her from every single threat in the same instance. With Eliza, he did. The big problem he faced?

He was her current threat. Because being with him would totally wreck her carefully ordered world, and he knew it.

Memphis forced his hand to move away from her. He even managed to take a step back, and, honestly, he felt as if he needed a round of applause for that effort. After clearing his throat, he asked, "What made you act that way last night?"

"A dare."

One brow notched up. "Now I'm curious."

"I, uh, I thought you were a new bodyguard. My friend Bethany challenged me to tell you to, ahem, fuck off, so I did."

Interesting. *Mental note, Eliza likes a dare.* "Did she also tell you to pour the beer on me?"

A wince. "No, that was a spur-of-the-moment decision. Sorry about your shirt."

He shook his head. "We are gonna break that habit."

Her brow furrowed at his words, but Eliza doggedly continued, "In my defense..."

Oh, good. She's defending herself. Do it, baby. Tell me that I was an arrogant ass and—

"You shouldn't have teased me and said you wanted to have sex with me. You shouldn't have implied that being with me physically was some sort of bonus perk that came with the job." She sniffed. "I didn't find your joke funny, but, obviously, I overreacted."

Yeah, they were on different pages. Maybe reading totally different books? Time to fix that.

"I wasn't teasing." He'd just be clear from this point on. "I don't do that. I say what I mean. Got a super low bullshit tolerance on my end. Honestly, you should try it. You tell more people to fuck off, and you will feel *so* much better."

"That's...not the way the world works."

"It's how my world works."

Her lashes fluttered. "And you weren't teasing?"

"Nope. I would fuck you right here and now if that was what you wanted." Outside in the garden, with all those judgmental, whispering pricks inside the building. They'd have privacy, he'd have her.

Her mouth opened, then snapped closed. Her eyes narrowed on him. "That's not a possibility."

He looked around. Considered his options. Definitely possible. All he had to do was shove up that cute dress of hers, get her panties out of the way and—

"Could we get back on topic?" Her voice held a brittle edge. "Or were you lying about hunting the person who abducted me?"

All amusement—and tempting thoughts of sex with her—vanished. "I'm not going to lie to you. Not my style. I will always tell you what I think. You might believe I'm an asshole, and you certainly wouldn't be the first with that opinion, but that's just how I am." He had no tolerance for lies. A habit he'd picked up thanks to his father. "How about we start over?"

"I..." She bit her lower lip. "Okay?" A question rife with nerves.

"I'm Memphis Camden." He extended his hand between them. "Back in the day, I made my living as a bounty hunter."

Her fingers reached out. Curled around his. "Eliza Robinson. I currently make my living working in the PR department at Robinson Corporation." A rueful smile tilted her lips. "When you were once *an extreme PR disaster*, you pick up some skills that help you to clean up messes in the future."

His fingers tightened around hers. "You were never a disaster. You were a victim. You should have always been treated that way."

She blinked.

Hell, had that been the flash of tears in her eyes?

She blinked again, and the glimmer—or flash or whatever it had been—vanished. Eliza's hand pulled away from his.

But he could still feel the heat of her touch against him. That heat had seared right through him. "When I was a bounty hunter, I learned how to stalk my prey. I learned how to slip into the darker side of life. To go *into* that dark and haul the monsters out." He'd made quite a bit of money with that career. Taking down the worst of the worst paid well. He'd also gotten pretty lucky with his investments. Lucky enough that if he'd wanted, he could easily buy his way into the country club lifestyle.

Not too bad for a kid who'd grown up wearing thrift store clothes and sweeping out shops for money so that he and his mom could make rent payments.

As for the country club lifestyle? Not really his thing.

"More recently," he said as her gaze seemed to see right through him, "I've been working with some rather talented individuals online." Their group contained members with all sorts of unique backgrounds and talents. "We call ourselves the Ice Breakers."

"Ice Breakers?"

"Um. Because our job is to break open cold cases. You know, all those crimes that were never solved? Murderers who weren't brought to justice? Missing people who vanished and were seemingly forgotten?" He waited a bit when her breathing hitched. "We focus on them. Happy to say that we've had a pretty successful run so far."

She edged closer to him. "You believe me?"

What in the hell kind of question was that?

"You're here...because you believe I was taken?" Her voice broke a little with excitement. "My family believes me. That's—that's why my dad and brother insist on the protection. Even though it's been years, even though...surely, there's no way he would come after me again—"

Memphis opened his mouth.

"But the cops couldn't find evidence. Nothing to point to the person who took me. Then stories started circulating on the gossip sites about the rich girl who faked her kidnapping. My dad's lawyers said it would be better to just go quiet. To make it all go away."

That had been shit advice.

"But it never went away." Her hand rose to press against her chest. "Not for me."

No, he didn't imagine that it had.

"You believe me?" she asked again.

"Yeah, baby." The endearment rolled from him. *She is going to matter too much to me.* "I do."

Eliza leapt toward him. Her arms wrapped around him in a fierce, tight grip. "Thank you."

His hands lifted, then hesitated and kind of hung in the air. *Since when do I hesitate?* His arms wrapped around Eliza and pulled her even closer against him. Memphis was jolted by just how *right* she felt against him. Heat filled him, but not just some sexual intensity, though, sure, that was there. But this was more, this was deeper, this was...

Probably big trouble.

Her head lifted. She gazed up at him. A dawning sexual awareness filled her dark eyes. "Oh, my."

So freaking cute. He started to—

"*Eliza*!" Nearly a screech of her name. "*What in the world are you doing with him?*"

She jerked from his arms.

Hell. Leave it to the brother to ruin a good moment.

CHAPTER FOUR

Get control of yourself, Eliza! You do not get to embrace strangers. Even if the sexy stranger in question was the first person to give her unwavering support in a very, very long time.

Benedict came to a shuddering stop right beside her. "Have you lost your mind?" he demanded. "One minute, you're getting security to throw out this—this—"

"Memphis," she said, a little surprised that her voice came out so unruffled and smooth. "His name is Memphis."

"Whatever!" Benedict obviously did not care. "You're trying to throw him out in one breath, and then you're embracing him in the next!"

The turnaround hadn't been *quite* that fast, but she could certainly see why Benedict might have gotten the wrong impression. Her right index finger tapped against the top of her thigh. "He's going to help with my case."

Pity flashed on Benedict's face. "No, Lizzie, he's not. He's just another in a long line of scam artists who will try to *make* you think he's here to help."

A long line? Since when was there a line?

"There have been others," Benedict revealed as he glowered at Memphis. "Plenty of people clamoring to help solve the big mystery of your lost time. But when it came down to it, know what they really wanted to help themselves to?"

She'd never been told about anyone wanting to help her. No one had reached out to her directly, and neither her father nor Benedict had ever said—

"Money. As much cash as we could give them. After dad foolishly paid two of the bastards and they up and vanished, he finally got wise to what was happening." He pointed at Memphis. "He's just another swindler."

Heat flared in Memphis's green eyes. "I'm not."

"No? Then you didn't tell my sister that for ten grand or twenty or maybe even thirty, you could find the man who took her? You could be the hero she's always wanted?" Disgust twisted Benedict's lips. "I have heard this story before." He spun away from Memphis. Focused on Eliza. "Let's walk away now. Do not ever talk to him again. Don't even think about him again."

But she couldn't seem to take her eyes off Memphis. He was just staring back at her. Not even trying to defend himself. So she was the one to say, "He didn't ask me for any money." He'd just said that he believed her.

"Yet," Benedict snapped. A long sigh escaped him as he lifted a hand to rub along the back of his neck. "He just hasn't asked for money *yet*. I probably interrupted before he could. It's a swindle that has happened too many times already." He positioned his body next to hers. "I didn't tell you about the others because what was the point? Giving you hope and then just dashing it as you realized the world was full of bastards who wanted to take advantage of you?" He jerked a thumb over his shoulder. "He is no different. He just wants to use you."

Her chest ached. She side-stepped so that she could see Memphis once again. "Do you want to use me?"

"Yes."

Eliza flinched.

"See?" Benedict muttered in disgust. "Though, at least I'll give this one credit for admitting—"

"I want to use you in order to help me find the SOB I'm after. I want to go back through everything that happened to you leading up to your disappearance." Memphis advanced on her. "I know it will be hard. Digging up the past can be a real bitch, but I think it is necessary."

Benedict swung toward him. "Stay *away* from my sister! I told you, she isn't going to fall—"

"He took other women."

Her finger tapped faster against her thigh even as a breeze lightly lifted the hem of her skirt. "You said that before." It was those words that had compelled her to stop him before the guards could lead him away.

"He can't *know* that, Eliza!" Benedict burst out. "He's manipulating you!"

"I can know it. I've got a profile on the perp, one that comes courtesy of a former FBI agent, a guy who has been working on this case for a very long time." The faint lines near Memphis's eyes deepened. "This is personal for me because I have a friend—her sister was taken five years ago. Taken by the same man that I suspect took you. Only her sister never made it back home. I am personally invested in this case. I want that bastard brought to justice. I *want* to stop him before he hurts anyone else."

"How..." Eliza stopped. Cleared her throat. Tried again. "How many others?"

"Counting you, I suspect seven victims."

She backed up. Her knees buckled because the shock hit her so hard. He was saying...six other women? Six women who might be *dead?*

Eliza would have fallen, but Benedict dove forward and caught her. "It's okay." His fingers tightened around her arms. "Breathe, Lizzie. Breathe."

She *was* breathing.

"He's a serial predator," Memphis continued, and each word pounded at her with the force of a hammer's blow. "One with a very specific MO. And I don't have the bodies..."

Goose bumps covered her skin, and Eliza feared she might be physically sick all over Benedict's favorite loafers.

"But I strongly suspect we are dealing with a serial killer," Memphis finished.

Serial killer.

Benedict's hold became almost painful as his fingers bit into her arms. "*Eliza.*"

Her horrified gaze met his.

"We are leaving," Benedict told her, the words bitten off. "Now."

She tested her legs. Made sure she wasn't going to do something like fall on her ass. Her legs seemed to be in working order again, but she just felt so very, very cold.

Serial killer. Oh, God. Serial killers were supposed to be on TV shows. Or they were supposed to be horrible characters who terrified readers in books. They weren't supposed to be in your real life.

They weren't supposed to be in her life.

"Stay the hell away from my sister!" Benedict blasted at Memphis. "If I see you—if anyone from my family or if any of our guards see you again—it will be a mistake that I can assure you...you will regret it for the rest of your life."

"I don't regret many things." Memphis's unconcerned reply.

He was so casual. He'd just imploded her whole world, yet he acted as if it was nothing. Just a normal day for him.

"He's lying to you." Benedict kept a hold on her elbow as he hurried with her away from the garden and toward the front of the country club. Toward the valet area where his car waited. He shoved a card to the attendant and didn't let her go. "He just made up that story to scare you, Lizzie, don't—"

"Maybe she should be scared."

Benedict jumped. Eliza didn't. She'd been aware of Memphis following behind her. Even though his steps had been nearly silent. For such a big guy, he could sure move softly.

Her brother whirled toward him. "What part of 'stay away from my sister' did you not understand?"

Memphis reached into the back pocket of his pants, and he pulled out a card. But it wasn't a card he handed to one of the valet attendants. Instead, he offered it to Eliza. "This is the hotel I'm staying at while I'm in town. And my number is on the back. Why don't you do some digging on me? When you see that I'm legit, you can call me or you can just come straight to me, and we can get to work."

"Oh, no," Benedict huffed even as his Benz was brought around the curve and parked near him. "My sister is not working with—"

"Your sister can make her own decisions," she told him, softly, coolly. Her control was in place, but she could feel it cracking along the edges. If what Memphis was saying was true...

Her body swayed.

No. Keep it together. Just for a little longer. She wasn't allowed to show her cracks in public.

She took the card from Memphis. When their fingers brushed, some of the unsteadiness she felt eased. The world stopped wanting to tilt and slide away from her, and she even stopped being quite so chilled. Warmth began to bloom in her hand. To travel up her arm. To flood through her.

"Don't you want to stop him?" Memphis asked.

She nodded.

"Then let's do it. Let's work together and we can stop—"

"My sister isn't a fucking superhero! She doesn't hunt down bad guys. And she isn't going to fall for some ridiculous story that you have concocted from thin air." Benedict locked tightly to her and pulled her toward his Benz. Pulled her *away* from Memphis.

She caught the faint narrowing of Memphis's gaze.

One of the attendant's held open the passenger side door for her. But she hesitated. Pushed back against Benedict's hold. Memphis was watching her, and she felt like there was something else—

"Don't worry, Eliza," Memphis assured her. "I will be seeing you again."

Her breath slid out. She eased into the car. Benedict slammed the door and spun back to confront Memphis. "The hell you will!"

Then her brother rushed around the car. Jumped into the driver's seat and had them leaving the country club behind with a squeal of his tires. But Eliza found herself looking back. She expected to see Memphis staring after her.

He was already gone.

"You should give me that card," Benedict said as his gaze cut to the rearview mirror. *He's looking for Memphis, too.* "I'll get rid of it."

Her hold tightened on the card. "I want a background check done on him."

"No need." An instant reply. "He'll turn out to be another con artist, just like all the others."

Her stomach twisted. "Why wasn't I told about the others?" She looked down at the card. The front of the card was embossed with the name and address of a well-known hotel in town. She flipped it over. Stared at the number. Memorized it.

"No need," Benedict said again.

Yes, yes, there was a need.

"They were just trying to cash in," he hurried to explain. "You were in a very vulnerable place. Dad thought it was best for us to protect you."

"Protect me or himself?" The question came from her before she could stop it. And she didn't mean it. Not...not really. Did she?

He braked at a stop sign. Turned toward her. "You, of course." Concern filled his gaze. "We are always trying to protect you. There are unscrupulous people out there, Lizzie. People who will use you and lie to you and try to bleed every bit of money from you that they can. You had enough to deal with as it was. No need to expose you to people like that." His hand reached out, and he plucked the card from her fingers. "Forget Memphis Camden. If that even was his real name. He's nothing but a fraud. You will never see him again."

But she remembered Memphis's steady gaze. The casual reassurance in his voice as he'd said, *I will be seeing you again.*

And she knew that her brother was wrong.

***

The knock at his hotel room came sooner than Memphis expected. He glanced at his watch. Only 6 p.m. He'd been about to head out and rustle up his dinner. But...

Change of plans.

He'd figured that Eliza would research him. Put some of the Robinson family resources to work and explore his background. Though, honestly, the woman could just pop his name in a search engine online and come up with plenty of info. Once she had a chance to see he wasn't there to scam her, he figured that she'd be making an appearance.

This is faster than I hoped.

Feeling a smile curve his lips, Memphis threw open the hotel room door. "Decided to come by for a friendly visit, did you—"

"No."

Well, hell. Eliza wasn't standing on the threshold of his room. Her brother was. The brother who gave off hard vibes that suggested he might just be a total asshole.

"This isn't a friendly visit at all," Benedict continued. "But it is a necessary one." A muscle jerked along his clenched jaw. "Do you mind if I come in?"

Memphis scratched his cheek. "Yeah, I do. You're not the one I wanted to see. The one I wanted to see is a whole lot shorter and one hell of a lot prettier than you, no offense."

That muscle jerked again.

"So, how about you show up with her," Memphis suggested, "then we'll talk—"

"Ten thousand dollars," Benedict announced dramatically.

Memphis waited.

Benedict frowned.

"Is that figure supposed to do something for me?" Memphis wondered. "Because I'm kinda confused. Maybe it's because I haven't eaten. I'm always a little confused when I haven't eaten—no, check that, I'm usually hangry."

"You think this is a fucking joke?" Benedict's hands fisted.

"No. If I thought it was a joke, I would be laughing." He stepped toward the annoying brother. Toe-to-toe. "Do I look like I'm laughing?"

Benedict swallowed. "You look like someone who is trying to take advantage of my sister."

"Nah. Not really the plan I have in place."

"Fifteen thousand," Benedict snapped.

Memphis's head tilted to the right. "You're trying to buy me off right now." Behind Benedict, he caught a faint movement in the hallway. Another guest, heading off to dinner? If so, *jealous*. Dinner would be amazing. But...

The movement came again. Almost furtive. He tensed.

"You're damn right I am trying to buy you off." Benedict huffed out a breath. "I don't want you anywhere near my sister. I told you that already!"

Memphis scratched his cheek once more. "Yes, I do recall you mentioning that fact to me a time or two."

Benedict leapt over the threshold. "You sonofabitch!"

Memphis moved to the side so the guy could barrel forward. When Benedict staggered past him, Memphis murmured, "Do come in." He looked into the hallway.

Didn't see anyone.

He almost smiled. Instead, he shut the door and turned to face the annoying asshole who was wasting his time.

You're not the one I want to see.

Eliza is.

CHAPTER FIVE

"I assume you checked out my background?" Memphis crossed his arms over his chest and propped his shoulders against the door.

"Fifteen thousand is a lot of money," Benedict gritted out. "Just walk away."

"If you *did* check my background—or get someone in your employ to do the work for you, something tells me you are a delegating type of guy—then you should really know that I'm not the type to walk away."

Benedict's lashes flickered.

Ah. So he did know that.

"Twenty," Benedict said.

How high would he go? Memphis was vaguely curious to know. "Yeah, sorry, not interested. I have a job to do, and I intend to do it."

"Job?" Benedict pounced on that word choice. "Someone else is already paying you? Who? Why?"

Settle down, bro. "I'm actually not getting paid. Just doing it out of the kindness of my heart." He smiled.

"Bullshit."

"Whatever." Like Memphis cared what Benedict believed. Now the sister on the other hand... "Where is Eliza?"

"Do you know what it would do to her to have this mess dragged into the public arena again? To have her face splashed on the news and to be clickbait on every online gossip site? Do you know how many nightmares she's had? Do you know how scared she used to be just to walk outside?" Rage vibrated in each word. "You're not stirring this mess up for her again."

The rage appeared genuine. Good to know. Memphis nodded. "So you do care about her. I wondered. Said to myself...*Memphis, is this asshat just trying to protect his image and his company or does he care at all about finding the man who hurt his sister*?"

Benedict's nostrils flared. "I don't like you."

"This may surprise you to hear, but I actually get that response a lot." His hands fell to his sides, and he leaned forward, as if to reveal a dark secret. "It never really matters to me. I do not give a shit."

Benedict's nostrils flared again. "Eliza is not going to work with you. She will not help you."

Maybe. Maybe not. "I intend to find this bastard with or without her help. Your sister isn't the only person who was hurt. Other families are out there, and they never got their loved ones back. They need closure. They need justice." He'd give it to them.

"Right. And like this isn't some publicity stunt for the Ice Breakers?"

"Ah. So you *did* thoroughly research me. Good for you."

For a moment, it looked as if Benedict might explode. His cheeks puffed out, his eyes bulged...

"The Ice Breakers don't care about publicity," Memphis said. "As for me personally, I don't want my name splashed anywhere. Not much for the limelight. My team is just trying to help the people everyone else forgot." He let his brows climb. "What I really don't get is why *you* wouldn't want him found. You did believe her, didn't you?"

"Yes." A hiss.

Good answer. "Dragging this bastard into the light will make everyone else believe her, too. And it will stop another woman from being taken. Because this bastard, it's not like he's just gonna wake up one morning and decide to change his life. He won't decide to stop being a monster. He will continue his pattern until he has no choice." *Until he's locked away or until he's buried in the ground.*

And instead of exploding, Benedict seemed to shrivel. The fire left his eyes and his breath rushed out on a sigh as his shoulders sagged. But he still said, "Twenty-five grand."

"No."

"Any price you *would* take?"

This guy was vaguely interesting. Not nearly as interesting as Eliza, but still...vaguely. "I don't think your heart is really into this whole buy-off scene." Sure didn't seem to be that way. "Who sent you to make the offer?"

Benedict's lips clamped together.

"My guess would be your father? He the one really pushing for this to all go away?"

Benedict didn't answer.

"Or maybe it's the stepmother?" A distinct possibility. "Heard she really didn't like all the publicity at the time. Stole the attention from her wedding."

Again, Benedict didn't answer.

So Memphis took another step closer to him. "I don't think you want to be here. I don't think you want to be buying me off."

Benedict held his stare.

"I think you learned that I am the real fucking deal," Memphis added grimly. "But someone else told you I still had to go away. So you came here and made your half-ass offer, and now that I've said no, part of you is happy because you think someone is finally going to help Eliza."

Benedict seemed to have been carved from stone.

"I will," Memphis swore, voice soft. "You might not like my methods, be warned about that. You might not like the way I work, but I do get shit done, and I will not give up. I will stay close to Eliza. I will watch her every moment, so I can promise she will not be hurt. But things are gonna get ugly. They always do. You need to be ready to handle the backlash that will come from whoever is trying to pull your strings." He waited a beat. "Think you can deal with that?"

And Benedict continued to hold his stare. "Yes."

Well, well... "Then you might not be such a giant dick, after all. Good for you."

Benedict shouldered past him and headed for the door. "Something tells me you *are* the giant dick."

He put a hand to his heart. "Aw, have you been talking to my exes? I mean, it's fairly impressive but I'm not one to normally brag about size."

Benedict glanced back. "You're fucking insane."

"Just crazy enough to be able to catch the bad guys. My track record speaks for itself."

Benedict yanked open the door. Marched away.

Memphis watched him head toward the elevator. That had certainly been an interesting conversation. Someone in Eliza's world wanted her past buried as deeply as possible—and that person didn't care that a killer was still out hunting in the world.

That person was *not* her brother.

Benedict might have plenty of faults, but he appeared to love his sister.

Benedict vanished into the elevator. Memphis kept standing in the doorway. "He's gone," he finally said. "You can come out now."

There was a small alcove just to the right. An ice machine nestled in the corner of that alcove and a drink machine—stocked with severely overpriced sodas—stood beside it. Not a very big area, but he realized it had been just the perfect hiding space for her.

Slowly, Eliza appeared. First, he saw her dark hair. Then her dark eyes. She wore a loose black top. Faded jeans that fit her like a second skin. Elegant sandals on her delicate feet.

He lifted an eyebrow. "Do you often hide in corners so that you can avoid your brother?"

She nibbled on her lower lip. Glanced toward the elevator, then back at him. "More often than you would probably suspect."

Dammit. There she went. Being all interesting again. "I like you way better than him."

Her steps were silent as she headed toward him. "Most people do. Or at least, they pretend to. I'm not sure most of the individuals we encounter honestly like either of us. There's a lot of pretending in my world."

He still stood in the open doorway of his hotel room. "I like you. I don't lie. Remember that about me. Life is too short to waste on bullshit."

Eliza glanced over her shoulder, as if she expected Benedict to pop out at any moment. "Why...why was he here?" Her gaze swung back to Memphis.

"To offer me cash to vanish."

She sucked in a quick breath.

"I refused, of course." She was truly fucking gorgeous. That skin of hers was flawless. And her lips—plump and full. Red.

He wondered how she would taste.

Later. "And then, your brother and I—after I told him to shove the money up his ass, but just so you know, I used much more refined terms—we came to an agreement. Of sorts."

A lock of her hair slid over her shoulder. "Do you think you and I can come to an agreement?"

He moved back and swept his arm out to indicate that she should come inside with him. "Abso-fucking-lutely."

But she didn't cross over the threshold. Just stayed in the hallway. Truly not the best spot to do business, especially if she was in the mood for privacy.

He wondered why she was—

"You scare me," Eliza confessed.

His heart seemed to squeeze. The damn thing needed to stop doing that shit. "Well, then we need to work on correcting that situation."

"I did my research on you. I know about all the criminals you've hunted. Dangerous, deadly people. The things you had to do in order to catch them..."

He rolled one shoulder in a shrug and tried to look harmless. When the tension didn't leave her gaze, Memphis figured he'd failed in his attempt. "I am dangerous."

She wet her lips.

"Definitely deadly." A nod from him. "But then I would have to be, or I wouldn't have been a very good bounty hunter. For the record, I made a habit of going after the worst of the worst. Want to know why?"

A nod.

"Because the worst ones are the ones who need to be stopped the most. The guy who took you? I will stop him. One way of another." He should probably try to soften his voice or something. Do some little action that made him seem less scary. But hell if he knew what that action should be. He'd never been the soothing or reassuring type.

She moved her head in another jerky nod. "Then I'm in."

Hell, yes. Hell, *yes*.

Her eyes darted over his shoulder, to the quiet hotel room. "Maybe we should talk? Come up with a game plan?"

He already had a plan. It was time for him to share that plan. In fact, they could actually get started on his master plan right now. The best way to do that?

Be seen with her.

"I do my best strategizing over dinner." He grabbed his keys and wallet from the nearby table. "Hungry?"

"I...sure?" More a question than an affirmation.

"Good. Then let's go, and I'll tell you everything I know."

***

This isn't a bad decision. Eliza told herself that for maybe the tenth time as she sat across the table from Memphis. He'd picked the place, a family-run Italian restaurant around the corner from his hotel. He strolled in with her as if they were on a date, even gallantly pulling out her chair before ordering some wine.

When the waiter came back with their wine, Eliza ordered chicken alfredo and Memphis decided—

"Same thing." He put down his menu. Leaned back in his chair, and as the waiter disappeared again, Memphis's eyes seemed to drink her in. "Do you want to know about the others?"

Absolutely, she did. Her head jerked in agreement.

"First, they don't look like you. I know there are plenty of stories that circulate saying serials always pick the same type of victim. Same hair, same eyes, same body type. And, I suppose, to a certain extent, there are some similarities...you are all young, attractive females. At the time of the abductions, you were either heading to a bar or you had just left one. You were alone at the time."

She could feel the goose bumps growing on her arms. "I was leaving the bar." She could remember that part so clearly. She'd been there with friends—Bethany had been at the bar with her. They'd been celebrating the end of the semester. Exams had been done, and they'd just wanted to let off some steam. "I-I felt sick."

His gaze sharpened. "What?"

"I was leaving because I felt sick." She didn't reach for the wine. Instead, her fingers curled around the glass of water, and she brought it up to her suddenly parched lips.

"That wasn't in the police report."

Report. She put the glass back down. A few droplets slid down the side of the glass. "You read a report on me?"

"Sweetheart, I have four manila files full of data on you. I believe in being very thorough. Research is my bread and butter." A hint of annoyance darkened his tone as he added, "There was no mention that you were sick before you left the bar."

"I told Bethany..."

The flash was in her mind. She could see herself. With one hand gripping the black-painted edge of the bar top. Another pressing to her overheated forehead. *"I have to go...It's way too hot. I...I don't feel..."*

"I'll need to go back and see if something like this wasn't reported with the other victims." His right hand balled into a fist and slid under his chin. His whole pose was like that of someone studying a puzzle. "At the hospital, you were tested to see if you were drugged, but the test results didn't show anything."

Her hands twisted in her lap. He couldn't see the nervous movement. "You're not the only one who can research. I did research on my own. Most drugs leave the body in twelve to seventy-two hours. It was over forty-eight before I made it back to my father's house. Forty-eight *lost* hours."

"You truly have no memory of that time?"

"Bits and pieces." Flashes that came and went in her head, like little clips from a movie. Something she'd seen. Not lived.

He absorbed that info. Kept studying her—not in a clinical way, his eyes held too much heat for that—but he looked at her as if he could see *into* her. "Ketamine can cause memory problems."

"Yes," Soft. She glanced around. The other couples in the restaurant were leaning close to each other. Whispering. Laughing softly. She was at a table with the most gorgeous man she'd ever met, and she was talking about murder and the monster who'd tried to destroy her. That seemed right. Her gaze flickered back to Memphis. "It can also cause a loss in your sense of time. It can make you unable to move." Wasn't that something that she feared? That she'd been helpless in those lost hours.

He leaned forward, a fast, jerking movement. "You weren't raped."

A shake of her head. "You did read my files."

"Told you, I—"

"Thorough, check." She remembered the testing. The way she'd stared at the ceiling as a tear had leaked down her cheek. *Sexual assault forensic exam.* "There was no sign of a sexual assault. No bruising. No tearing. I was still wearing all my clothing that I'd had on the last time anyone saw me."

His eyes darkened to an even bolder green. "I can kill the sonofabitch for you."

Her breath froze in her lungs. "Excuse me?" He had not said—

"You heard me."

She looked around to see if anyone else had heard him.

"I hate that he hurt you. I hate that he left you scared. And I will end him for you."

Her stare whipped back to Memphis. "I—"

"I have bread for you," the waiter announced.

She nearly jumped out of her chair.

"Fresh from the oven," he continued with a wide smile. "And you must try our special honey butter to go with it. Absolutely divine—"

"Yeah, so..." Memphis didn't look away from her even as he addressed the waiter. "There's an extra fifty in it for you if you only come back when the food is ready, and you make sure no one disturbs us."

The waiter practically flew away.

"That was a little rude," she chided.

"Was it? How about that? I think I'm a little rude." A shrug as if that wasn't any big concern. "But he'll still get the extra money and we'll get our privacy, so I really believe it's win, win for everyone."

"You threatened to kill him."

"The waiter? Nah. I bribed him. There's a big difference." He helped himself to the bread.

She kept twisting her hands beneath the table "I'm talking about the man—the man we're after."

"I didn't threaten. I offered." He glanced up at the ceiling as he seemed to consider his words. "Maybe I promised." He mulled that. Chewed some bread. "Yep, it was a definite promise."

"Why?"

His stare came back to her. "Because I find that the idea of anyone hurting you—in any way—makes me feel even more savage than normal."

She leaned toward him. "You're in a public restaurant." Her voice was hushed. Whispery. "You can't just threaten to kill someone over—over bread."

He leaned toward her. Smiled. "Sure, I can, princess." *His* voice was deep and rumbly and darkly sexy. They were leaning so close that it probably looked as if they were about to kiss.

She wondered what it would be like to kiss him.

The thought had her jerking back.

He moved back, too, only much, much slower. "Rohypnol also leads to memory loss." He lifted a hand and started ticking off items one finger at a time... "Also leads to loss of muscle control, issues talking, nausea. Your blood pressure can bottom out." His lips thinned. "Then, of course, there's GHB. Another contender we can't overlook. When you're drugged with GHB, you can't remember what's happening. You get nauseous, you sweat, you can have tremors."

Her hands curled, and her short nails bit into her palms. "There are also plenty of other drugs out there that can cause memory loss. But, uh, not everyone believed my lack of a memory was due to being drugged."

His lips thinned. "You're talking about the asshats who said you faked everything?"

"Actually, no." A slow exhale. "My dad made me see a therapist. She suggested I was just unconsciously blocking the memories because it was such a traumatic event. She said I didn't have to be drugged in order for the memory loss to have occurred. The therapist suggested that my mind shut everything out as a way of protecting me. She thought I might be better never knowing."

He took more bread. "That what you want? To never know?"

Absolutely not. "I want to know *exactly* what happened. That's why I'm here with you now."

"You're here with me because you're a fighter. It's the same reason you got away from him. He didn't realize he'd taken a fucking hellcat, did he?"

She froze in shock. "That's...that's not what I am. Not who I am." He was completely mistaken.

"Um. I think it's exactly who you are. I think you gave him the fight of his life, and you got away. After you, he had to be a whole lot more careful. He probably learned from you. Fixed it so that no one else *could* get away."

Cold air seemed to blow over her skin. "I want to hear more about the others."

"Amelia. Casey. Layla. Drew. Tameka. Stephanie."

The names seemed to echo through her. No, they seemed to *pierce* her. Sinking into her body like the plunge of a knife's blade.

"I have pictures of them in my files. Like I said, you all look different, but you had certain similarities in common. You were all young, female, and alone. And..."

The waiter was approaching. She could see him darting toward them with a tray in his hands.

"Each year, a new woman has gone missing either around—or in most cases *on*—the anniversary of the date you were taken."

For just an instant, the restaurant seemed to spin.

That night...that terrible night...

The anniversary was coming up again. So soon.

The waiter put their food in front of them. Asked about adding cheese. Said some other things that she couldn't hear over the ringing in her ears.

"It's two weeks away," Memphis said bluntly as soon as the waiter stepped back to attend to other customers. "That means he's going to be hunting again. It means we have to stop him before he takes someone else. The day is damn significant for him, and we have to figure out why—"

"I know it's significant," Eliza said. She didn't touch her food. Couldn't. Her appetite had vanished as soon as he named the other women. "He never lets me forget."

"What?" An alertness seemed to sweep over Memphis's strong form.

The lump in her throat felt huge. With an effort, Eliza choked it down. "He doesn't let me forget. Every year on the anniversary, he sends me flowers. Flowers just like the ones I can see in some of my flashes."

Memphis dropped the fork he'd just picked up. "You are fucking kidding me."

If only. "No, I'm not. He sends me flowers every year on the anniversary." Very specific flowers. "Sunflowers. And I—I can remember running through a field of sunflowers. Can remember it...can see a flash of it..." Sunflowers were supposed to be beautiful and happy. But she hated them. *Hated them.* "Just a brief image. A moon shining down on the flowers. They are *everywhere.* I slip and fall into the dirt, and the flash is gone."

"Sonofabitch."

Eliza couldn't seem to stop talking. "There's never a card with the flowers. But I know it's him. Doesn't matter if I change my address. Doesn't matter where I go—I can be out of town, and the flowers still make it to me. Every. Year. He knows where I am. Like he's keeping tabs on me."

"Fucking hell."

"Yes." Very definite from her. "It has been fucking hell." She had the feeling Memphis was the first person who truly understood that. "The first time I got the sunflowers, I...I hadn't gotten the flashes before that point. I went into my office at work, and the sunflowers were just sitting on my desk."

A muscle flexed along his clenched jaw.

"I smiled." She hated this memory. "I thought my brother or father—I thought they were trying to cheer me up because I had been dreading the anniversary. I walked across the room. Touched a petal, and then in my head, I could see the sunflower field. The field beneath the full moon." Her hand lifted. Slid to her right temple. The faint scar she carried—one she tried to hide by parting her hair to the side. "I fell. Hit my head on the desk."

A low curse.

"I told my father that I remembered being in a field of sunflowers. I told the cops. But..." She just trailed away.

"But the dumbasses didn't believe you? They didn't know a sensory memory when they saw one staring them straight in the face?"

Her gaze darted around the restaurant. For the longest time, she'd hated going out in public because so many people would whisper and stare at her. Eliza still felt the stares sometimes. That uncomfortable awareness of someone watching her, but she'd learned to live with it. After all, it wasn't as if she could hide away forever.

So she'd learned to lock down her emotions. She smiled politely in public. And she went through the motions...

"Eliza."

Her gaze swung back to him. "They looked." She had to defend the cops and her father. "Daniel—Detective Jones—he searched the area for a potential sunflower field that I could have been running through that night."

"Detective Jones." A twist of his lips. "Interesting that he didn't mention the field to me in our chat."

"What chat?" But she shook her head, banishing the question for now. She needed to explain everything. "He wasn't a detective when I was abducted, just a beat cop who was trying to help."

"I bet. The fact that he wanted in your pants had nothing to do with it. Guy is a total helper."

"Wh-what?" Her hand flew up and out. Hit the glass of water beside her and sent the glass wobbling back and forth and—

His fingers curled around the glass before it could fall and spill. "Easy."

She shook her head. "H-he wasn't helping because he wanted to..." Her voice dropped to a whisper as she finished, "Have sex with me."

His eyes gleamed as Memphis leaned toward her once more. "Princess..."

"I am not a princess."

"You seem like one to me."

"I'm *not.*"

He leaned ever closer. "True story time. Your cop buddy Danny wanted to have sex with you back then. He wants to have sex with you now. Helping you on your case—hell, *solving* the mystery for you—he would have thought that gave him a definite in with you."

"You're saying he only wanted to help because he wanted to get me in bed?" Her breath huffed out. "What about you? Are you only sitting here with me right now because you want the same thing?" The words just burst out, and, too late, she heard them seem to echo in the air around her.

Too intimate. You never should have said something so personal—

A slow smile curled Memphis's mouth. "Make no mistake, I would absolutely love to get you in bed...That is a definite goal for me."

CHAPTER SIX

She leapt to her feet.

Anticipating that she was about to do a very graceful—yet still angry—rush away from him, Memphis casually threw out his hand and curled his fingers around her far too delicate wrist. "But your extreme sexiness aside, I am here because I want to find the bastard. I want to stop him. I intend to see justice served."

Her pulse point raced beneath his touch. "You're mocking me."

"No. I'm being dead serious with you. Told you already," his head tipped back as he stared up at her, "I don't waste time on bullshit. I say what I think. I think you're incredibly attractive. Do I want to take you to bed?"

Her cheeks flashed that faint pink as she nervously glanced around the restaurant. Worried someone would hear his confession about her?

He didn't give a damn who heard him.

"Absolutely," Memphis told her as his fingers tightened just the tiniest bit around her wrist so he could draw her attention—and those fabulous eyes of hers—back to him. "I would love to have you in my bed. That's one thing. A completely separate item from my business in this town. The business in question? I want to drag this piece of shit who took you—and all of those other women—out of the shadows and make him pay for what he did. Hell, yes, I do want that." He lightly tugged on her wrist. "Now that we've cleared that up, will you please sit down? There's more we need to discuss." And she hadn't eaten. Not even a bite of bread. Eliza should eat something.

Her jaw tightened, but she sat.

He had to reluctantly let her wrist go.

He picked up his fork, thinking she would do the same.

She didn't. Eliza sat, stiff and nervous, across from him. He had so many questions that he wanted to ask, but he knew those questions were going to terrify her. She'd just made one seriously big reveal to him, and that reveal changed the game completely.

The perp was keeping watch on her. Something that Memphis had never expected. Suddenly, he was incredibly glad her overprotective father had gotten guards for her, even if those guards weren't the best. *Better them than nothing else.*

But things had changed with her revelation. Now, she wouldn't have subpar protection. She'd have the best out there. She'd have him. "Game changer."

"Excuse me?"

He wolfed down more chicken alfredo. "You're not eating."

"I don't...I'm not very hungry."

She needed to fucking eat. "How are you gonna help me track down the bad guy if you're not eating right? My mom always said you can't run on an empty tank."

A furrow appeared between her eyebrows. "Well, no, you can't—"

"Then eat."

She reached for a fork. Took the tiniest bite in the world.

"Why didn't they find your sunflower field?" Memphis wanted to know.

"Because there wasn't one. Not according to Daniel. From the look of things, wherever I escaped from...I *walked* home. My bare feet were bloody and covered in dirt. No one ever came forward and said they'd given me a ride. When I arrived at my father's reception, there was security footage of me just walking out from the darkness. So Daniel said..." Another small bite. "He said if there was a sunflower field, it would have needed to be in the radius that the cops had calculated for me. There are several fields just outside of Houston, but he said there were none close enough that would have fit."

This news just pissed him off. "Or they didn't have a big enough radius for you." Dumbasses. "Maybe you traveled farther than they thought. You were gone for over forty-eight hours. For all they know, you escaped right away. Maybe you were traveling that whole time. Maybe you snuck on the back of a truck and the driver didn't even know you'd hitched a ride—that could be why someone didn't come forward to talk about helping you. It could have been an unaware good Samaritan."

Her gaze never left him.

"Hell, you could have stolen a fucking bicycle and ridden it. That would have let you travel faster and farther than being on foot. I can think of a dozen different scenarios that would change things for you. Daniel should have taken you to those fields. Let you look around. He should have gotten crime scene teams out there—"

"He said that he did go and talk to a few of the owners of the fields. They didn't have anything to contribute to the investigation." Her long, dark lashes lowered to shield her eyes. "And I did go out there, too. Without telling Daniel. I just wanted to see if I would have another flash."

His gut tightened. "Did you?"

She put down the fork. "No. The sunflowers had all been cut when I was at those fields. Nothing looked familiar. Nothing *felt* familiar. There was no sense that I'd been there before." A long exhale. "Look, I'd really like to talk more about the other women." Her lashes lifted, and she bit her lower lip.

I get that, baby, I do. Because you want to know what happened to them. But she was the one who could give him clues, and with the anniversary of her abduction less than two weeks away, they didn't have a whole lot of time.

Before someone else vanished...

"The friend you mentioned," Eliza began. "You said her sister was taken?"

Yes. "Delilah's fraternal twin sister went missing. Layla Darrow. It's been five years, and there has never been any sign of her. No real leads in her case. Not until you." Almost five years to the fucking day, and he knew each of those years haunted Delilah. His friend had just married, and even at her wedding, he'd seen the sadness that clung to her as she thought of her sister.

But now things have changed. Because of Eliza.

Delilah was a first-rate reporter. She wrote her stories under the name of Lila Darrow. Most of her friends even just called her Lila. He didn't usually, though, because he was an ornery bastard who liked to be different. Life was more entertaining that way.

"I'm not a lead."

"Yes, prin—uh, Eliza, you are. You're the only survivor. That makes you one hell of a lead."

Once more, her hand flew up and jerked, hitting the water glass. This time, he didn't move quickly enough to stop the accident, and the glass fell onto the table and spilled. The water soaked the linen tablecloth.

The waiter rushed forward.

Memphis gazed into Eliza's pain-filled eyes—eyes that had gone even darker. He nodded. "Know what?" Memphis addressed the waiter. "We'll take the check. And maybe some to-go boxes." Because it was past time to get her the hell out of there.

You're the only survivor.

***

"You really didn't have to follow me home," Eliza said as she turned toward Memphis.

"I did." He pushed his hands into the pockets of his jeans. "And now I need to come inside, too."

She took a step back. They were in her building—a building with absolute top-notch security. A guard was always on duty downstairs, and every floor was equipped with cameras. She lived on the top level, in the penthouse. The place gave her amazing views of the city, and it was pretty much as close to a fortress as her father had been able to create.

He owned the building. One of his many properties. So he always made sure it was extra safe.

"Are you coming in so you can tell me more about the other victims?" Eliza asked. Those women were already haunting her, and she'd never seen their faces. *I could have been lost, too. Never returned home.*

"I'm coming in..." A roll of one powerful shoulder. "Because I'm staying with you."

She sucked in a quick breath. *Oh, no. No, no. Bad idea.* "Look, I don't know what you *think* is happening here, but—"

"I think you're in far more danger than I originally realized. I think I'm probably about to scare you to death, but there are some important facts you need to understand."

A chill skated down her spine. "Excuse me?"

He looked toward the elevator. "You're the only one on this floor."

"Yes."

"Daddy's building?"

She didn't like the way he said that, even if, dammit, yes, it was true. "I pay rent just like every other tenant."

"Sure, from the job you have...at your father's company..."

Eliza took a hard step toward him. "I work *hard* at that company. Often fifty-to-sixty-hour weeks, so don't dare imply that I am some spoiled rich girl who—"

"Ah." A smile. "There she is. Bet if you had a beer in your hand, you'd be dumping it on me, wouldn't you?"

"What?"

"I don't think you're some spoiled rich girl. I did my homework on you. I know you work your ass off, that you should probably be the VP at Robinson Corporation instead of your brother—a brother I am guessing you actually *help* a whole lot behind the scenes—and I know when you're not at the family business, keeping the empire in order, you're working with a half a dozen charitable groups. I honestly don't see where you find time to have a social life." He squinted at her. "Or *do* you find time?"

Eliza straightened her spine. "My social life is none of your concern."

"Wrong. It is. One hundred percent."

He was making no sense. "Are you trying to drive me crazy?"

"Absolutely not. Unless, of course, I'm driving you crazy with desire for me."

Why did he keep saying things like that? Her breath shuddered out.

His gaze darted around the corridor once more. "I am curious about just how close of a watch your father is keeping on you—and your safety. This building could be breached far too easily. I'll have to talk with him about that situation. Then I'll want to look at your workspace. See what we can do to strengthen security there, too."

She was getting such a bad feeling in the pit of her stomach. And that feeling got worse when he said...

"I really don't think it will be hard at all to convince your father that I should be put in charge of your protection. Instead of attempting to buy me off tonight, your brother should have just hired me." Memphis waved away the issue. "No matter. I'll be in charge from here on out, and I'll make the necessary changes."

"*No.*"

He blinked. "No?"

"I have enough guards. I don't need more. I need less. I need—"

Memphis stepped right up to her. He towered over her. Seemed to surround her. His rich, masculine scent teased her nostrils, and his voice rumbled—all dark, deep, and commanding, as he told her, "Hard truth time, princess. You need *me*. You need me because the sonofabitch who abducted you before? He's still locked on you. That is a very dangerous thing. So far, he's moved on to other victims, and those poor women never came home. But he hasn't forgotten you. I don't think he ever will. He sends you the flowers either right before he takes a new victim or right after—

I don't know which yet, but I will figure it out. He does that, though, because he wants you connected to what he's doing. You're a part of this for him, and I don't see him ever completely letting you go."

Memphis couldn't know all that. "You're not some profiler, you don't know—"

"I mentioned before that I had a friend who was former FBI. Elijah Cross was the best when it came to getting in the heads of serials. Though, technically, he wasn't called a profiler. Went by the title of behavioral analyst. That was his job. And he was very, very good at analyzing the behavior of serials."

A serial killer. It just still didn't seem real.

"Elijah is on my team. He helped me to learn as much as I could about the SOB that we're after, and I can tell you now, when I report on what's been happening with your fucking sunflower deliveries to him, Elijah is going to flip the hell out."

She backed away from Memphis because he seemed to be taking over her space. Big and strong and hot. The heat from his body stretched out to wrap around her even as his words caused fear to lodge deep inside of her.

I am so tired of being afraid. She was so tired of looking over her shoulder. She wanted this to end. "I don't have a social life." Her chin lifted. Why had she gone back to that question? He'd asked if she found time, and the answer was, no, she didn't.

"Seems a crying shame," he murmured.

Was it? "I haven't been with a lover in several years." *Oh, dear God.* Why had she said that? Eliza turned, gave him her back, and unlocked her door. She slipped into her home and disabled the security system so the beeps would stop.

He shut the door softly behind her. The flipping of the locks seemed very loud. Maybe he wouldn't say anything about her last statement. Maybe he would just pretend she hadn't blurted out that ever-so-personal detail.

"Are the men in your life just dumbasses?" Memphis wanted to know.

She walked toward her windows. Didn't turn on any lights because there was no need. The curtains were open, and the city shone brightly. "It's not easy getting close to me."

His steps were certain as he crossed to her. His arm brushed against hers. "Seems like I'm close right now. Got here easy enough."

He was close. Memphis—big, bold, confusing, terrifying, dangerous, and sexy—he was *very* close. Eliza slanted a glance his way. "I don't know what to make of you."

His rumble of laughter wrapped around her. "I get that a lot."

Her head turned toward him. The better to study Memphis. "I don't know how to play the games that men and women play."

One eyebrow quirked. "Something tells me you can figure that shit out."

"No, no, I—" She blew out a breath. "I don't want to play games. Lovers want more from me than I can give. They want to know my secrets. They want for me to laugh and flirt and be carefree and let down my guard for them and I just—"

"Can't." No more amusement. The teasing light had vanished from his eyes almost as suddenly as it had appeared.

She looked back out at the city. "Can't," she said. Why was she telling him all of this? Why was she opening up so much to this stranger? Except Memphis didn't feel like a stranger. "Before I came to your hotel room tonight, I talked to five different cops who had worked with you on previous cases." Not beat cops. Lieutenants. Chiefs. "Want to know what they said?"

"Probably that I was incredibly charming. A true gem of a human being."

Her gaze slanted back toward him. "You joke a lot."

"Who is joking? I am charming. And a gem. Bet the people you spoke with wish they knew more guys like me."

"Actually, yes." Her hands pressed to her thighs. Her index finger tapped quickly, then stopped. "That was a refrain from them. More guys like you would make their jobs easier. They told me you were one of the most dangerous, single-minded individuals that they'd ever met. That when you were focused on a target, you never gave up, not until you'd taken down your prey. They told me..." *Take a breath*. She did, then finished, "They said I could count on you."

"You can."

"I want that to be true." No, more than just that... "I *need* it to be true." Once more, she faced him. "I will give you all my secrets. I will let you past the walls I've made, but I want to count on you. Completely. I don't want you doing this for fame, for some challenge, and certainly not because you're...you're looking to get hired by me or my family."

He never glanced away from her.

"Because all of those reasons..." She swallowed. "They mean that you can turn on me. That you can sell my secrets. That I can become just another tabloid story again. And they mean that I can put all my faith in you, but then, in the end, I can wind up with nothing."

His arms remained loose at his sides. "Why do you want me to be doing this?"

Because you just want to help me. Because you believe in me. Because someone finally does.

"Fair enough." A nod from him even though she hadn't spoken. "I'll tell you why *I'm* doing this—hell, I already did, but I'll say it again. I owe my friend Delilah."

Right. Delilah. And an uncomfortable feeling—an odd tightness—unfurled in Eliza's chest. *Was it...wait, am I jealous?*

"She's a good person. Never let me down, not even once. So when she asked me to find out what happened to her sister, I said I would. See, one thing you should know about me, I never break a promise."

That was something easy to say. Hard to do in real practice, though.

"I'm going to stop him because he's a sonofabitch who needs stopping. I swear, I'm not doing this for fame. Fuck that. I'm doing this because monsters live in the world, and if I'm not going to use my talents to hunt them, then who the hell will?"

She could accept that answer. "What do I have to do?" In order to help him.

He extended his hand to her. "Start by shaking. You and I—we'll be partners from here on out."

She'd never had a partner before. Her fingers curled around his. A lick of heat pulsed through her. That seemed to always happen when she touched him.

"You'll trust me completely," he added. "After all, five cops said you could, right?"

They had. Eliza nodded.

"You'll tell me all your secrets. I'll stay at your side. We'll hunt the bastard. And when danger comes, you will follow my orders exactly, no questions asked."

The last part gave her pause. "I generally have questions. Especially when it's *my* life that's involved."

He was still holding her hand. Actually, his index finger had slid out and was lightly stroking along her pulse point. "Every order I give would be designed to protect you. Not just fired out because I'm an asshole. You'll follow my lead because it's the safe thing to do when danger is around us."

His touch was making her nervous. No, *he* was doing that.

"When you were doing your research on me, Eliza, I'm sure you saw that my little group and I—we've managed to close quite a few cases that stumped the authorities." Again, his finger stroked over her pulse.

She shivered. "Ice Breakers." That was what he'd called his group. What she'd seen them referred to online. And, yes, they had closed cases. They'd managed to find missing people that everyone else had seemingly forgotten. They'd brought killers to justice.

"I will do everything possible to find him. When it comes to tracking monsters, I know what I'm doing."

Yes. She believed that statement. "It's...it's getting late." Honestly, she had no idea what time it was. But the longer she spent standing there, staring into his eyes and feeling his fingers against her skin, the more tension she felt. The more awareness. She had been telling him the truth when she said that she hadn't been with a lover in years. Unfortunately, she'd developed a bit of a reputation in her circle.

She will freeze you if you make a move on her. Like she hadn't heard the whispers and mocking words a time or ten. But trust just wasn't easy for her. It never would be.

She tugged to free her hand. He let go instantly.

And she missed his touch. *Get a grip, woman.* "We should pick up our conversation tomorrow. I'm free in the morning." The next day was Saturday.

"We can definitely pick up the conversation tomorrow." He turned.

Eliza exhaled in relief. She followed quickly on his heels, thinking he was going for the door.

He marched toward the couch. Sat down. Wiggled a bit. "A little small, but it will do."

She stopped. "Do for what?" But, oh, no. Oh, *no,* she knew his answer...

"Sleeping, of course."

Impossible. "You're not sleeping here." She had *not* invited the man to camp out on her couch.

"Eliza..." A sigh of her name that came out sounding oddly sexy. Intimate. "Didn't we just cover that you were going to follow my lead in this situation?"

"You said I was supposed to follow your lead in *dangerous* situations." This didn't feel dangerous. "We said nothing about you spending the night!"

"I'm being a gentleman." He didn't get up. He did wiggle more. "I'm taking the couch. Not even asking you to share your bed with me." He turned, looking a bit toward her hallway as he craned his head. "Though knowing you, I bet you have silk sheets and the bed smells like heaven." A disappointed exhale. "A lavender heaven."

First, he didn't *know* her. Not like that. Not...not intimately. "Why do you keep joking about sex?"

His head swiveled back toward her. "Why do *you* keep thinking I am joking when I am one hundred percent serious?"

"You aren't."

Slowly, his gaze swept over her. From the top of her head to the bottom of her feet. Then back up, until he met her stare once more. "Got to circle back to this. What kind of dumbasses have you been hanging out with, sweet Eliza?"

"I—" She clamped her lips together.

"You're fucking beautiful. I wanted you from the instant I looked across the bar and saw you sitting on that stool. So do let me be clear." He rose once more. Towered over her.

Her head tipped back.

"I would like nothing more than to take you back into your bedroom, put you on your silk sheets, and fuck you long and hard on the bed that smells like heaven."

CHAPTER SEVEN

He'd probably overstepped. Memphis could see where he *probably* should have held back a little instead of just announcing that he wanted to fuck Eliza. Sure, he did like to say what he thought but...

He'd sent her running. Truly. *Running*. She'd mumbled something about the couch being fine for him and then she'd bolted on him. When her bedroom door had slammed shut, he'd actually felt the vibrations.

Memphis supposed he could take that as a sign that Eliza wasn't interested in his offer. Fair enough, he certainly would not push her, but he had wanted to be honest. When he was close to Eliza, his dick stood up and saluted and all he wanted was to put his hands all over her body and—

Creak.

A low sound, and if the penthouse hadn't been so still and silent otherwise, he might have missed it. But he didn't miss it, and Memphis knew the sound of a door opening when he heard it. The hinges on Eliza's bedroom door had just creaked open.

Best case scenario? She was coming out to seduce him.

Worst case? She was coming to try and kick his ass out. Not something that he wanted to happen because he truly did hope to keep her safe.

As she advanced on him, he caught the faint pad of her footsteps. Closer, closer…

"What will we tell people?" Eliza asked.

He'd settled on the couch, and he'd also kept open her curtains because he liked looking out at the city. A soft illumination spilled into the room, courtesy of the city's glow.

He sat up, pushing down the cover that he'd found in her hall closet. He'd plundered. That was his nature. He'd discovered a guest room but opted against using it because it was on the other side of the penthouse, and he wanted to be close to her front door.

Memphis had stripped off his shirt, shoes, and socks, but he'd left on his jeans and boxers. For her. So she wouldn't stumble onto his naked ass in the middle of the night. "Tell them about what?"

"About why we're together? About why you spent the night here with me?"

His hand rubbed over his jaw. She stood about five feet away, wearing a black slip of a gown that was pure sexy perfection. Tiny little straps on her shoulders. All silk. Stopped right at the middle of her thighs. *Give me strength.* "Fuck me."

"Excuse me?" A quick step toward him. "We're going to tell people that we're…ah, fucking?"

And the way the word came out of her sweet, prim mouth...

Yeah, baby, let's tell the world. If possible, his dick got even harder. And it had already been plenty hard.

"Are we..." Another tentative step from her. "Are we supposed to pretend to be in a relationship?"

He looked her over. More like drank her in. Then he rose. Advanced until they were nearly toe-to-toe. "I don't do the fake relationship bit. Goes along with my low tolerance for bullshit."

"Oh." Her tongue swiped over her lower lip.

"Don't get me wrong." *I want to touch her.* "Sometimes, I can see that deal sure as hell working out. Take my friend Delilah, for example. She pretended to be involved with Archer Radcliffe in order to draw out the perp who'd made Archer's ex vanish years ago, and the trick worked. Like a freaking charm. The killer came to the surface..." Though Delilah and Archer had both wound up facing one hell of a lot more danger than they'd anticipated. "And, end bonus for them, their pretend relationship resulted in them getting hitched."

"Archer," she breathed the name.

Breathed it with a little too much familiarity for Memphis's peace of his mind. "You know him?" Then, shit, he realized she probably did. Archer was rich as hell, and a lot of his business involved travel to Houston. He'd probably crossed paths with Eliza plenty of times. *If they dated, I will have to kick his ass.*

The thought gave him pause. Hold up. Was he...jealous? God forbid.

"I do know Archer. Though it's been a while since we've seen each other. I, um, stopped going out as much after the abduction, and, well, I'm sure you know what life was like for him in the last few years."

Half of the world *had* thought that Archer was a killer, until Delilah helped him prove his innocence. So, yes, Memphis knew what life had been like for him. "Tell me you didn't fuck him."

Her eyes widened. "Excuse me?"

His hand raked through his already disheveled hair. "There's been an unexpected complication with your case. I'm finding that I'm jealous and possessive. Weird, but, it is what it is."

"I have never had sex with Archer."

Memphis released the breath that he'd been holding. "Excellent to know. Because the guy is desperate to be my best friend, and if I'd found out that he ever so much as put a hand on you, those plans would have definitely been altered." More like permanently derailed.

Her head tilted. "I don't understand you."

"Get that all the time," he assured her.

"You and Delilah," Eliza began, voice halting. "Since she's with him, I take it that the two of you never, ah..."

"Yeah, never. I'm single in case you were wondering."

Another quick lick of her tongue over her lower lip. "What makes you think I was wondering?"

Because I'm hopeful. "Because you came out to me wearing the sexiest damn negligee I've ever seen. If you wanted to send a hands-off message, I suspect you would have put on a robe before taking your stroll. Or maybe you just wanted to make me drool a bit?"

Her shoulders straightened. "Or maybe my clothing choice has absolutely nothing to do with you and everything to do with what *I* like? And I happen to like sleeping in short gowns because they give me freedom of movement."

He loved the fire in her voice. "Then let me just say that I heartily approve of your fashion choices."

A huff from her. "We're not pretending to be lovers."

"Nope." Because that would be torture, and he wasn't into that. Being close to her every day, touching her, kissing her and knowing everything was just pretend? *Hell, no.*

"Then what will we tell people?"

"I like the truth. We're hunting the bastard who took you."

"Won't that—will that make him be even more on guard?"

Potentially. "Could also make him sloppy. Don't know what option will win yet." He paused. "Or, since I'm taking over your security, if you prefer, you can tell everyone I'm the new bodyguard. Another true option that works for me."

"But it's not true."

"Oh, it is. The guards your family hired aren't gonna cut it. I'm taking over. We'll be hunting together, and I don't want some wannabe heroes in my way. So they need to take a backseat for the case." They could stay in the periphery, but he would be running the show.

Her head moved in a nod. "Yes, I would hate for them to get in the way. I don't want anyone hurt." Another nod, as if she'd made a decision. "You're my bodyguard. That's exactly what we can say." She spun on her heel. Began to head back to her bedroom. Fast, quick steps.

"Aren't you a little bit curious?" Memphis called out.

She stilled. "About what?"

"About what it would be like to kiss me."

Her shoulders stiffened. She took a step forward. He thought she'd keep walking away.

Then she whirled back toward him. "I know what it would be like."

"You do?"

"Yes."

She fascinated him. "And what would it be like?"

Eliza took a step toward him. "I'm sure it would be...intense."

Fair enough. "I have been known to be an intense kind of guy."

Eliza crept closer. "Hot, of course."

"Hot?" he repeated.

"You know, very sensual."

He smiled at her. "You think I have skills."

Another step. "I think...I think kissing you would be quite pleasurable."

His jaw almost hit the floor. He yanked it back up and glowered. "Hell, no, it wouldn't be."

"No?"

"It would be a whole lot more than just 'quite pleasurable' for us, I can promise you that." The very idea was insulting. "My kiss would be so good that you'd want to rip off all my clothes. To rip off yours. So good that you'd want to have sex with me immediately. So good that you'd pretty much never want to kiss another man for the rest of your life because you would know all those other bastards would just forever disappoint you because they weren't *me*."

She...laughed. An oddly sweet, musical sound that stroked right over him. "Someone has a high opinion of himself," Eliza murmured. Another slow glide of her feet that brought her right back in front of him.

"Not bragging. Just stating facts." He wanted her mouth. "Kiss me." Low, husky. A dare. He remembered that she liked dares. "See if I'm worth the hype."

He could feel her hesitation. She wasn't going to do it. She was going to turn away and—

"Go ahead," Memphis pushed her, voice rumbling. "I won't bite, unless you want me to, that is."

Eliza surged toward him. She shot up onto her tiptoes and her hands wrapped around his shoulders. Her mouth crashed against his.

Her movements were fast, hurried, and a little awkward. Overall, sexy as fuck.

Because this moment mattered, because he wasn't just a hype guy, his hands curled slowly and carefully around her hips. He brought her even closer against him so that their bodies brushed. His lips parted, and his tongue slid out to press lightly to her mouth.

Let me in, baby. Let me in.

Her mouth opened. The seduction began. Memphis knew how to kiss. He knew how to kiss very well. So he savored and caressed and he took his time so he could have her pushing eagerly against him. So he could have her tongue meeting his with fierce need. So he could have her opening her mouth wider to give him better access. So he could have—

She moaned. A low sound in the back of her throat, and her short nails bit into his skin. The moan did something to him. The hungry, soft, little sound ratcheted up his desire.

And his hold stopped being quite *so* gentle. His grip tightened even as his kiss became more demanding. Desire drummed through him. Lust heated his blood. He lifted her up, and when her legs wrapped around his hips, it just seemed like the most natural movement in the world.

Her nightgown had hiked up. He could practically feel her heat, and Eliza rocked her hips against his. Once, twice...

Another little moan came from her.

Fuck, yes. He could feel the sharp peaks of her nipples pushing against his chest. He tore his mouth from hers and began to kiss a hot path down her neck. His ultimate goal? *Getting to her perfect breasts.*

"Memphis..." A gasp of his name.

He *loved* the way she said his name. With need and want. So much desire. He took some lurching steps forward and pinned her to the nearest wall. Her back hit the smooth, white surface and her nails bit deeper into his arms.

He lifted her higher. Positioned her just so he could—

"Memphis?"

He took one nipple into his mouth. Sucked it through the silk and felt the absolute jolt that went through her. He kept her pinned with one hand on her waist. The position she was in had her straddling his hips, and it was so easy to move his other hand around…to dip it down toward…

"A kiss," she breathed. "It was just—just supposed to be a kiss."

He froze.

"But…I want you to touch me," she admitted, voice a husky temptation. "Touch me, Memphis."

Oh, hell, *yes. Hell, yes.* He took her nipple again, pulling it and the silk into his mouth. He laved her with his tongue, then forced his head to lift. "Where do you want to be touched, sweetheart?" But he knew. His fingers slid between their bodies. Eased under the silk of her nightgown. The silk—and the panties he could feel—were between him and his ultimate goal. "Right here?"

"Yes."

He stroked her through the silk. Strummed her. Rubbed the center of her need and just had to go back and kiss her mouth again because her lips were parted and she tasted so damn sweet.

This kiss wasn't careful. This kiss wasn't about seduction. It was just about taking. About need. About the lust that churned and burned inside of him, and as he kissed her, his fingers kept stroking her. He worked her clit through the silk, moving his fingers faster and a little harder even as he kissed her deeper and—

She gasped against his mouth. Her body tensed against his. He knew an impending release when he felt one, and his fingers just worked her ever faster because he wanted her to go over the edge. He kept stroking her. Pressing hard with his fingers. Hard and fast and giving Eliza just what he knew she needed until—

Her body quaked. Jerked. Her mouth pulled from his as she cried out with her release, and that breathless cry just made his savage lust all the stronger.

She shuddered. Shivered.

He watched the pleasure wash over her face, and he kept his fingers on her hot core as she came for him. *Hell, yes, baby.*

Her breath panted out. Quick and hard. Her legs had tightened around his hips. Fucking beautiful.

She was the most responsive partner he'd ever had. She'd gone up in flames beneath his touch, and he wanted *more*. Over and over again. He wanted his mouth on her when she came the next time. Wanted his tongue in her. Wanted to drive his dick into her over and over again.

He wanted to give her the kind of orgasm that would have her clawing at his back and *screaming* his name. His next goal, that was for sure.

For now...

Memphis locked his jaw. He carefully eased her legs down until her feet touched the floor. Her nightgown fell back into place.

"That was..." Her words trailed away.

So he finished for her. "One hell of a first kiss?" And, more than that, what he wanted to ask was...*Am I the first man who made you come with a first kiss?*

She cleared her throat. Her lashes fell to conceal her gaze. "I was going to say...that was the first time I've come just from a partner touching me. And, oh, God, you did it through my panties..."

Because you are responsive as fuck. Your body is ready to ignite for me. This time, he was the one to shudder. Need burned him up. "Baby, you really are hanging out with dumbasses."

Her lashes lifted. "I've, ah, taken care of myself, and the partners I had tried, but I-I couldn't let go enough to just feel. Not since—not since the abduction."

She felt pretty fucking fantastic to him. And her honesty was pushing him to the edge. "Let me get this straight. Just so there is no confusion on my end."

Eliza wet her lips.

"Are you telling me that you haven't come with a lover in—"

"A very long time," she finished quickly. Her words tumbled over each other.

Yep, she definitely has dumbasses in her life. As far as her coming... "I can do more." Not to brag but...yeah. Way more.

"What?"

"That release was like a little pop. Too fast. Not nearly strong enough."

"It felt pretty strong to me," she muttered.

"No. The next time—when we're both completely naked—and I'm buried in you, the climax will be so strong that you scream my name. That you nearly buck off the bed. That your nails tear into my back..."

She shook her head. Offered him a weak smile. "That sounds really fun..."

Fun? He had to laugh. "It will be plenty of fun for us both, trust me."

"But I've never been the type to do all of *that* before. At least, not since..." She stopped. Squared her shoulders. Slipped around him.

Memphis let her go because he knew when to push. And when to wait and fight another day. So his dick would just need to settle down because this was important.

"I think you would have liked me more if we'd met before I lost all that time. Before I disappeared." She bit her lower lip. "I used to be a lot more adventurous. Bethany said I was the one who would dance on the bar, and she was right. Back in those days, in college, I was the life of the party. I was up for adventure, and I was never shy or scared." Her hands twisted in front of her. "Like I said, I think you would have liked me more back then." Her head tipped forward as she seemed to find something on the floor absolutely fascinating to study.

He looked down, making sure he wasn't missing something. Nope. Nothing valuable down there. His hand curled under her chin. She truly had the softest skin in the world. He lifted up her chin, tipping back her head. "I like you plenty right now. Even if you did just give me the most severe case of blue balls ever."

Her eyes widened. "I—" Immediately she looked down—not at the floor this time, but at his swollen dick—then her gaze flew back up to him.

"Totally worth it, though," he added with a wry grin. "And there is no way I will ever forget the first kiss I shared with you." His thumb brushed over her lower lip. "You taste sweeter than any candy I've ever had. Actually didn't think I had much of a sweet tooth. Guess I was wrong." He forced his hand to fall. Forced himself to back away. A man's control could only last so long. His was down to the last thread. "Good night, Eliza."

She didn't move. "I don't understand."

"Understand what?"

"Why do you want me?"

"Seriously?" He gaped at her.

"Is it because I'm some kind of challenge? That's happened before. Someone wanting to prove that I could be seduced but I have to tell you, I'm not interested in games."

"You're a very honest, very blunt person. And I respect the hell out of that." She didn't pretend or try to hide her emotions. No bullshit, just like him. "You've got a lot more tact than I do," he decided. Understatement. But she didn't like BS.

She stared back at him.

Yeah, he hadn't answered her question. So he would. "If I wanted a challenge, I'd climb Mt. Everest." He considered that option. Grimaced. "Nah. I wouldn't. Don't like the cold and can't climb for shit."

Her lips curled. A faint smile that made his heart feel a little weird. "You're beautiful," he growled.

Her smile froze.

"You're strong. And you're determined. You also burn hotter than any lover I've ever had before. No one has come that fast for me, and I've got to tell you, all I want to do is make you come over and over again. Harder each time."

Eliza swallowed.

"And we'll get to that. When you're ready for me." He was the one to take a step back. "Until then, how about you do me a favor? How about you take that sweet ass of yours to bed..." *Before I pounce.*

"And do what? Have sweet dreams?" Eliza turned away.

He waited a beat. "No, baby. Screw sweet."

She looked back at him.

"Have hot dreams. Scorchingly hot dreams about me."

Eliza sucked in a deep breath. "Good night, Memphis."

"Good night, princess."

Her steps padded away from him. The door closed a few moments later. Not a hard slam. Soft. Just a little creak of the hinges.

Memphis exhaled. Then he glanced down at his damn dick. "Yeah, we will *not* be having sweet dreams." All night long, he knew Eliza would be haunting him.

She might just haunt him for the rest of his life.

He marched back to the couch. He'd put his phone on the coffee table earlier, so he grabbed it. Memphis had turned it off, and when he powered it up, he wasn't surprised to see the line of texts waiting for him.

His team would be wanting an update. He had planned to check in with everyone sooner, but he'd been distracted.

Eliza was a major distraction that he hadn't predicted.

The first text was from Delilah. *Any news?*

The second was from Elijah. *Working on the profile updates. Did Eliza tell you anything new I can use?*

The third was from Tony. Dr. Antonia Rossi, Tony to her friends. Her text read, *If you get a lead on a potential location for the bodies, call me. Banshee and I are ready to go.* Tony and her dog Banshee were an inseparable team. When it came to finding the dead, no one could beat their skills.

He didn't bother responding individually. They'd all want the update so...His fingers flew over the phone's screen as he prepared a group text. *Made contact with potential first victim. She's agreed to help. Working together now.* He frowned at the screen, remembering what Eliza had told him. *She thinks she remembers running through a sunflower field, but cops said none were close enough to fit with timeline.*

He saw the three dots appear on his screen to indicate someone was replying...

It was Elijah. *I'll dig on the field. See what I can find. Got some associates who can get me aerials from the time of her abduction.*

He didn't push to see who those associates were. Elijah still had contacts at the FBI, so they were probably people who'd be using some unofficial channels to get the intel. Lots of interesting people owed Elijah favors.

Just as plenty of dangerous people owed favors to Memphis.

He stared at the phone's screen and knew he had to tell them all the biggest discovery he'd made. Fuck. It was such bad news, but...His fingers swiped over the screen. *Every year, she says the SOB sends her sunflowers on the anniversary of her abduction.*

Memphis knew that was bad. So very bad. Every instinct he possessed told him it was—

Fucking hell. A fast response from Elijah. Elijah knew his monsters. Knew exactly how those bastards thought—and how they could get obsessed.

A long breath escaped Memphis. *That was my reaction, too.* His reply.

Elijah fired off another message. *He's keeping tabs on her. Shit. He could be someone in her life. Someone she sees every day. If he's locked on her, he would want to be close. He could want to feel like they have a relationship. If he stays close, if he talks to her, sees her...dammit, even dates her, he would feel like she never escaped him. That he always kept control.*

His grip nearly shattered the phone. Memphis took a few more breaths. Then even more.

The next text that came was from Delilah. *Is she in danger?*

It was Elijah who said, simply…*Yes.*

CHAPTER EIGHT

"I want to read all your files," Eliza said crisply as the elevator opened. Memphis stepped out first, but she quickly followed on his heels. "I want to read everything you have on the other victims. I want to see what data you've compiled and review any leads that you might have."

"Yes, ma'am," he told her, the faintest hint of the south sliding through his voice. "I will give you everything you want...and more. Just let me get in my room."

They were back at his hotel. The morning had certainly been interesting so far. She'd woken feeling excruciatingly embarrassed about the previous night's events. *I came with our first kiss!* And then after that sensual moment, she'd had to go and overshare about how she hadn't been able to climax with anyone in...ages. Talk about need-to-know info. And Eliza still didn't know why she'd felt as if Memphis needed to know that info. *He didn't.* But now he did and...

Things were a tangle.

She'd slipped out of her bedroom, fully dressed in jeans, a red shirt, and her black sandals. She'd figured there would be some awkward morning-after talk. But instead, she'd found him in the kitchen, breakfast already made for two, and just sipping coffee as he waited on her. Like being in her place was the most natural thing in the world.

And, craziest of all, it *had* felt natural to have breakfast with him. It had almost felt like they were a normal couple. He'd smiled his lazy, wicked grin at her, and she'd had an image of them together, doing—

"The lock is broken." Low. Angry.

She jerked to a halt as his words registered.

"Someone has been in my room," he rumbled.

For all they knew, someone could *still* be in there. When he started to lunge forward, she grabbed his arm. "Wait!"

His head jerked toward her. "Why?"

"Because...what if someone is in there now?"

"I hope the fuck he is." He pulled away and rushed inside.

Well, sure, that was one way of dealing with things. An extremely scary, bold, reckless—

"Sonofabitch!" His snarl carried easily to her.

She poked her head inside. And saw chaos. Papers littered the floor. His clothes were thrown everywhere. It looked as if the room had been ransacked.

"No one is here. He tossed the place, took my laptop, and left this mess behind." His jaw locked. "Does he think he's dealing with an amateur?"

Her heart pounded far too fast as she stared at the scene around her. "What if you'd been here last night?"

He stalked back toward her. Caught her hand with his and didn't even slow as he pulled her back into the hallway and toward the elevator. "Then I would have kicked his ass right then and there."

The elevator doors opened. They slipped inside. She could feel his fury.

She could also feel plenty of her own fear. "Do you have a lot of enemies?" Eliza blurted.

"More than I want to count." He jabbed the button for the lobby.

"So this...it could be from one of your old cases? Your bounty hunter work?"

"No, baby, those files that were tossed were all about *your* case and the other victims. This is about you. Someone watched me leave with you last night, and then the SOB came back to search my room. He wanted to know exactly what intel I had. This is about *you*."

She'd been very afraid that would be the answer. "Do you think it's him?" Him. The man who'd taken her.

His stare jumped to meet hers. "We're about to find out exactly *who* it was." His left hand still held hers. "Tracking down bastards is my specialty, remember?"

"Ah—"

The elevator doors opened. He kept his grip on her hand, and they double-timed it toward the check-in desk. She more triple-timed it, actually, because his stride was so fast and long. When they reached the counter, a man in a blue suit turned toward them with a welcoming expression.

"Mr. Camden," he began, "I trust you slept well last—"

"Security footage. My floor. I want it. Now."

The clerk blinked and seemed nervous as his gaze darted to Eliza, then back to Memphis. "Why would you want that?" A tentative smile. Weak around the edges. "Our guests do not normally make such requests."

"They do when someone breaks into their room, trashes everything, and steals a laptop. This is supposed to be a *nice* hotel, and I saw the security cameras on my floor, so I want access to the footage, now."

The clerk—his name badge identified him as Rodney—swallowed. "You'd like to report a break-in? I am so sorry. We take security very seriously here, and I can assure you that sort of thing does not normally happen at our establishment."

"Security cameras. Now," Memphis snapped.

"Is anything missing from your room? And are you certain that you didn't give the key to a friend or an associate?"

"I'm fucking certain, and yes, my laptop is missing. So cut the bullshit—"

"There is no need to curse at me." Rodney reached for a phone. Pressed a button. He lifted the phone to his mouth. "Yes, ah, I have a Mr. Camden in front of me, and he seems to be highly agitated."

Memphis turned to her. Gave her a quick smile. It wasn't reassuring. It was scary. "This is the part where I'm gonna have to threaten to kick his ass."

She felt her eyes widen. "Excuse me?"

"He's stalling me. Calling his manager. They're both trying to figure out what the hell to do. Because they were in on it. That just pisses me off." A disgusted shake of his head.

A sharp gasp from Rodney. "I was certainly *not* involved! Why would I break the lock on your room when I had a key?"

"Never said the lock was broken, did I? But I didn't have to say it because you already knew that part." His head swung back toward Rodney. "Because this *is* a nice hotel. Because security guards were monitoring the floors. They saw what happened. They reported to you. I've been in town long enough to know your schedule, Rodney. You've been on duty all night, and you *should* be leaving in about thirty minutes. That means you were probably on the premises when the break-in occurred. You were informed of what happened, but you didn't do anything because...?" Memphis waited.

Rodney put the phone back in place. Once more, his gaze darted to Eliza. Only there was something in his stare...

"Why the hell are you looking so hard at her?" Memphis wanted to know.

"I-I thought this problem would have been handled by now."

"Problem?" Memphis seemed to pounce on that word. "You have not even *seen* me be a problem yet." His hand flew across the counter. He grabbed Rodney's yellow tie and yanked him close. "How much were you paid to look the other way?"

"Oh, God, you're going to hit me!" Rodney squeaked. He sucked in a breath, then expelled it as he called, "Security, security—"

Eliza glanced around, thinking security guards would be swarming, but they were nowhere to be seen.

"You're pissing me off more and more. Who paid you?"

Once more, Rodney's gaze darted to Eliza. She blinked. There was guilt in his stare. But, more, it was almost as if he was saying…

"Don't even try it," Memphis snarled at him. "She was with me. Eliza had nothing to do with what went down last night."

And that was when the twist in her stomach got even worse. "I want to see the security footage." This man knew who she was. She could clearly see his recognition. And the way he was acting… "What will it take to get that footage?"

"I don't want to make an enemy of your father!" Rodney cried.

"No, buddy," Memphis fired back. "You don't want an enemy of *me*. Get the footage."

***

The sonofabitch in the video just strolled right up to Memphis's hotel room. Didn't even try to hide his face. Took a moment to smirk at the camera, then he kicked in the door.

Or tried to kick in the door. The first attempt wasn't successful. The second wasn't, either. On the third try, the lock broke, the door flew open, and the man with the dark hair, black pants, and white dress shirt sauntered inside.

A few moments later, the video footage showed Rodney and a security guard rushing into the room, too. "Well, look at that," Memphis drawled. "The cavalry." He shot an annoyed glance at a heavily sweating Rodney. Both Rodney *and* the hotel manager, a woman named Vivian Parker, were currently sweating bullets.

"This isn't what it seems," Vivian hurried to say.

"It *isn't* your hotel staff members rushing to stop a break-in..." His gaze slid back to the monitor. "Only to head back out of my room a few moments later *without* the bad guy?" Sure as hell looked like that to him. "Though I do wonder, did he pay you right then and there to walk away, or did he promise to give you money later?" Anger burned in his gut. His hands balled into fists as he watched the SOB stride out of his hotel room a few moments later, the laptop gripped under his left arm. *Such a fucking annoyance*. "Tell me why..." Each word rumbled with his fury. "Why I shouldn't call the local news channels and let them know just what a shady-as-hell operation you're running at this place?" His gaze returned to Rodney and Vivian as they huddled together. "I'm tracking a potential *murderer* and you let my suspect walk—"

"Oh, God." Rodney's hand flew to his chest as he took a hurried step back. "No one said anything about murder." And *his* gaze jumped to Eliza. "Not a word. I-I thought I was helping, if-if you do a favor for the Robinson family—"

"Favor?" Memphis latched onto that slip. "Explain. Right the hell now."

But it was Eliza who cleared her throat. "I know the man in the video."

Memphis's head whipped toward her. "You're shitting me."

Rodney tried to sidle out the door.

From the corner of his eye, Memphis caught the movement. "Nope. Rodney, get your ass back here. We're not done."

Rodney froze. Then sidled back to stand with Vivian.

Memphis concentrated on Eliza and the miserable look on her face.

"I'm so sorry," she said.

"Why?" They'd talked about her not needing to—

"Because the man in the video is Alec Davis." A fast exhale. "One of the bodyguards hired by my dad." She winced. "Actually, he was *the* main guard for a while, but I thought that he was now mostly doing security for the company." Eliza reached for his hand. "I swear, I had no idea he was coming to your place. This should *never* have happened."

Of course, it shouldn't have happened. "When people commit crimes, their asses should get punished. Breaking and entering and *theft* damn well count as crimes in my book." He sent a glare toward the hotel staff. "You two are complicit."

"I am not made for jail," Rodney whispered. His eyes seemed to water.

Vivian lifted her chin. "Before you call the cops, perhaps you want to meet with Prescott

Robinson? Because I talked to him last night. He is the one who assured me this situation would not come back to bite me in the ass."

Prescott Robinson. Eliza's father. Definitely past time for a chat with that SOB. *You will not get in my way.*

Memphis rolled back his shoulders, but the move did nothing to chase the tension from his body. "Consider yourself bitten."

Rodney whimpered.

Eliza's fingers pressed harder to his arm. "I am so sorry."

He looked down at her hand, then back up at her face. "You didn't know."

"I swear, I didn't."

He caught her fingers. Brought them to his mouth and brushed a kiss over her knuckles. "Then don't apologize. Your father is a controlling bastard, I get it. Not like it's the first time I've come across one of those guys, but it *is* past time for us to have a one-on-one chat. He needs to understand that I'm not the kind of man he's used to having in his life. In fact, I'd wager that your dear old dad has never quite met someone like me."

"Memphis..." Worry threaded through her voice.

She shouldn't be worried. He could handle her dad any day of the week. Arrogant, rich bastards didn't intimidate him. Come to think of it, no one intimidated him.

"Are you calling the reporters?" Vivian asked tentatively.

"Clean up my room. Comp my full stay. Make sure that not a damn one of my possessions was destroyed." A hard incline of his head. "Pack all my bags and have them waiting for me. And *if* my laptop comes back to me in perfect working order, then we'll consider this matter closed." He tugged on Eliza's hand. "Let's get the hell out of here."

Vivian shouted reassurances, and Rodney appeared close to fainting in relief as they passed him.

Anger still burned in Memphis's blood, but most of that anger was directed at one person. No, make that at two people.

The dick bodyguard who'd seemed to enjoy trashing his room.

And Eliza's dear old dad.

"You didn't call the cops or the reporters because of me," Eliza said softly.

The hotel doors opened for them, and they stepped outside. Automatically, he glanced to the left and then the right. Surveying his environment was second nature to him. Had been, for years. "You were certainly a factor." His lips pressed together as he considered the situation. "That what it's been like for you since your abduction? He does whatever the hell he wants, no boundaries, no one to stop him because your dad is filthy rich?"

"He thinks he's protecting me."

Maybe, but what he's really doing is protecting the perp. "Good thing I'm in charge of that particular protection routine now because, not to throw shade at him—oh, wait, yeah, I do want to throw shade—but he's been doing a piss-poor job of it."

***

He didn't like the towering SOB who stood so close to Eliza as they left the hotel. Didn't like the way he held her hand. Didn't like the way his body brushed against hers, as if he had some right to touch her.

He didn't have the right to touch her. No one else did.

Eliza had spent the night with the jerk. They'd gone into her building together and hadn't come out again until the next morning. Not like it was the first time that Eliza had taken a lover. She'd done so before. Men she'd dismissed soon enough from her life.

This guy was just another mistake. Eliza would send him packing in no time. Because deep in her heart, Eliza knew the truth.

I am the only one who is right for her.

He was the one who had been there for her ever since that incredible night so long ago. He was the one who would never, ever let her go.

Never.

CHAPTER NINE

"He's on a conference call! You can't just burst into his study! Stop! Eliza, you have to stop him—"

Eliza ignored her father's assistant because she had no intention of stopping Memphis. If anything, she wanted to help him tear into her father. The fact that her dad had sent one of his men to *search* Memphis's hotel room infuriated her. And that Alec had *stolen* Memphis's laptop was just too much.

Memphis threw open the door to her father's study. They'd made it to the Robinson estate in record time, and as soon as they had arrived, her father's ever-present assistant Miranda Locke had tried to block their path.

She hadn't succeeded.

Memphis marched inside her father's study, and Eliza rushed in right on his heels.

"What in the hell?" Prescott boomed. Behind the massive desk, she saw her father surge to his feet. He was *not* on any conference call. "What is the meaning of this?"

"I want my laptop." Memphis stalked right toward the desk. Slapped his hands down on the gleaming surface. "Then I want an apology. A beautiful, deep, heartfelt apology—followed by your promise to keep your interfering ass out of my business."

Her father's jaw dropped.

Eliza was one hundred percent certain that no one had ever spoken to her father in quite that way before.

"How *dare* you..." Her father snarled as red filled his cheeks.

Memphis just leaned closer to him. "How dare *you?* How dare you get your asshat goon to break into my hotel room?" Fury. "How dare you steal my laptop?" Even hotter. Even rougher. "And fucking *how dare you* try to interfere when you know I'm here to find the bastard who took Eliza?"

There was a gasp from behind Eliza. She looked back to see Miranda gaping.

"Excuse us, would you, Miranda?" Prescott said, voice oddly cordial under the circumstances. "I need to talk to my daughter and her...acquaintance privately for a moment."

Miranda backed up and hauled the door closed. As far as Eliza knew, Miranda had never refused an order from Prescott.

Silence. One beat. Two, then...

"You want to talk to me," Prescott said, voice *not* so cordial any longer, "then you do it like a gentleman. You come to me with—"

"Oh, screw that." Memphis still had his hands flat on the desk. He still loomed toward her father. "I'll do whatever the hell I want. And right now? I will be giving *you* a tip. You want to know what I've discovered about the man who took Eliza?"

I want to know. Eliza wanted to know everything, but her father had slowed down their investigation.

"Then you *ask* me," Memphis growled. "You don't send your son to buy me off and you don't send some SOB to *trash* my room and steal my laptop."

She saw the slight stiffening of her father's shoulders. "No one was supposed to trash your room."

Eliza noticed that he didn't deny the other actions. He had sent Benedict to buy off Memphis. He had ordered the laptop stolen.

"Alec must have gotten overzealous in his search. He is very protective of Eliza." Prescott sniffed. His gaze darted to her. "Isn't he?"

She pulled in a breath. Released it. Walked slowly toward her father. Kept her chin up and her shoulders back. "Alec Davis is interfering and controlling. Those are the two main reasons I demanded that he be pulled from duty with me."

But her father shook his head. "You were just tired of having the guards around you. But it was—still *is*—necessary. I am only trying to keep you safe—"

"No worries," Memphis cut in to say. "Because I have taken over that position. The position of always watching her ass and keeping her safe. I will be viewing it as a twenty-four, seven role."

Her father's jaw tightened. The lines around his eyes deepened. His nostrils flared. All three warning signs that an explosion was imminent. "Who the hell do you think you are?"

"I think I'm Memphis Camden, former bounty hunter extraordinaire. And I don't think Eliza should spend her life locked away. I think she should be out there with me, hunting this perp. Stopping him before he can hurt anyone else." A pause. "I think Eliza should be making her own choices about who she wants around her and what she wants to be doing with her time."

"You don't know my daughter. You don't know—"

"Stop," Eliza said because the shade of red that her father was becoming couldn't be good for anyone. His blood pressure always ran high, and the last thing she wanted was for him to start having a dizzy spell. "I know exactly what I want. It's the same thing I've always wanted."

Both men looked at her. Fury still covered her father's face, but Memphis—his expression seemed almost tender as he stared at her. The tenderness made her feel nervous.

"Tell us," Memphis invited as he finally lifted his hands from the desk. He crossed his arms over his chest and watched her.

She swallowed. "I want to know what happened during that missing weekend." *What happened to me?* "I want to find the man who took me." *You can't scare me anymore.* "And I want him to be locked away so that he can never, ever hurt anyone else."

"Damn straight." An approving nod from Memphis. "Let's make all those dreams come true."

"He hasn't been found," Prescott gritted out as he fired a glare at Memphis. "Do you think I haven't looked? That the cops haven't looked? The man vanished without a trace, and the absolute best thing for my daughter to do is move on with her life. She doesn't need you to come back in and drag up the most painful time she experienced."

"I haven't moved on, Dad." Quiet. True.

But he flinched, as if she'd shouted at him. His head swung toward her, and he suddenly seemed older. Thinner. Not the larger-than-life tycoon that so many people knew.

"I have nightmares," Eliza confessed. "I'm always looking over my shoulder. Sometimes I wonder if the stories are true...did I make it all up? Am I going crazy?"

"Lizzie, *no.*" He hurried from behind the desk. Came toward her.

She was conscious of Memphis watching them with a hooded gaze.

Her father's palm curled around her shoulder. "You aren't crazy. Don't say that."

"Because Mom wound up in an institution? Because she took her own life at the end?" Their deep, dark secret. One that had never managed to work its way into the press. Because her father's money had been able to keep that part secret. "Because you're afraid I'm like her?" That was Eliza's deep, dark secret...no, her fear.

His hand tightened on her. "You *are* like your mother."

Her lower lip wanted to tremble, so she caught it with her teeth.

"You're smart, you're kind, and you're beautiful. But I have *never* thought that you were crazy. And I never thought your mother was, either. I do not think you will wind up like her. That is not in the future that waits for you. You are going to be happy and safe, no matter what the hell I have to do in order to assure that ending for you." Now both of his hands squeezed her shoulders.

Her father didn't get it. He couldn't control the world. He couldn't stop the danger or the bad things out there. She was certainly proof of that.

"He's been contacting her," Memphis announced.

A cloud swept over her father's features. "What?"

"Each year, he sends her sunflowers. He's been keeping tabs on her."

"The sunflowers," Prescott whispered. His hands spasmed around her.

"My team and I suspect," Memphis continued in a careful voice, "that he's been inserting himself in her life in other ways. We believe that he's wanted to stay close to Eliza all this time. To put it bluntly, he thinks she's his."

Her father shook his head. "No. *No*."

"On that, we are in total agreement." Memphis paced closer to them. "I hunt perps like him. I find them in the shadows, and I haul them into the light of day—kicking and screaming. I am going to hunt this bastard, but I don't want you in my way. No more sending dumbasses to go through my stuff. You want to know what I'm doing? Try asking me. Eliza is going to work with me because that is what *she* wants to do. She's the only one who got away from him. The others didn't."

And, again, her father seemed to age before her eyes. "I looked at the files on your laptop." He let her go and walked back to his desk. Opened a drawer. Hauled out the laptop. "All those other women—you really think the same man took them?" He put the laptop on the desk.

"I do." No hesitation from Memphis.

Her father sat down, hard. "How will you find him?"

"Eliza is going to take me back through the moments before and after her abduction. She's going to show me everything that she remembers. That's our starting point. We're going to review every detail of her case, then the cases of the other women. Because maybe something from their stories will trigger a memory for her. We are going to dig and dig until we find something we can use."

"The cops tried..." Her father's shoulders slumped. "*I* tried. When that wasn't good enough, I paid off the tabloid companies to stop running those damn stories. Enough time had passed that the blood finally left the water. The sharks left her alone."

Eliza positioned her body right next to Memphis's. She wanted her father to see them as a united front. A team working together. "Memphis says that a woman has been abducted each year on or near the anniversary of my disappearance."

"Sweet Christ...I read that in his files..." Her father's shaking hand flew over his face.

"We have to stop him before he takes someone else," Eliza said. Determination filled her. "We *will* stop him."

But there was not much determination reflected in her father's eyes. If anything, he just looked sad. "I hope you can," he admitted gruffly. "But no one else has, and I fear you are just setting yourself up for heartbreak. If the cops couldn't find him, if the private investigators I hired couldn't do it, why should we believe this guy can?" A dismissive glance toward Memphis.

Memphis opened his mouth to reply.

She moved in front of him.

Her father's lashes flickered the smallest bit.

"Because when he was a bounty hunter, he had a case closure rate of one hundred percent," Eliza stated. Something she'd discovered when she did her digging on him. "Because Memphis isn't working this case to get paid. He turned down Benedict's offer, as I'm sure you heard. Memphis cares. He wants to help people, and he is not going to give up."

And, from behind her, Memphis said, "Damn straight."

***

"Are we going to have a problem?" Prescott Robinson asked.

Memphis stood in the doorway. Eliza had just vanished up the stairs with her stepmother, a woman who barely looked to be five years older than Eliza. The stepmother, Kathleen, had appeared moments before. She'd said she desperately needed Eliza for a moment.

I need her, too. A stark thought. One that came straight from his core.

Satisfied that Eliza was safe upstairs, Memphis turned to face her father. "Hell, yes." He pointed to the laptop. "Don't ever touch my shit again."

"And what if I were to tell you not to ever touch my daughter again?"

Battle-ready tension flooded through him. "Excuse me?" But what he meant was... "Nah, check that. Excuse the hell out of yourself." He stalked toward Prescott. "If Eliza wants me touching her, then I'll touch her." Was he supposed to be intimidated just because the man pretty much owned the whole freaking state? Not happening.

"You spent the night at her house last night."

"Saw that on the security cameras, did you?" Like he was gonna be shocked by her father's knowledge of where he'd been last night. "Yeah, I know that you have the whole place wired, but there are a ton of upgrades that we need to make at her home. With this creep keeping tabs on her, we can't afford any mistakes. Honestly, you've gotten lucky so far. I'm not going to count on luck protecting her forever."

"You act as if you care about Eliza."

"I do." Hell. That had been a fast admission—

"Good." Prescott nodded, as if pleased. "Because I like you."

"What?" Memphis did a double take as real surprise flooded through him, but he rallied quickly. "You don't need to like me. You need to stay the hell out of my way. You need to let me protect Eliza. You need to—"

"From the minute I learned you were nosing around my daughter, I made it a point to discover as much about you as I could."

"Good for you." Memphis glanced down at his watch. Time was ticking away. Maybe he should ditch the guy and go after Eliza...

"Your father abandoned you and your mother when you were six years old."

His eyebrows climbed as his stare returned to Prescott. "Someone is thorough."

"Your mother worked two jobs, sometimes three, and when you turned sixteen, you immediately went to work, too. But still graduated high school with honors."

"I don't like to brag," he muttered. He also didn't like to walk down memory lane.

"Started at the police academy—you were doing great there—but you dropped out. Joined the military instead." A narrowing of Prescott's eyes. "Your record in the military is sealed."

"Was I in the military?" He wasn't confirming or denying. "Hmm. Imagine that..."

"When you got out, you started bounty hunting. One of the first people you brought in? Your father."

Where was this tale going? And what was the point? Other than to waste his time. "I remember everyone I brought in, but thanks for the history lesson."

"He was a bank robber, a drug dealer, and sometimes an arsonist."

"He was an asshole, a liar, and a criminal, and it gave me savage satisfaction to personally drag his ass to jail. Totally on my highlight reel." Was he supposed to be embarrassed because his father had been a crook? Not likely.

Prescott's eyes were a glacial blue, not deep and dark like Eliza's. He was tall, wide at the shoulders, and had a widow's peak in the middle of his high forehead. "You made quite a reputation bounty hunting, and you created a fortune for yourself, too. Courtesy of some good investments."

"What can I say?" His hands lifted and fell. "Always been great at math. Probably came from my bank robbing daddy. He liked math and money, too." True story.

Prescott didn't change his expression. "You bought a house for your mother in Florida."

"She likes the ocean." Impatience bled into his voice.

"And then you started working with the Ice Breakers. And, yes, I know all about them, too."

Give yourself a cookie. "Am I supposed to clap at this point? Be impressed?"

"I suspect it takes a great deal to impress a man like you."

"Your suspicion would be correct."

"But my daughter has impressed you, hasn't she?" Almost sly.

Sonofabitch...I walked right into that one.

"Impressed you, charmed you, touched that hard, hard heart of yours." A nod of Prescott's head. "The giveaway was in your eyes when you looked at her."

"Would you get to the point? I hate wasting time."

Prescott smiled. "You don't care about who I am, do you?"

"Nope." He looked at his watch again. Yep, too much time wasted. The meeting was over. He stepped toward the desk. He would be taking his laptop with him.

"Do you think she'll fall in love with you?"

He didn't take his gaze off the laptop. "What in the hell kind of question is that?"

"You're right. My mistake."

Hell, yes, it had been. His phone vibrated, so Memphis pulled it from his pocket. His finger slid over the screen as he read the update and noted the locations that Elijah had sent to him.

"Do you think *you'll* fall in love with her?" Prescott asked him.

Memphis's head jerked up. Automatically, he shoved the phone back in his pocket.

"Ah. Got your attention. Good. Because I believe you're the type of man who would fight hard for someone you love. I think if you fell for my daughter, you would never let anyone on this earth hurt her. You'd kill to protect her, am I correct?"

I would kill to protect her now. But Memphis just stared back at the other man.

"That kind of devotion can't be bought. You can't pay a bodyguard to take the risks and to go to the lengths that a man in love will."

"What the hell are you saying? You asking me to go marry Eliza?" Was he in the Twilight Zone?

"I wouldn't object."

What. The. Fuck?

"But you'd have to convince Eliza first. Get her to fall for you, then we'll talk business."

Business? Screw that.

The door opened behind him before Memphis could ask the guy if he'd gone off his meds, and he looked over to see a tight-lipped Benedict poking his head inside the room. Sure. Why not have him appear? Seemed about right.

"This is becoming incredibly unfun, so I'll be leaving now, and I'll be taking Eliza with me." Memphis walked toward the desk and scooped up his laptop. "Ask next time," he growled.

"Take care of my daughter," Prescott fired back.

Their gazed locked. "Count on it. But I don't want your goons in my way, understand? They can watch from a distance, but if they get in my path, they'll regret that move for the rest of their lives."

"I'll make sure they receive that message."

"Fabulous. You do that." He took his laptop and headed for the door. Benedict blocked his path.

Of course, he did.

"What are your intentions with my sister?" Benedict snapped.

Ah, so he *had* overheard the last bit with Prescott. Now he was in protective-brother mode. Figured. "I am not in the mood for this."

"What are your—"

Seriously? Fine. "To seduce her. To make her need me more than she needs anyone else. And, once we've stopped the bad guy, to convince her to run away with me and ditch all you idiots. There. Happy?"

A strangled gasp came from behind Benedict. Oh, hell.

Benedict glared, but he moved to the side—moved just enough for Memphis to see Eliza's stunned face. But Eliza hadn't been the one to make the gasping sound.

That had been the stepmother. The blond woman with her mouth still stretched open, and her blue eyes wide with a mix of shock and horror.

He inclined his head toward her. "Hi, there. I'm Memphis."

"You...you..." The blonde couldn't seem to come up with more words.

Okay, probably best to leave. He offered his hand to Eliza. "Ready to run away, I mean, ready to go with me?"

She stared at him, not his hand.

"Friend came through for me," he added softly. "Got some potential locations to scout for that missing sunflower field of yours."

Her hand rose. Touched his. His fingers immediately curled around hers. He sent her a smile. "Great. Let's get the hell out of here."

And they did. Stares were on them. A heavy silence filled the air behind them. As they neared the front door, a tall, muscled figure emerged from the room on the right.

A figure that Memphis recognized so he paused. Memphis squeezed Eliza's hand and told her, "Just one minute, sweetheart. I need to have a word with, ah, Alec, I believe it was?"

At the endearment, he saw Alec's eyes narrow. So the bodyguard didn't like that, did he? Too fucking bad. Memphis began to pull his hand from Eliza's—

But her hold tightened on him. "Do not hit him, Memphis."

Alec stiffened. "I'd like to see him try."

"No," Memphis assured him. "You wouldn't. Because once my fist made contact with your face, you'd be on the floor."

Alec surged toward him.

And Eliza stepped between them. Oh, the hell, no, she had not. That prick of a bodyguard could have hit her. His fists had been clenched and ready.

"Eliza," Memphis began, voice dropping and going ice cold. *Do not ever put yourself between me and danger*. Not ever.

Eliza's free hand pressed to his chest. "I want to get to those fields. I understand that you're angry, but..."

He took a breath. Two of them. He and Eliza would be having a very important talk, very soon, a talk about her *not getting between me and a threat*. For now... "Oh, princess, don't worry. I'm not about to get violent." Not at the moment. But he also wasn't about to forget what Alec had done to his hotel room. "I just wanted to go over the new ground rules with the goon—guard."

A muscle flexed along Alec's jaw.

Memphis brought Eliza's hand to his mouth. Kissed her knuckles. "Relax."

Her eyes widened. Over her shoulder, he saw Alec's narrow even more.

Oh, he is going to be a problem. Memphis pulled Eliza to his side. He'd be keeping her there.

"You trashed my place," Memphis said to Alec, aware of the others still watching. They'd slipped out of Prescott's study. "Total dick move. I'll get around to paying you back for that very soon."

Alec's jaw notched up. "I was following orders."

"Don't remember telling you to trash anything," Prescott responded, voice carrying easily. "Just to search."

"I was being thorough," Alec groused. "Usually, you appreciate my thoroughness. You've called it a bonus before."

Thorough, my ass. But Memphis kept a genial smile on his face, and a go-to-hell glare in his eyes. "I get that you used to be in charge of Eliza's security so maybe you still feel somewhat protective of her. But no need to worry. From here on out, I've got her."

Alec didn't respond.

"So don't get in my way. If you do, I can assure you, we will have a major problem." With that, he made his leave. Mostly because Memphis figured if he stayed much longer, he might give in to his more primitive urges...

And take a swing.

Eliza didn't speak until they were back in his SUV and on the road. In fact, it took her a little too long to talk. The silence stretched and hummed and just when he was about to break it, she said—

"Was that really necessary?"

"Telling the prick to back off? That I was covering your protection? Absolutely. You know, I think he may have a crush on you and that shit just makes me—" *Jealous.* Nope. Not time to go into that bit. "Uncomfortable. I don't like the attachment he has." *I don't like him.*

"I meant what you told my father. About s-seducing me."

He shot a quick glance her way. Found Eliza staring out the window.

"Seducing me and then convincing me I needed you more than anything else." Her voice was very careful. Almost stilted. "Then adding that you were going to try and get me to run away with you. Did you truly need to say all that? I thought you weren't into bullshitting people."

"I'm not."

Her head swung toward him. "Then why did you say those things? Were you just mad because of what happened at your hotel?"

"Break-ins do have a tendency to piss me off. You are not wrong on that part."

"Memphis..."

He let a low laugh slip out. "I wasn't bullshitting, sweetheart." He braked at a light. Turned to look straight at her so there would be no mistake. "Those are my intentions."

Her eyes widened.

She didn't say anything else, not for a long time...

***

"I don't like him," Alec Davis said as soon as he shut the door to Prescott's office. "The guy obviously just wants to fuck her. He's not interested in her protection."

Prescott lifted a brow. "Watch the tone. You're talking about my daughter."

Alec snapped his teeth together.

"Memphis Camden will be in charge of her security for the foreseeable future. He has assured me that he will be staying with Eliza, twenty-four, seven." Prescott pointed at him. "But that doesn't mean I don't still want eyes on her. But any other guards are to stay in the periphery. Make sure everyone understands. And *you* are included in that group of everyone."

Looking more than a little displeased, Alec jerked his head in acknowledgement of that order.

"Good. Memphis thinks he may be able to find the man who started this nightmare. I'm going to give him a bit of time to see if he can get the job done."

"But, sir—" Alec began.

"That's all. It's Saturday, Alec. You're not even supposed to be here. Go enjoy the weekend. Eliza is covered." He made a quick, waving motion with his hand.

Alec spun for the door. When he was gone...

"You're quiet," Prescott noted as he studied his son. "You and Eliza—you both always go silent when you're troubled."

Benedict kept staring out of the window. "I think most people get quiet when they're troubled. Not like it's a family trait or anything."

"You think I made a mistake with Memphis?" He wanted Benedict's opinion.

Benedict swung toward him. "I don't want her hurt."

"Memphis assured me that he would keep her safe."

"No, I mean..." He jerked a hand through his hair. "I don't want him to break her heart."

"You think he could?" Since her abduction, Eliza had made a point not to let herself get close to anyone. Not physically. Not emotionally.

"I think he doesn't strike me as the kind of guy who believes in forever and happily-ever-after BS. I think he likes hunting monsters, probably is addicted to adrenaline, and I think Eliza is his complete and total opposite. She's been sheltered for years. She can't handle someone like him." His hand fell.

"You're being a protective big brother. That's good."

"No!" A sharp retort as his hands fisted. "I'm not. I've never been good for her. If I had been, this shit would never have happened. You think I don't know? You think I don't get that it was all my fault? I do. I always fucking knew that." And he practically raced from the room.

When the door closed behind him...

"You knew," Prescott said softly. "But Eliza didn't." *She still doesn't.*

Would she ever remember that particular detail? He hoped not. Eliza loved her brother. Prescott would hate to see that love vanish.

CHAPTER TEN

"So, the first two stops were busts, but, you know, everyone always says that the third time is the charm." Memphis turned to survey the dirt field around them. "Though I have to tell you, this place doesn't exactly scream charm to me."

Or to her. Eliza lifted a hand to shield her eyes from the glare of the sun. One of Memphis's friends—Elijah—had gotten access to old aerial photos that had been taken near the time of her abduction. He'd managed to find three areas that he said could have potentially worked as locations for sunflower fields. At various times in the past, sunflower fields *had* grown on these sites. The first two stops had been closer to her father's home. But they hadn't stirred any memories for her.

She'd stared at them, searched around the old properties—under the watchful gaze of the owners that she'd seen Memphis pay—and recognized nothing. "You bribed the other owners to let me look."

"Seemed like the easiest thing to do. Bribed them *and* questioned them covertly, even though Elijah had texted and told me those lands had changed hands multiple times since your abduction."

The ground was so dry that it crunched beneath her feet. "This location is too far from my dad's house." No way could she have walked from this spot.

"Is it?" He turned to look at an old, dilapidated barn that sat to the right.

"It took us two hours to get here." She looked at her watch. "And you were driving at least forty miles an hour. That's eighty miles. Even if I managed to walk five miles an hour, that's—"

"Sixteen hours. Totally possible for you to do if you consider that you were gone for over forty-eight hours. And we had no idea how long your captor actually held you. For all we know, you could have escaped from the bastard right away." He took a step toward the barn.

She did, too. The ground crunched beneath her sandals once more. "I didn't have on shoes, Memphis. My feet were cut and bloody, but if I had walked for sixteen hours, they would have been even worse."

"Maybe you didn't walk the whole time..."

He kept heading for the barn.

Sighing, she trudged after him. Her gaze darted to the right. She could see where the sunflowers had once been planted. Clean, straight rows...

The moonlight fell onto them, and she staggered past the sagging sunflowers as they—

Music.

Eliza stiffened.

She heard the faint chime, and her whole body shuddered to a stop. Wind blew her hair over her cheek, and the faint sound came again.

Gentle. Soothing.

Terrifying.

Sweat broke out on her body.

"There's a wind chime near the barn door," Memphis called back to her. "Weird as hell because it looks as if no one has been here in years. Elijah is still digging to find out who owns the property. Last owner was listed as dying right before your disappearance."

She tried to take a step toward him, but she couldn't. Her feet had locked into the dirt.

Shadows stretched around the wilting sunflowers. The chimes called to her. But she didn't want to go back. It wasn't safe. She wouldn't go back in—

"The barn!" Eliza choked out.

Memphis spun around. "Eliza?"

"I..." *Help me.* She clamped her lips together. Swallowed twice. A shudder traveled the length of her body.

He bounded back to her. "What's the matter?" His hands flew out and curled around her arms.

"I...I remember that sound." How could she have forgotten it? How could the chimes still be there after all of this time? *How?* The place was abandoned, but the chimes kept swaying in the faint breeze. *How could they still be here after all this time?* "I think I was here." Fragments came to her. Flashes.

Running. Falling near the sunflowers.

Have to get home. Have to get home—

"I think I was in the barn." A whisper.

His hand slid under the back of his shirt, and Memphis pulled out a gun.

"Where did you get that?" Eliza felt dazed. Battered.

"Glove box. Got it out every time we stopped to search. Just didn't want to scare you so I waited until you were out of the vehicle before I snagged it."

She was scared. Terrified to her very soul.

"You want to come in that barn with me?" Memphis asked her.

No. "Yes." *No. I want to get far away. I never, ever want to come back here.*

"I will be with you every step of the way," he promised.

She lurched forward with him, and he stayed with her. Every step. The wind chime grew louder, and as they got closer, she realized that it didn't look worn from time. Not like the faded, wooden barn door. The chime appeared to be new. The wood of the chime gleamed as if...

"Someone really likes that fucking wind chime," Memphis muttered. "Likes it so much that he keeps coming back to take care of it."

Eliza was afraid she'd be sick. One arm curled around her stomach. Memphis was at the barn door.

I don't want to be here. I want to leave. I need to leave.

The door opened with a long, ragged groan. It hadn't even been locked. Just swung open when Memphis pushed lightly against it and revealed the deep, dark cavernous space that waited. Dust fluttered in the air, and holes gaped in the barn's walls and the loft. The barn smelled stale. Old.

Familiar.

No, no, it had been nearly seven years. *Seven years in just a few days.* Surely, she wouldn't recognize a smell. But...*I recognized the chime.*

"See anything that stirs a memory?"

Her gaze flew around the barn. Nothing was there. The stalls were empty...

*Fingers digging in the dirt. Looking, searching for a way to get free. Yanking at the cuff that locked me to the...*She stumbled forward as if pulled by a magnet. This couldn't be happening. This was a nightmare and a dream all in one. To remember...To be...

"When they found me, I was still wearing a handcuff on one wrist." She didn't recognize the hollow sound of her own voice. "I-I always wondered why just one wrist had the cuff on it." She passed the open stalls. The first. The second. The third...

Third time is the charm.

A tear slid down her cheek as she stopped before that stall.

Memphis's hand curled over her shoulder, and Eliza jumped. "You recognize something?" His voice was low, almost soothing.

Nothing could soothe her.

Her breath came faster. Harder. "I think I was cuffed to something in here."

He slipped past her. Went into the stall. Toward the right wall. Only it wasn't a full wall like in the other two stalls. This wall had wood that went from mid-level down to the floor. And in the top section, there were long, thin bars that ran up to the ceiling.

"For keeping horses," Memphis said as he moved deeper into that stall. "The bars would allow for air flow and interactions with the horse beside him..."

One of those bars had broken. The wood was jagged, only going up about four inches.

Her heartbeat thundered in her ears.

Memphis didn't touch that broken bar, but his eyes had locked on it. "Could have put one cuff around this bar. The other would have been closed around your wrist. He left you in here thinking you were secure, but you pulled and pulled until the bar broke and then you ran—"

She *was* running. Eliza couldn't stay in that barn with the familiar scents and the thick, suffocating air surrounding her for another moment. She couldn't *breathe*. Her feet kicked up the dirt as she raced for the open barn door. She had to get outside.

Get away. Get home. I have to get—

The sunlight hit her as soon as she shot outside. Bright and blinding—

No, it should be dark. The moonlight should show me the sunflowers.

She ran toward the right. Where the sunflowers should have been.

"Eliza!" Memphis shouted.

But he shouted for me, too. He shouted my name because he was trying to find me. He chased me. And he—

He grabbed her.

She screamed. A high-pitched, utterly terrified cry, and then she fought him. Twisting, shoving, punching and kicking in his arms. "No! Let me go, let—"

"Baby, you are ripping out my heart," Memphis rasped.

She slammed her fist into his jaw.

He winced.

And...

"Oh, God," Eliza gasped. "What am I doing?" Her heart nearly burst from her chest. "I'm so sorry. I'm so—"

He wrapped her in a bear hug. One that was incredibly gentle. "Don't apologize for a damn thing to me. We talked about this." Gruff. Rough. "And what you're doing—you're remembering, aren't you, sweetheart?"

Not clearly. Just images. Just feelings. Just...

I think I was here, and I was terrified.

"This is a lead, baby. This is what we want."

Yes, it was. One hundred percent. She wanted to know. She wanted to remember.

"We're not touching anything else. I'm calling my contacts. We're getting the cops out here."

Would the cops even believe her? Her arms wrapped around him. Held him tight. She had vague flashes and a consuming terror. Not like that was gonna be enough to get a warrant.

"Don't worry." Memphis seemed to read her thoughts. "They'll search. If the cops don't fucking do it right, I'll handle it myself." He eased back. Stared down at her face. "*This is a lead. This is good. We are going to get him.*"

***

Eliza had come back to him, but she was in another man's arms. A man who didn't deserve to hold her. A man who kept touching what he should not.

She stood near the field that had once bloomed with sunflowers. Stood near the barn. He'd left the music playing...for her. For them.

A memory.

Something sweet from that night.

What all did she remember? If she'd come back to this spot, the time they'd spent together had to be returning to her mind.

He slowly lowered the binoculars. Not like he could get too close. Not with that bastard with her. Eliza's family had made sure someone was always close. They guarded her, like the treasure she was. But what they didn't know...

He could get close to her. Whenever he wanted.

***

"Eliza, I can't go to a judge and get a warrant on a hunch," Detective Daniel Jones yanked a hand through his hair. He'd arrived at the scene—with his partner Camila Perez—just moments before. It had sure as hell taken the cops long enough to get there. Eliza had insisted on calling in the ones from Houston because they'd been familiar with her case. So Memphis had gone along with things...

But the detective was just an utter disappointment as he roughly added, "I want to help, you know I do, but—"

"Then help," Memphis said flatly as he cut through the other man's words. "Do it. We've given you the crime scene on a silver platter. Waited in this hot-ass sun for hours so your slow selves could arrive. Now do your job and search for clues."

Eliza had wrapped her arms around her stomach. Her gaze remained steady and clear, and she'd stopped crying long ago. Not that she'd ever been doing any dramatic crying. Hell, he didn't think she'd ever been aware of the tear drops that had slid down her cheeks when she'd stood in that barn. No gasping or moaning. Just silent tears.

Those tears had made his chest ache.

Daniel and his partner shared a long look. Then Camila—a brunette who wore her hair in a high twist and proudly displayed the badge on her hip—cleared her throat and said, "Just because you randomly picked a spot on a map and you found an abandoned barn, it doesn't mean—"

"I was here," Eliza stated. Clear. Calm. A little quiet. "I remember being in the stall. The third stall. There's a broken bar in there from where I was handcuffed. I can remember the wind chime. Remember running outside."

Sympathy flashed on Daniel's face, and his hand reached out, as if he'd touch Eliza.

Memphis casually stepped into his path and Daniel wound up giving *his* arm a reassuring squeeze. "Aw, thanks, man," Memphis told him. "But I'm good."

Daniel frowned.

"Know what would make even me better though?" Memphis continued. "For you to do your job. Actually, you know what? Scratch that. I called you out here because Eliza thought you'd be the best point of contact with the police." He still disagreed, but he'd played *nicely* for Eliza. Because her tears had thrown him off his normal game. Memphis would not be making that mistake again. Fuck, it was hot out there. "This is out of your jurisdiction. Feds handle the serials. They know how to work them. You don't. Should have started at the top to begin with."

A sputter came from Daniel. "A serial? What are you talking about?"

"I'm talking about a killer who murders multiple times." What else would he mean?

Eliza hugged herself even tighter.

"That's what you think we're dealing with here?" Camila shook her head. "Look, with respect, just because you found an old barn doesn't mean that you've suddenly cracked the case and discovered a serial killer." She rolled her eyes. "A serial killer, seriously? And day one on the job and you just figure out where his lair is? Because you're Mr. Magnificent?"

"Thanks for noticing," he drawled without missing a beat. "Usually takes people some time to register the fact that I'm incredible. And, for the record, it's not day one. We're seven years into this bitch. Seven years and, as I told Detective Jones the other night, there are other missing women."

Camila glanced at her partner in surprise.

"Daniel, please," Eliza said.

Memphis stiffened. *Baby, you don't beg anyone.*

"Search the place. Do whatever you have to do, but this is it. I'm telling you...I have been here. This is *it*. He brought me here. He handcuffed me in that barn. I got free, and I ran out to the sunflower field."

A field that was long gone.

"And he chased after me," she added, voice haunted. "He chased me...but somehow, I got away." Eliza swallowed. "I was *here*."

***

"I wanted to stay." Eliza's left hand fisted on top of her thigh.

"Yeah, totally get that," Memphis slanted a fast glance in the rearview mirror. The vehicle behind him had been tailing them for a bit, something that made him edgy. Could be one of the guards on her father's payroll. Could be trouble. Could be nothing. "But if the cops are turning it into a crime scene..." And, yes, that was exactly what he thought the location was, "then we have to play by their rules. For now."

"I didn't take you as a rule follower."

He wasn't. Guilty. He'd already sent off several texts to get his team on the move. The very first message he'd sent? It had gone to Tony. He needed her and her dog Banshee down there, ASAP. But it was already dark, and there wasn't much that could be accomplished during the night.

They needed to regroup. Get back on the hunt in the morning. And it was going to be a long drive back to Eliza's place.

The vehicle behind him zoomed closer. Memphis tensed at the flash of headlights.

"What is it?" Eliza asked as her voice notched up in alarm.

"Nothing." Not yet. "Just some asshole who needs to pass." It was a two-lane road. No other traffic around. No street lamps. No houses. Just darkness.

Memphis eased off the pedal, just a bit.

The vehicle immediately slid into the other lane and started to whip past him.

But Memphis's instincts screamed.

Empty road. Aggressive driver rushing up behind me. Flashing his lights in the middle of damn nowhere.

Except, it wasn't nowhere. The road was close to the crime scene.

And now he saw that the other driver was in a truck. One of those trucks with the giant tires and a big grill on the front and—

The truck slammed into the side of Memphis's SUV. The other driver hit him hard and then swerved away.

Eliza screamed.

Oh, the fuck he was there to play. "Hold on, baby," Memphis shouted.

The truck's motor revved. It was still in the lane next to them. Memphis knew the bastard was about to hit them again.

Not gonna happen.

Memphis slammed on the brake pedal.

The truck flew in front of him as it crossed over into his lane.

"That's right, asshole," Memphis snarled. "You missed." Then he punched down on the gas because *you don't fuck with me. And you sure as hell don't come at her.*

But he wasn't fast enough. And the truck's engine roared as it hauled away from the scene. *No damn license plate.*

Memphis pulled his vehicle to the side of the road. Tightened his two-handed grip on the steering wheel. None of the air bags had deployed, but fear still pumped through him as he jerked his head toward Eliza. "Baby, you okay?"

A frantic nod. "What just happened?"

Well, either they had really shitty luck and some road raging SOB had just taken aim at them or...since he didn't believe this was some random bastard coming at him for shits and giggles.... "I think you may still have his attention."

"His?" she breathed.

The bastard who'd taken her. The perp they were hunting.

Baby, I think you always had his attention.

CHAPTER ELEVEN

A sharp knock came on the door. It sounded just before the door flew open. "*Eliza*! You alive in there?"

She spun around, her hand automatically flying up to cover her breasts. The shower water beat down on her, pouring in a steady rush, and, thank goodness, the heat from the shower had steamed up the glass door so that Memphis wasn't being given a show. "I'm fine!" She even sounded it. Maybe. "And you don't get to burst in on someone's shower!"

"I do when the someone in question has been in the shower for as long as you have. I wanted to make sure you were all right."

He was *still* in the bathroom. A shadowy form behind the glass door. She could see very little of his actual features. That meant he couldn't see her, either. But she still had one hand over her breasts and the other over the juncture of her thighs. Like that was going to help. Her hands dropped. "Get out, Memphis."

He took a step closer. "It's okay to be scared."

No, it wasn't. She was sick to death of being afraid.

But before she could tell him that, he turned away. His shadowy image vanished, and Eliza realized it wasn't as if she could actually tell him those words, anyway. She wasn't supposed to tell anyone those words, was she?

Her hand flew out and jerked off the spray of water. Eliza toweled off. Shouldered into her robe. A big, white, fluffy robe that normally made her feel safe and comforted.

A lie.

She wasn't safe. Hadn't been safe. Because it seemed the bastard had been watching her for years. She'd only thought that she'd gotten away from him. The stark truth was that she hadn't escaped at all. Not really.

Her wet hair trailed over her shoulders as she yanked open the door. It was close to one a.m. Or maybe it was after one, she didn't know for certain. After that hit and run on the road, they'd had to call Daniel again. Had to speak with the local cops, too, and fill out a report.

It had taken forever to get home. She should just want to crash in bed. Instead, Eliza felt wired. At any moment, she was sure she'd be jumping out of her skin.

Or jumping Memphis.

That shouldn't be an option, but it was. A very, very tempting one.

She hurried through her bedroom and rushed down the hallway and into the den where Eliza found him on the couch. He'd showered in the guest bath, and his wet hair had been casually shoved back. He wore jeans and nothing else as he sat there and seemed completely and totally at ease.

She didn't stop walking, not until she was in front of him.

He stared up at her.

Say something!

"All done?" His voice was as mild as could be. As if the events of the day and night had no impact on him.

"This happen a lot in your line of work?" Her hands shoved into the pockets of her robe. "You find crime scenes. You nearly get hit by random people in trucks—"

"You know I don't think there was anything random about the hit."

She flinched.

"You don't think there was anything random about it, either, princess."

Anger—hot and bracing—pulsed through her. "You know I've asked you to stop calling me that."

His head tilted back. "Is it the adrenaline? Burning through you? Making you feel like your body is electric?"

Her breath came faster.

He kept reclining on the couch. "Or is it the fear? You tried to hide it all these years, tried so hard to push it back, but the idea that he has been here all this time...it's making you realize your nice, ordered life is just a lie."

Everything felt like a lie.

"Or maybe..." He leaned forward. Kept his eyes on her. "It was going back to the scene. Did it stir up too many emotions?"

"You think you know everything about me."

His gaze hardened. "No, I don't know everything."

"Oh, really?" She couldn't stop. She wanted to push him because she felt so out of control. "And what don't you know?"

"I don't know how good you'll taste when I make you come with my mouth."

She stumbled back.

"Or how good it will feel when I'm buried balls deep in you. Two very important things, and I have no idea what they will be like." A pause. "Though I can imagine, and in my imagination..." A sigh. "Amazing."

"Are you playing with me?" An almost painful question to voice.

"Never." Sounded like a promise. "I am giving you an option for the night. You're practically shaking in front of me, sweetheart, and I want to push all that fear and anger away. I can do that for you. I can give you something else. Pleasure instead of any pain or fear."

She blinked quickly because stupid tears had wanted to fill her eyes. "You're offering to let me use you?"

His hands lifted as he shrugged. "Use me all night long, if that's what you want."

"That's *not* who I am. I don't use people." She spun away. Hurried for her bedroom. She'd get in her room. She'd shut the door. She'd sleep. When she woke up, this ridiculous, unnerving rush that filled her—that wanted to shake her apart—would be gone.

"Don't you get tired of being good?"

Eliza's steps faltered.

"Seems like you have to be perfect all the time. And, yep, I *know* because I did so much research on you. You never take a misstep..."

She'd *just* taken a misstep. Nearly fallen on her face.

"Always saying the right things and doing the right things in public. Doesn't that get old for you? Don't you just want to let go?"

Yes. But she couldn't. The last time she'd let go, something bad had happened. *The worst thing*. She had to be careful. There was no room for—

"Of course, we're not in public. So you don't have to worry about anything being right or wrong. It's just you and me, and if you want to be wrong with me, I can be so wrong that you'll scream with pleasure."

Do not look back at him. Because if she looked back at him, Eliza knew that she would go to him. She'd return to that couch. She'd drop her robe. She'd climb onto his lap.

She'd be wrong with him. Over and over again.

But what if it felt right? What if it finally felt right?

"Think about it, Eliza."

She lurched toward her bedroom.

"The offer will always be open," he promised.

***

He'd probably screwed up that scene. Memphis exhaled on a long breath. Did Eliza have any idea of just how much self-control he'd been exerting? Probably not. He looked down at his hands and saw the tremble in his fingertips.

He wanted her more than he'd ever wanted *anything*.

Eliza wasn't the only one riding an adrenaline high. And, sure, he knew all the signs and symptoms of that surge. If she'd said yes, they could have ridden out the surge together. Could have wrecked the couch. Her bed. Could have found oblivion together.

But it's not just the adrenaline driving you. Pure, savage lust burned in his blood when he was near Eliza. The longer he was with her, the more he wanted her. The more he noticed small things about her, like the way her nose would crinkle or how her dark eyes would gleam when she was angry or how—

Fuck it. He needed to get his head in the game and stop drooling over her. Memphis surged off the couch and grabbed his phone. He dialed Elijah, and, yes, it was late as hell, but Memphis needed to tell Elijah about the accident.

"Beauty sleep is a necessary component of my life," Elijah told him by way of answering.

"Yeah, mine, too," Memphis growled back. "Know what else is a necessary component of my life? *Staying* alive. Not having some dick in an oversized truck attempting to run me and Eliza off the road when we're leaving the crime scene."

"*What?*" Now Elijah sounded completely awake.

"Oh, you heard me." He'd texted Elijah hours before to tell him that Eliza had recognized that barn and the old sunflower field location. But he hadn't gotten to tell the former Fed this particular detail yet. "I swear, I think he was waiting for us. Or maybe he followed us *to* the field. But when we left—and it was nice and dark then for the bastard—he slammed into my side of the vehicle. He was coming in for a second hit, but when I braked, he shot past me."

Elijah swore.

"Exactly." He looked out of Eliza's windows. "Local authorities tried to feed me some crap about it being an aggressive driver, but my instincts say it was him. He knows Eliza remembered that spot."

"You think he is watching her now."

He stared out at the city. Looked across at the other high-rises. So many buildings. He was looking out, but what if someone else was looking back at him? Eliza thought she was safe in this castle of her father's, but really, it just gave someone else the opportunity to watch. *Give me a pair of binoculars and a place in the building across the street, and I can watch you all the time, Eliza.* "Isn't that what you believe?" Memphis responded.

"Yes." Grim.

His stomach clenched. "Then what do we do?" Because Elijah was the one who could get into their heads, he was the one who—

"You don't let her out of your sight."

The creak of the bedroom door seemed incredibly loud. It was the same creak he'd heard last night, right before Eliza had come to him. Memphis turned away from the window and gazed toward the darkened hallway.

The lamp still glowed beside the couch. The light spilled toward those shadows.

"Did you hear me, Memphis?" Elijah blasted in his ear.

"Don't worry," he assured his friend, voice going gruff. "Got my eyes on her right now."

"Good. If evidence is discovered at that old field or barn—evidence that can tie this guy to her kidnapping or to any of the other cases, the Feds will be called in. I'll touch base with my contacts and see who is available to help out. And Tony is on her way?"

"Yes."

"If bodies are out there, she'll find them."

Tony always did.

Eliza crept forward, but didn't step out of the shadows.

"You need backup," Elijah continued adamantly. "I'm getting on a plane to come—"

"Got backup already. The Robinson family has an army of guards at my beck and call."

"You need someone you can personally trust to watch your six. You trust them?"

No. "Don't worry. There's someone else I know who I can bring in." Someone who enjoyed fighting dirty and hard and brutally. "Stay with your wife."

"My wife will understand. You know she will. Of all people, Penelope will get this."

Because Penelope had once been targeted by a serial killer. When Elijah had worked at the FBI, Penelope had been the last victim he'd saved. "If I see I can't handle things, I will tell you. Not like I ever play the hero. Not really my thing, you know?"

Eliza...turned away. It seemed that she was heading back to her bedroom.

"Got to go," he said abruptly to Elijah.

"Wait, Memphis—"

"We'll talk tomorrow. Update everyone else, will you?" He ended the call. Shoved the phone down on the nearby table. "*Stop.*"

Her shadowy figure stilled.

"Did you want something, Eliza?" Had he managed to keep the need out of his voice? Probably not. Screw it.

"Yes." So low that he had to strain in order to hear her.

But then she came forward. She stepped out of the darkness. The big, fluffy robe was gone. In its place, she'd slipped into another one of the gowns that had surely been designed to drive him insane. Pale blue, with the smallest spaghetti straps in the world. Silky, almost see-through, and with a slit in the right thigh.

Every bit of moisture dried from his mouth. "What is it that you want?" *Do not pounce. Do not.*

"I want to be wrong with you."

Hell, yes. He practically flew across the room and hauled her into his arms. His mouth crashed onto hers even as a distant part of his mind shouted...*Slow. Go slow. Take care. This is Eliza! This is important—*

Her nails bit into his shoulders as she pulled him closer. She tasted so sweet. Her mouth had opened for him, her tongue met his in a greedy dance, and his dick shoved eagerly toward her. He could feel the pert peaks of her nipples pushing against his chest. He would be kissing those nipples. Sucking them. Tasting them.

He would taste her everywhere.

But not here. Not with the curtains open. Not somewhere that the sonofabitch might be able to see...

Her mouth tore from his. "I don't...want to disappoint you."

Memphis shook his head because he must have misheard.

"I tense up. I can't let go. I get too lost in—"

"Baby..." Tenderness flooded through him. Such a sharp, stunning contrast to the greedy lust that made him want to take and take and take. "You'll get lost in me. Before I'm done, you'll let go of everything else." She'd forget everyone else.

"But...what if I don't? I shouldn't...we shouldn't, I—"

"Trust me."

The faintest nod.

That was all he needed. Memphis scooped Eliza up into his arms. A cry of surprise spilled from her as he carried her back to her bedroom. He kicked the door shut. Did a quick visual to make sure all the curtains were closed. A light spilled from the bathroom she'd been in earlier, and he liked that bit of illumination. *I want to see her.* But he sure as hell didn't want anyone else getting the view.

He carried her to the bed. Big, a four-poster, and, yeah, it smelled like heaven.

Like her.

He lowered her until her feet touched the floor. Then his fingers swept under the straps of her gown. First, he pushed down the right strap. Then the left. The gown fell to the floor with a whisper. Memphis took a step back. Stared down at her. Drank her in. Her hair was still wet. Her eyes huge. Her body perfection. Full, pert breasts with tight nipples. Flaring hips. Long legs. And between her legs, the spot that he would be taking...He was almost drooling. *Get a grip, man.* Not like this was his first time. Not even close.

So why do I feel like it matters more than anything else? "Get on the bed."

Her breath hitched, and she climbed onto the bed.

"Do not *move,*" he ordered her. Then he spun for the door. He practically ran out.

"Memphis?" Confusion notched in her voice, but he didn't stop.

Memphis rushed back to the den. Then turned for the guest room. While he'd planned to bunk on the couch again, his bags were actually in her guest room. He'd wanted to be on the couch to be closer to her.

So if anyone came through the front door, they'd have to face me before getting to her.

When they'd returned to her place, a quick phone call had gotten the bags sent over courtesy of the extra-helpful staff at his hotel—staff who'd still been worried about impending legal trouble. He went straight to the bags and snagged the foil packets that he needed. Then Memphis double-timed it back to Eliza's room and—

"What in the hell?" He froze in the doorway and glared.

She was tugging back on her gown. She was *not* in bed.

"What are you doing?" Memphis surged forward. "Baby, the goal is to get you in less clothing, not more."

Her head jerked up. "You...you left me—"

Memphis opened his hand. Showed her the condoms. "I went to get protection for us while I still had a little sense in my head." He put the condoms on her nightstand. Tugged her nightgown down again. "*Nothing* can make me leave you." The words seemed to echo through him, and Memphis realized he wasn't just talking about this night.

Unsettling. World changing. And...

He'd deal with that problem another time.

"On the bed," he directed her.

She slid onto the bed. Then crouched there, on her knees.

The fear in her eyes had to go. That uncertainty needed to vanish. She was the sexiest woman he'd ever seen, and he needed her as hungry, as desperate, as he felt.

His hands went to the top of his jeans. He jerked open the snap. Hauled down the zipper. His dick sprang out as he ditched the jeans.

Her lips parted. A little gasp.

"I'm sure men have told you that you're beautiful a thousand times," he growled.

She shook her head.

No? Again, he had the thought...*dumbasses.* "I'm not those other bastards, and I'm not here to just say you're beautiful."

Her gaze snapped back up to meet his.

"I'm here to tell you that I want to break your control, Eliza. I went to see you go wild in my arms. I want you wild for me." *Only me.* "I want you to know just how incredibly sexy you are." He put a knee on the bed. Leaned in. "Because I have never wanted anyone as much as I want you. And before we're done, you're gonna want me the same way. More than you've ever wanted *anyone* else."

Her hand lifted out to him. Touched his cheek. Scraped over the stubble. "I already do."

Fuck me. His head turned, and he pressed a kiss to her palm. The last bit of gentleness he had because...

Want her. Need her. Will take her. Because he knew that Eliza was absolutely meant...

To be mine.

He tumbled her back onto the bed. Kissed her deep and hard. Her legs slid down, pressed on either side of his hips. His dick lodged at the entrance to her body, and he swore he could feel her heat against him.

It would be so easy to drive into her right then...

To sink into paradise.

Not yet. Not...yet.

Because he hadn't been lying when he said she'd need him more than anyone else. And he was certainly a man of his word.

Memphis kissed a path down her neck. Loved her little moans and gasps. Down he went, and his mouth closed over one tight nipple. He sucked and licked and loved the way her body twisted beneath his. As his mouth savored her, his hand rose to tease her other nipple. His fingers squeezed, plucked, and her hips shoved up hard against his.

And down he went...down more...Memphis kissed a scorching trail over her stomach. Repositioned his body and spread her legs wider. He took a moment to just stare at her. This was a memory he would not be forgetting anytime soon.

“Memphis?”

“This is the fun part.” He put his mouth on her.

She nearly shot off the bed, but his hands clamped around her hips, and he held her down. Held her while his tongue licked over her clit, then dipped into her. He tasted and he savored and he knew he was getting drunk because she was so good. So fucking perfect. He lapped her up. Feasted on her, then went in hard on her clit, knowing that he could push her and push her until...

Her nails dug into his shoulders. Her hips shoved toward his mouth. And she came with a choked scream.

He kept tasting her. Didn’t let up until the trembles had stopped rolling over her body. Then and only then did he lift his head and ease up.

The ragged sound of her breathing filled the room.

"Memphis?" Stunned. Hushed. She licked her lips. "You...ah, you haven't...yet..."

No, but he would. He grabbed a condom. Tore it open. Rolled it on. Speech was beyond him. The lust was too strong. Too primitive. He'd tasted her. Brought her to release, now he needed to be buried *in* her.

He eased in, just pushing the head of his dick inside of her.

Her body tensed.

So tight.

"It's...I told you...it's been, a, um, while..."

She'd take him. She'd been fucking made for him. His fingers slid between them. Stroked her in just the right spot...

Her hips surged toward him. He sank into her. All the way. Slammed into heaven. And there was no holding back. No more soft touches. No more restraint. There was just lust. Desire. A driving, savage climb toward release. Faster and harder and she was with him. With him as she moaned and arched against him. As her legs locked around his hips. As she met him thrust for thrust, no matter how powerful or fast. With him as they wrecked her bed.

And as his orgasm barreled down on him, she was *with* him. He felt the clench of her inner muscles. The tell-tale contraction of her climax as she came hard and long around him. He emptied into her. Shoved deep and exploded.

I will never let her go.

***

Memphis jerked awake. The dream—damn *nightmare*—had his heart racing. He didn't normally have nightmares. He *was* the nightmare. But this time...

This case was different. His head turned. Eliza slept beside him. She'd snuggled up against him like it was the most natural thing in the world.

He didn't usually stick around to sleep with partners. Dick move? Yeah, but the lovers he'd been with before had known the score. They knew he wasn't playing for keeps. They hadn't been, either. The sex had been satisfying. The arrangements mutually beneficial. No one ever got hurt. All they got was pleasure.

Tonight, with Eliza, the pleasure had nearly decimated him.

Her arm curled lightly over him, and, carefully, he lifted it up and slipped from the bed. He stared down at her for a moment, oddly aware of how innocent she looked.

In his world, he'd seen innocence destroyed too many times. Eliza had already faced more horror than most people could imagine, but she still had that haunting innocence about her...

I would kill to protect that light in her.

No, he'd just kill to protect her.

Kill for her.

Memphis turned away. Marched back to the den. Scooped up the phone he'd put down before taking Eliza to bed. He tapped the screen. Sent the text.

I need you. Simple. Straight to the point. *Calling in the debt you owe.* He included Eliza's address and sent the message. He'd told Elijah that he had backup in mind. He just hadn't mentioned exactly who his backup would be. Mostly because he knew the man's identity would freak Elijah the hell out.

And it took a lot to freak out Elijah.

This man can do it. To most people, the backup that Memphis had just requested was the boogeyman.

But when you were fighting a monster, you needed the right kind of help.

He put the phone down. Padded soundlessly back to Eliza. Slipped back into bed with her. Then he was the one to curl his arm around her and pull her close.

His eyes closed, and the nightmare whispered through his mind.

A nightmare where he was running through a field of sunflowers, screaming Eliza's name over and over again...

And he couldn't find her.

***

Eliza waited until she heard Memphis's breathing deepen and slide into a gentle rhythm. Then she carefully opened her eyes. Darkness surrounded them. It took her a moment to be able to adjust to the dark so that she could see him. His arm was a warm, strong weight around her stomach. She wanted to stay right there with him. To be safe and secure in his arms but...

But there was something she needed to do. Something she should have already done.

Carefully, she lifted his arm. Eased it off her so that she could crawl out of bed. Then she tiptoed to the door. Slipped into the hallway.

A few moments later, she was pushing open the door to the guest room. She flipped on the lights. His laptop waited on the desk in the corner, and Eliza bit her lip as she headed toward it. Eliza pulled out the chair, sat down, and—

A note had been written on the pad near the laptop.

Eliza, I figured you would come in here. My password is Fuckyou1234. Don't be afraid of what you find. We will stop the bastard. -Memphis.

She raised the top of the laptop. Booted the machine.

Fuckyou1234.

She held her breath and waited and...

A vivid background appeared to show waves crashing onto a shore. Turquoise water. Foaming surf.

And one file in the top left-hand corner of that beautiful scene. A file with the name of...*Six Victims.*

She clicked on the file.

Amelia Lake. The victim taken on the first anniversary of Eliza's abduction. The notes on her case came up first. Notes. Her picture. The image of Amelia filled the screen. A vivacious redhead with sparking blue eyes and a dimple in one cheek. She wore a college cheer uniform and had a red star painted on her cheek as she grinned in her photo.

Memphis had compiled detailed notes on her. Eliza read through the material. Parts of the research burned in her mind. Amelia had been twenty-two years old when she went missing. She'd vanished on her way home from a bar in Tuscaloosa, Alabama. At the bar, she'd had a fight with her boyfriend. Told him that she would be finding another ride back to her sorority house.

She had never arrived at the sorority house.

The police had conducted an exhaustive search. No one could remember seeing her leave the bar. No one could remember anything to help find her.

The second anniversary of Eliza's abduction...*Casey Carter*. Eliza swallowed as she gazed at Casey's picture. Brown hair, shot with red highlights. A mischievous smile. She'd been working at a local bar in Galveston as she dreamed of being a singer. She'd been scheduled to close up the place for the night. The next morning, when the owner had gone in, the bar had been unlocked, and Casey had been nowhere to be seen. The owner had thought that maybe she'd hooked up with a customer, so he didn't report her disappearance, not until the next night when she didn't show up for work and no one could get her to answer her phone.

The third anniversary...*Layla Darrow*. The next victim. A pretty blond. One with soft gray eyes. A fragile build. No red star happily painted on her cheek. Just a slightly silly grin on her face. She'd been eleven months younger than Amelia.

She was younger than me.

Layla had taken her sister's car while Delilah Darrow finished up work. They'd planned to meet at a bar to let off steam as soon as Delilah was done.

Layla hadn't made it to the bar.

The abandoned vehicle she'd taken had been found the next day. Layla hadn't. Delilah had searched and searched. But Layla hadn't come home.

Fourth anniversary...*Drew Salters.* A brunette with green eyes. Wearing a trim business suit and staring back at Eliza with her steady gaze. Twenty-six at the time of her disappearance. She'd been planning to meet friends for a bachelorette party at a bar in Atlanta. When she hadn't shown up, they'd just thought she got tied up with work. So they didn't report her missing. Not that night. Not the next day. And Monday, when Drew didn't show up for work, it was her assistant who finally realized something was wrong.

By that time, Drew was long gone.

She didn't come back.

What had their families thought, Eliza wondered, when the women never came home? When they just vanished? Did they think they might still be alive? Did they think there was hope?

Delilah did. Eliza knew that with certainty. Delilah was still searching for Layla. After all, she'd gotten Memphis to take the case. She'd hadn't given up.

But is there any hope left?

Eliza went to the next name even as she felt a tear slide down her cheek. *Tameka Williams.* Taken on the fifth anniversary of Eliza's abduction. *Tameka...*Dark hair swept back from her forehead. Killer cheekbones. Sparkling eyes that tossed out a challenge to the world. In the photo, she wore gold hoop earrings and a small cross necklace.

Twenty-seven when she vanished. Recently divorced, Tameka had met a guy on an online dating app. She'd gone to a bar to meet him. Her friends had said that she'd deliberately picked a public spot for their first meeting.

Only five days later, when authorities were hunting for Tameka, when her brother and mother were desperately begging the public for help, when her preacher father called on everyone to find his precious daughter...

The bouncer at the bar would say that she'd never gone past the door. Security footage would back him up. Tameka never entered the local bar in Tallahassee, Florida. But her car was found in the bar's parking lot.

Eliza blinked rapidly. She could taste the salt of her tears, and she wanted to stop. She wanted to stop looking at these women and imagining what it had been like for them...

But I don't have to imagine. The nightmare comes to me all the time.

The last woman...*Stephanie Stone.* Taken last year. On the sixth anniversary. Twenty-four. Brown hair. A small mole near her lip. Stylish glasses. Eyes that seemed a little sad behind those lenses. Just a little lost. She'd gone to a bar in

Biloxi, Mississippi. The bartender remembered several men approaching her, but he'd said that Stephanie politely dismissed them all. He'd been called away by other customers, and when he went back to check on her, Stephanie had been gone. She'd left her payment and a tip on the bar top for him.

Eliza swallowed as she read more of the details that Memphis had collected.

Two weeks. It was over two weeks before anyone realized that Stephanie was gone. She'd worked from home but had been scheduled to take a vacation. Her mother and father had been deceased.

The police were only alerted when her mailbox began to overflow, and neighbors grew concerned.

Eliza leaned forward as she read the notation Memphis had made...

By that time, her case was already cold. No cameras at the old bar. She disappeared, and no one noticed.

Eliza's breath shuddered out. *I did this.* If she had just been able to remember who had taken her, if she could have just stopped the man who'd taken her...If she could have *found* him...

Those other women would never have vanished.

"Eliza..." Low. Rough. "Baby, I'm trying to give you the time you need, but your tears are ripping out my heart. Pretty shocking, honestly, because until you, I wasn't sure I still had a heart."

A sob tore from her.

"Fuck." Memphis bounded toward her.

She couldn't stop the tears. Couldn't slow them. They just rained down as the images of those women rushed through her mind. "My...fault. I-I did—"

He hauled her out of the chair and into his arms. "No. Absolutely not. Don't say it. Don't think it."

She was saying it. She was thinking it. She was—

"The sick prick who took you is the only one we blame. *He* did this. Not you."

But if she could have just remembered—

"*Not. You.*" Fierce, but his hold was gentle. "You didn't do this. He did. You got away. You survived. You lived. Sweetheart, you went to the cops. You told everyone what you knew. You did everything you could."

The women were still gone. Their families devastated. Their lives...lost?

"He will pay. We will find him. We will stop him. We will make him pay."

The guilt and pain tore through her.

Memphis carried her out of the guest room. Took Eliza back to her bedroom. Carefully, tenderly, he tucked her into the bed. Then his shadowy form hovered over her. "Don't move." Gruff. "I know you like to hop out of bed when my back is turned, but just don't do it. I'll be right back."

She squeezed her eyes shut. She couldn't stop seeing those women. *I'm so sorry.* Sorry for their pain. Sorry that she couldn't help them. That she hadn't stopped him.

"Here, baby." A warm cloth pressed to her left cheek. He wiped away her tears. Moved the cloth to her right cheek. "If crying makes you feel better, then do it all night long. But if it doesn't...can you stop? Because watching you cry is like taking a knife to the chest."

Eliza pulled in a shuddering breath. "Tell me..."

"Anything."

"Tell me that w-we'll stop him."

"We'll stop him."

"That h-he won't hurt anyone else."

"We are going to lock the bastard away. I am not going to give up. I don't care how long it takes, we will stop him." He eased down into the bed. Pulled her into his arms. "I fucking swear it, princess."

CHAPTER TWELVE

When she opened her eyes again, the night had ended. Sunlight streamed through her curtains and lit the room.

Her eyes felt grainy and rough, and Eliza couldn't remember how long she'd cried. Memphis had held her, and eventually, she'd drifted to sleep. His vow had followed her.

We are going to lock the bastard away.

Their goal. Their plan.

Eliza trusted Memphis. She trusted him completely, and maybe that should have surprised her. She'd known him such a short period of time, after all, but...

But it didn't matter. It was Memphis, and he was going to help her.

She dressed carefully, putting on designer jeans and a pale gray top. Matching sandals. Her hair fell loosely around her shoulders, and she took a few moments to apply mascara and even a splash of red lipstick. Eliza added a little concealer beneath her eyes to try and hide the puffiness.

Look like you're in control. That had been her mantra for years. *Look like it even when you aren't. Because no one will know the truth but you.*

She strode down the hallway—and remembered being carried by Memphis. She entered the den with her shoulders squared and her spine straight.

He wasn't there.

"Uh, Memphis?"

"In the kitchen!" he called, and the man sounded *cheery.*

She wet her lips and made her way to the kitchen. She didn't want him to think she was weak. Didn't want him to think that she couldn't handle—

Eliza drew up short at the sight that greeted her. Memphis had made her breakfast, again.

"Morning, sunshine." He shoveled eggs onto a plate. "You are absolutely gorgeous in the morning."

How could he say that? "You haven't even looked at me yet."

He put down the pan. Looked up at her. "You were the first thing I saw when I opened my eyes. Absolutely gorgeous. Like I said before." His green gaze seemed to heat. "I wanted to gobble you right up."

You did last night. Nope. She would *not* say that. Not going to do it. It was better not to rehash all of the previous night's events. Not the insane sex. Not the breakdown after.

"You look great now, too, but got to say, I prefer you when you're completely naked and curled around me."

So...he was focusing on the sexual events. Not the shuddering tear scene. Was that better? Worse? "You...you shouldn't just say things like that." Her kitchen felt too warm.

"Why not?" He winked before she could respond. "Because that stuff makes you hot?"

Maybe. Yes. "We should talk."

"Um. Aren't we talking?"

"I meant about what happened last night."

"You meant about the phenomenal sex. Sure. We can talk about it over and over again."

Frustration had her jaw hardening. "Do you take anything seriously?"

His gaze seemed to burn. "When it comes to you, my intentions are one hundred percent serious, be assured of that."

The racing of her heartbeat filled her ears.

"I take you—I take us—very, very seriously. So we can talk about the sex we had. Do it all day and night long." A muscle flexed along his jaw. "Or we can talk about the victims. But I'd rather not see you cry again so I am trying to distract you."

He was? That was oddly sweet of him.

"Either way, I will one hundred percent *not* allow you to blame yourself for what happened to them. That shit isn't going to fly on my watch, so don't even try it."

Some of the heavy weight around her heart—it didn't ease, but it seemed to shift.

"You should eat. I should eat. We can talk while we eat. Talk about sex. About the other things I take seriously. About our hunting plans. Whatever you want." He pulled out a chair for her. Waited expectantly.

Sighing, she sat down. Inhaled the utterly delicious scents. "You're quite the cook." A surprise that she'd discovered yesterday.

"That's because one of my first jobs was at the diner down the street from the apartment my mom and I shared in Tennessee. Grew up in Memphis, by the way, in case you were wondering about my name."

When it came to him, she wondered about a lot of things. If she'd had her way, Eliza would learn all of his secrets.

"I started by sweeping and bussing tables at the diner, then got bumped up to the kitchen." He sat across from her. "Realized then that if you could be a passable cook, you could always get a job."

She dug in and ate the breakfast, realizing vaguely that she was famished. *Must have been all that activity last night.* The fork nearly slipped from her fingers at the thought.

Memphis laughed. "You do this partial blush thing that is so damn cute. Your cheeks don't go red. More like they pinken a little. And I do have to wonder, what caused that sweet pinkness?"

You did. Or rather, remembering what she'd done with him. "If I...hurt you last night, I wanted to say—"

"What are you talking about now?" He squinted. "How would you have hurt me?"

She ate more food. Ridiculously, insanely good. How had he made *eggs* taste so good? After swallowing and carefully sipping some orange juice to buy herself more time, Eliza finally said,

"Because I believe I left scratches down your back." She distinctly recalled that act.

"Oh, yeah, baby, you did." He winked. "Told you we'd get around to that part. And to think, you were trying to act like you weren't the kind of person who ignites in bed."

"I'm not. Normally." She still couldn't believe how intense things had been last night. They hadn't just had sex once. Had it been three times? At the end, she'd just been lost to pleasure that seemed to never end. "I've got one ex in particular who will tell you that I'm as close to frigid as it's possible to—"

His fork hit the plate with a clatter. "Want me to teach him some manners for you?" Suddenly, all signs of playfulness were gone. His voice had become low and lethal, and his eyes blazed not with a sensual heat, but more like with the barely banked fires of hell.

"That's certainly not necessary." Her grip tightened around the handle of her fork.

"Name."

"Excuse me?"

"Tell me his name," he gritted out.

Now she was suspicious. "Why?"

"Because if I encounter the prick, I want to be sure and give him a few useful life lessons."

"I...think you want to kick his ass."

He laughed. "God, I love it when you say things like that in your prim tone. Future reference, it drives me crazy when you say 'fuck' in that polished voice of yours. Love it." He leaned toward her, as if imparting a secret. "And, yes, I do want to kick his ass." His gaze traveled over her face. "I find myself very protective where you are concerned."

"Is it because we had sex?"

One shoulder rolled in a shrug. "I was protective before that."

"Oh. So it's because we're...partners?" Or maybe it was because of her past. He felt bad because of what had happened to her—

"I think it's just because...it's you." Another shrug. "Name."

"I don't want you to kick his ass."

"Are you sure? Because it sounds to me like he said things that hurt you." Memphis pursed his lips. "How about if I just promise to kick his ass a little bit?"

"If you get thrown in jail for beating up one of my exes, how are we going to find the man we're really after?"

A muscle flexed along his jaw. "Fair enough." He settled back against his chair. "But I will need the names of your exes. All of them. And your friends. Work associates. Everyone who is close to you."

She'd just finished eating, and the meal suddenly felt very heavy on her stomach. "Because you think the man who took me has been in my life this whole time?" The man who'd taken her—and all those other women.

"I notice that you keep saying man. Is it because you remember him?"

Her lashes flickered. "I-I remember him calling to me. He was chasing me when I got out of that barn. Yelling when I was near the sunflowers. It was a strong, hard voice." God, she wished she could remember more. Remember something to *help*.

"And you don't think you recognized that voice?"

The flash she had of the voice—just a hard yell. Almost a thunder. Not like someone's normal, everyday voice. Eliza shook her head.

"Cops are supposed to be searching for the truck that swiped us last night. Haven't received a damn word yet from them and—"

She heard the chime of her doorbell.

"Well, well. Isn't that timely?" He tossed down his napkin and rose. "You expecting some company this morning?"

It was Sunday. She didn't expect anyone.

"Right." An incline of his head. "Then let's just see who decided to drop by for a visit."

She jumped up and followed on his heels. He took a second to glance through her peephole, then Memphis swung open the door.

"Morning, Detective," he drawled.

Detective Daniel Jones took a step back. "You're...what in the hell are you doing here?"

"Uh, where else would I be?" Memphis questioned in return. "Got to watch out for the hotel rooms in this town. People break in when you least expect it."

Daniel took in Memphis's jeans, his shirt, and the fact that he wasn't wearing shoes. "You spent the night here."

"Ah, sure, and I intend to—"

"Memphis has taken over my security detail," Eliza rushed to say as she stepped closer to his side. "He's moved in with me for the time being."

"Has he now." Daniel's hands went to his lean hips. He still wore his badge and had his gun holster under his arm.

"Yes, *he* has," Memphis replied. "That's what she just said."

Eliza put her hand on Memphis's chest. His very hard, strong chest, and pushed back. "Let Daniel come inside." For Daniel to be visiting this early, he must have news.

Memphis backed up so the cop could come inside, and once Daniel had paced toward the den, Memphis shut the door and locked it. Eliza strode to stand near Daniel. "Did you find information that we could use? Out at the barn or—or did you find the driver of the truck?" She could hear the hope in her own voice.

He spun toward her. "We found some information, yes."

Why was he being so slow to talk? Her stomach twisted. Maybe breakfast hadn't been such a great idea.

"Eliza, why did you pick that particular area to search yesterday? What led you to that land?"

"I—" She darted a glance over at a watchful Memphis.

"Eliza remembered sunflowers," he said. "A field of them. She told you that before though, didn't she?"

"Yes." Daniel's stare slid between them before returning and focusing solely on Eliza. "But you know that I looked before. Back then, we didn't turn up anything we could use."

That didn't mean that she'd just been going to give up. "I remembered the sunflowers." On this, she was adamant. "Memphis got a friend of his to do a search for us. His friend came up with some old aerial photos that were taken around the time of my abduction, and those photos led us to search several locations." A quick breath. "The place we showed you was our third search site. When we got there, I *remembered* that wind chime. I remembered running from the barn. That place was familiar to me. I had been there before." She surged toward him. "We have to find the owners of the property. Get them to allow you to search it. Or if they won't, I know there are legal means that you can—"

"The owner was buried beneath a ton of red tape, but we tore through that tape last night. My partner is talking to him right now. While she questions him, I thought it would be best if I broke the news to you."

Broke the news to her? Why was he phrasing things that way—

"Eliza, your dad owns that land."

What?

"He bought it under one of the Robinson Corporation's umbrella companies years ago. He bought it, then didn't do a damn thing with it. Now you're here, telling me that you were held captive on that land. That you escaped from that old barn."

Her cheeks felt hot. Then prickly. Then cold. So very cold.

"Doesn't make a damn bit of sense to me," Daniel continued gruffly. "Why would your father buy that land? Why hide the acquisition?" The questions came out, rapid-fire, just like an interrogation. "What in the hell is going on?"

***

"I don't understand what's happening."

Memphis didn't like the lost tone of Eliza's voice. When she'd first appeared in the kitchen, pain had flickered in her eyes. The victims had already started to haunt her. He'd tried to tease her during the meal. Tried to lighten her mood. He'd been making a little bit of progress, until the detective had shown up.

As for what was happening... "Things got easier, that's what happened." He spun into the driveway and looked back to the see that the detective was right behind him. Daniel had been trailing him ever since they left Eliza's place. The cop could have just gone ahead and passed him at any point—they were headed to the same damn location.

The Robinson estate.

He drove past the big gates and stopped in front of the curving drive. Eliza started to spring from the vehicle, but his hand flew out and curled around her wrist. "This development means that we can search the property to our heart's content. Your father owns it, so he'll give the go-ahead."

"Why does he own it?" She shook her head. "There is no way that can be some coincidence. My God, I was held there. *Trapped.* And the place belongs to my dad?"

No, he didn't think for a second that it was a coincidence. "It's a lead," he said grimly. "Another link in the chain that will help us to find the perp."

"But no one is finding him." She swallowed. "Daniel said no one found the truck. It didn't have a tag so he can't pull it up in the system."

"*I* can track it. I can do a search on the make and model, the full description of the vehicle with its big-ass tires and grille. It won't vanish on me. I will find him." He had plenty of connections that he could use in his hunt. He'd actually already started on that hunt. He'd texted a description of the vehicle to his friends in the Ice Breakers, and he knew that with their contacts, someone might hit pay dirt for him.

A door slammed behind them. He looked back and saw that Daniel had exited his vehicle. Daniel's movements were stiff and angry, but the guy had been angry from the moment Memphis opened the door of Eliza's penthouse.

You didn't like that I'd spent the night with her.

Daniel had a personal attachment to Eliza. Daniel had been in her life—in one form or another—ever since her abduction. So that meant, hell, yes, Daniel was on his suspect list. "Did you ever sleep with him?"

"*What?*" Her voice notched up. "This is *not* the time for that!" She yanked away and jumped from the car.

It actually *was* the time to learn as much as he could about Daniel, but Eliza was storming—rather elegantly but definitely still storming—her way up the stone steps that led to her father's house. And Daniel was already right on her tail.

Locking his jaw, Memphis climbed out of his rental. A new one, not the scraped-up ride he'd had before. He'd pulled a few strings and had this vehicle waiting. He slammed the door and stalked up after Eliza and Daniel. He could hear the raised voices before he even got to the top step—

"What in the hell do you mean that you'll get a warrant if you have to do so?" Prescott bellowed. "Do you know how many lawyers I have? Do you think talk of a warrant is going to scare me?"

"They don't have to get a warrant, Dad," Eliza's cool voice cut in to say. "Because you're going to give them your full permission to search the entire piece of property."

He spun around—Prescott had been going toe-to-toe with Camila in his study, but now he looked over at Eliza. "Have you heard what they're saying?" he demanded.

Memphis made his way into the study, too. Looked around at the assembled group. Prescott, the new wife, Kathleen, and the guard he really didn't like—Alec. They were lined up together and facing off against Camila. Camila, and now Daniel. Daniel had taken up a spot right next to his partner. And in the middle of those two groups?

Eliza.

Memphis crossed his arms over his chest to watch the scene.

Eliza faced her father. "Why did you buy that land?"

"I buy *thousands and thousands* of acres every year! I don't even know which piece of property Detective Perez is referring to!" A frustrated exhale. "She comes in here, demanding that I give her full access. Hell, no, I'm not giving her full access to anything, not until I know—"

"We were searching for the sunflower fields," Eliza said.

"Yes, yes, I know." He jerked a hand through his hair. "Did you find the right spot?"

His voice was...off when he asked the question. A tangled mix—hope, reluctance, fear.

"We did," Eliza replied.

Because Memphis was watching the little group so closely, he caught the surprising reaction. The fast gasp. The flash of anger...

On Kathleen's face.

But Eliza's stepmother quickly put her mask back in place even as Prescott advanced on his daughter. "You...did?"

"I did, Dad. And it's the property that the cops want to search. *Your* property."

Prescott shook his head. "That's not possible."

"I *remember* it. I remember being there. It's the place, I know it is."

"Eliza..." Kathleen's voice. Filled with sympathy and sadness. "You're upsetting yourself, dear. Didn't I warn you about this very thing yesterday? Didn't I tell you not to get overwrought?"

Overwrought? Memphis's brows snapped together. Overwrought, his ass. And Eliza could be whatever she wanted to be. *Be all you can be, sweetheart. I got your back.*

Kathleen shouldered Prescott to the side and curled her hands around Eliza's shoulders. "You need to call Dr. Kendall. She can help you. You can't just pick some random place and then magically make it into the spot you need for—"

"I hate bullshit," Memphis said. "Hate it."

Everyone looked at him.

"Yep, hi, there." He gave them a little wave. "Came with Eliza. Don't know if you realized it yet, but we're a package deal." Why did they all look so surprised? "Thought we covered this before. Guess you missed it?"

Alec glared at him. "You're giving her false hope. You're getting her—"

"Not really in the mood to talk to you just yet, so how about you wait your turn?" Memphis asked with a lazy grin. "Thanks. Now, back to Eliza. Because I am always in the mood for her." He advanced on the stepmom. "How about you stop grabbing on her, yes?"

Frowning, Kathleen let her go. "I was...comforting her."

Whatever. "There is nothing 'magical' about the location Eliza found yesterday, so let's begin by not using that word." Because it pissed him off. "And she's not having some spell, some delusion. She's not working herself up over anything. I was with her. I saw her reaction. It was genuine. She recognized that place. The first two stops did nothing for her, but number three was it because Eliza had been there before. The fucking wooden bar in the third stall of that barn was still broken from where she'd fought so hard to get free of her handcuffs."

"*Jesus.*" Prescott slumped.

"She recognized the wind chime that still hung outside the barn." A slant of his gaze toward Camila and Daniel. "Not to tell you how to do your job..." Oh, wait. Yes, he was. "But that would be the first thing I took into evidence. Someone has been keeping that all nice and shiny. Odd, isn't it? For an abandoned piece of property. To have one thing out there in mint condition. Seems weird, but what do I know?"

"*Jesus,*" Prescott repeated. "I...I own it?" His gaze jumped to Camila. "You're sure, Detective Perez?"

She nodded.

"Funny thing," Memphis continued, and he was now standing with Eliza. Cops on one side. Her family—and former bodyguard—on the other. "When we were leaving that location, some SOB side-swiped us. He was coming back for a second hit, so not like it was an accident, but I braked and he missed us." Memphis let his gaze travel over to Alec. "Didn't happen to witness that attack last night, did you? I know you like to keep a close watch on things...I mean, on Eliza."

Alec's chin lifted. "Mr. Robinson told me to stand down. He gave me the day off yesterday. Said I was to inform the guards that you were handling Eliza's protection from now on." He surged forward. "Are you telling me that your first day on the job, you put her in danger? That she was almost seriously injured in a car accident with you?"

"Everyone should take a breath and settle down," Camila announced in a rather impressive I'm-in-charge tone.

It was a tone Alec ignored as he blasted, "I watched over her for *years!* During all that time, I never had a single threat get close to her. You're here, and day one of your job, you already fuck up?"

Memphis had to laugh. He could tell by the way Alec's face mottled that it wasn't the response the other man had expected.

"You think that's funny?" Alec snarled. "You think Eliza's safety is some kind of joke?"

Nope. Not any day of the week did he think that. "Keeping Eliza safe is my number one priority," Memphis assured him.

"I don't think it is." The low words came from Kathleen.

He'd almost forgotten about her.

"I don't think that protecting my stepdaughter *is* your priority." She sniffed. Shifted from one high-heeled foot to another. "I read my husband's report on you."

Fabulous. Nice to know his info was being passed around like free candy at a school party.

"You're on this case because you're helping one of your—your Ice Breaker friends. That is what you call yourselves, don't you?" Kathleen asked, voice hesitant, but her gaze was hard. Aggressive. "You're here because your friend—*her* sister went missing and didn't come back. You promised to help her find her lost sister, and you're willing to do whatever it takes in order to keep that promise, even if it means using Eliza."

He sucked in his left cheek as he considered her. "You know someone in Archer Radcliffe's circle." Delilah's new husband. "It fits. After all, Eliza knows him, so stands to reason that you would, too." He nodded as he analyzed the possibilities. "You heard that he recently married my friend, and you got some gossip on my relationship with her."

"You're denying nothing," Kathleen noted as she curled her hand around her husband's forearm. "Your priority *isn't* Eliza's safety. You were a hunter once, and you're a hunter now. All you want to do is find this man, and you don't care who you hurt in the process." Her head turned toward Alec. "You need to take over her security once more."

The two detectives shifted uncomfortably. "About that property..." Daniel said determinedly.

"That's not even in city limits." Katheen's hand tightened on her husband but she tossed a questioning glance at the two detectives. "Is it even your jurisdiction? Shouldn't someone else be investigating out there?"

"I was taken from Houston." Eliza had not moved from her position in the middle of them all. "And I'm sure the detectives are cooperating with other law enforcement personnel." Her stare lasered on her father. "Give them permission to search that property. Sign whatever legal documents you need to sign. We do not have time to waste."

No, they didn't.

Eliza's index finger tapped against her thigh. "According to Memphis, the man who took me will take another woman on the upcoming anniversary of my disappearance. That's what he has been doing—taking different women each year. If we search, if the police search your property, maybe there is a clue out there that can lead us to him. Maybe we can stop someone else from vanishing."

Looking ten years older, her father nodded. "Search it," he told the cops. "I didn't even know...we have so many holdings. I don't think I've ever been out there. Just property for the future..."

A future that was tied to Eliza's past.

"I'll make sure my lawyers know that you have the all clear," Prescott added.

Kathleen's curved jaw set. "He's *using* you, Eliza," she said. "Don't you get it? Or are you just so desperate that you don't—"

Memphis moved his body in front of Eliza's.

"It's okay." Eliza's hand brushed over his shoulder. "I don't care."

Those words were wrong. Frowning, he looked back at her.

She sent him a smile that didn't touch her eyes. "I don't care if you're using me. I don't care if you dangle me like a worm on a hook for him. As long as you catch him, as long as you bring him in, I don't care what you do."

CHAPTER THIRTEEN

"Are you sleeping with him?"

Eliza turned off the sink. She'd been splashing water on her face in one of the *many* guest bathrooms in her father's house. *His* house. A giant house with too many rooms and not enough people inside. It always felt too empty to her.

Eliza grabbed a hand towel and glanced over at Kathleen. She didn't really think of the other woman as her stepmother. She was just...Kathleen. The woman who'd appeared in her father's life from seemingly nowhere. Her father had always enjoyed his lovers over the years. He'd sworn, though, that he wouldn't remarry. Not after her mother's death.

Then Kathleen had appeared.

Kathleen who often wore a smile that never reached her eyes. Kathleen who was often excruciatingly polite in public, but could cut a person dead in private. Kathleen who always seemed so watchful.

"Answer the question, Eliza," Kathleen ordered.

She turned off the water. Took her time rearranging the hand towel. Then looked toward the other woman. "It's rude to interrupt someone when the person is trying to have a moment of privacy."

"The bathroom door wasn't closed. You were just splashing water on yourself." Her head tilted. "Were you trying to make it look as if you were crying?"

No, quite the opposite. She'd been trying to get rid of any tears. To push away the burn that wanted to fill her eyes. "Of course, not."

"You can't trust him."

Sighing, she advanced on Kathleen. "Why does it matter to you?"

"Because I don't want you hurt, obviously! I am your stepmother. I *care* about you."

Okay. Her temples throbbed. "You've never been concerned about my personal relationships before."

"That man stood in this house and admitted that his plan is to seduce you! To get you obsessed with him."

"I don't remember him using the word 'obsessed,'" she murmured.

"And then he wants to take you away! It is so apparent that he thinks he can get his hands on your money, but if you run off with him, your father will—"

Eliza couldn't help it. She laughed.

"Are you laughing at me?" Kathleen bit out.

Not *at* her. "I'm laughing because the idea of Memphis caring about my money is ridiculous. He doesn't give a damn about any money that my family may have."

"Oh, is that what he's told you?"

"He has his own money."

"Does he?"

This was an absurd conversation. "There are bigger things going on in my life than this." She headed for the door.

Kathleen jumped in front of her. "He will dangle you in front of a killer. You do not matter to him. Hunting does. Bagging another monster. That's all he cares about."

Eliza's head tilted. "I know he doesn't care about me." Why would she be surprised by that? "He has been very honest about his goals all along."

She heard the groan of the wooden floor. The sound came from near the guest room's entrance, but Eliza didn't look that way. Not yet. "My goals are completely aligned with his. Memphis and I both want to bring the man who abducted me to justice."

"Even if you get hurt along the way? You were attacked last night—"

"And Memphis handled things. I trust him. He can hunt and protect me at the same time." Not like those things were mutually exclusive.

"And screw you?" Kathleen challenged, as her expression tightened. "Can he do that, too?"

"*Ahem.*" From the doorway. From Memphis.

Kathleen's face went white. Eliza had known that Memphis was there, but Kathleen, very obviously, had not.

"I'm thinking Eliza's isn't the kissing-and-telling type. Just something about her that strikes me that way. She's all proper-like. Restrained. I'm not. So how about I *tell* you something?"

Kathleen did an about-face that would have done a soldier proud as she looked at him.

"What Eliza and I do together is none of your fucking business." He smiled.

Kathleen sputtered.

Memphis offered his hand to Eliza. "Ready to go?"

She was always ready to leave this house. Eliza sidestepped around Kathleen and took his hand. He led her down the stairs, and as they passed her father's study on the ground floor, she saw Alec watching them from the doorway.

"Do you just live here or what?" Memphis paused to ask him. "Because you are always skulking around."

"He lives in the guest house around back," Eliza supplied.

"Really?" Memphis frowned at Alec. "Isn't that cozy?"

Alec surged forward. "Watch her every moment. If Eliza gets hurt while under your guard, I will—"

"Alec, I appreciate your concern, but I am perfectly safe with Memphis," Eliza cut in to say. There was no sign of the detectives.

Alec's hands fisted at his sides. "You have my number, Eliza."

Yes, she did. She'd had it memorized for years.

"If you need me—day or night—you call. I will come running."

Memphis swept a dismissive glance over him. "Why don't you run along, now? I'm sure you have things to do, and other people to annoy."

But Alec smiled. And he positioned himself even closer to Memphis.

The air was thick with tension. Too much testosterone. Time to diffuse the situation. "Guys, just calm down—

"If she gets hurt, I will kill you," Alec promised.

Her mouth nearly hit the marble tile floor. "*What?* Alec, you can't say—"

"You can certainly try," Memphis invited. "Not like you're the first one to threaten me."

"It's not a threat. If something happens to Eliza, I will come for you." Alec's gaze shifted to Eliza. "Day or night. You call me." Then he walked away.

She watched him in shock.

Memphis's fingers lightly slid under her chin. "Sweetheart, I'm afraid I have to ask ..."

Her head turned toward him as his fingers brushed over her skin.

"The man's attitude does make me wonder..." Memphis's tone roughened. "Did you sleep with Alec?"

"No. No, there has never been anything personal between us."

"Not on your end." Once more, his hand brushed over her chin. "What about the detective?"

Anger stirred. Seriously? "I don't sleep with every man in my life. I get that I jumped into bed fast with you, but that's—that's not normally me."

"Oh, sweetheart, jump into bed with me as fast—and as often—as you like. You will never, ever hear me complain." He leaned toward her. "I need to know who you've been personally involved with."

Yes, he kept asking for a list. The thing was—she didn't have a long list. Super short. She'd barely been in contact with her previous lovers over the years.

"The perp is close to you, baby. I can feel it. I have to see who I am up against."

"There hasn't been *anyone* in a long time. And certainly nothing passionate or dramatic or—" She stepped back from him.

His hand fell away.

"I would *know* if he was close to me." She'd have to know. "I would know if a man who kissed me or touched me was the same man who'd abducted me. *I would know*."

Sympathy flashed in his eyes. "No, you wouldn't. He could walk right straight up to you, and you wouldn't know, and I think, deep down, that's the part that terrifies you the most."

She could feel her lower lip trembling. Eliza backed away. Then spun for the front doors. She wrenched one open, and sunlight hit her in the face as she hurried down the stone steps. The detectives were out there, huddling together and talking softly.

"I'm coming to the search site," she announced.

Daniel shook his head. "It's not a good idea."

"My family owns the area. I won't touch anything. I want to be there. I just want to see what's happening." She needed to be involved. "And I might remember something else. I might think of something that can help you."

Daniel and Camila shared a long look.

"We can keep a uniform on her," Camila murmured. Her head tilted. "But if we find remains..."

Remains. Eliza sucked in a breath. "You think those missing women are out there?" On her father's land?

Another long look between the detectives. She wished they would *stop* doing that. Every time they shared a long look, worry knifed through her.

"We certainly can't speculate about that," Daniel's tone was censuring, as if Camila had overstepped and said something that should have remained private.

"Speculate all you want," Memphis declared as he joined their group. "Then when you're ready to really search for the missing, you can use my friend."

"Just how many friends do you have?" Daniel wanted to know.

"More than you would probably expect," he returned.

"I didn't expect any," Daniel muttered.

"Then, see, that's more than you expected." Memphis seemed casual, unconcerned, but she caught his stare dipping toward her. When it did, there was a flash of a dark, hard intensity in his eyes...

She took a step away from him.

His eyes narrowed right before Memphis squared his shoulders "Dr. Antonia Rossi. That's the friend in question. Don't worry. I already took the liberty of alerting her to the events taking place, and she should be arriving to join the fun at any moment. When it comes to finding the dead, no one beats her skills. The FBI uses her as a freelancer all the time. If you want that area searched for bodies, then you want Tony."

Surprise slid through Eliza. "You already told her to come down here?"

A soft sigh. "Yeah, sweetheart, I did." His hand lifted, as if he'd touch her, but then he stopped. His hand fell back to his side. Memphis seemed to focus on the cops once more. "She'll be checking in with your boss first. Tony is big about following official channels, though I've told her plenty of times that can be boring as hell. But she's the one always called to testify at trials, so she likes to play things by the book." His lips twisted into a half smile as he waved his hand toward the detectives in their suits. "You'll both probably love her."

Eliza's gaze darted to the rental that waited. When she'd gone downstairs, Memphis's SUV had been gone. He'd told her that he'd made arrangements to get the vehicle repaired—and to get someone he knew to do evidence collection on the vehicle since the cops hadn't been too active.

Another ride had just been there, and, at the time, she'd wondered a bit about his seemingly endless connections.

Now another connection was appearing. A woman who hunted the dead. Who else would be showing up?

And who would be coming out of the ground? Would this Tony really find bodies on that land?

She realized silence stretched around them. Everyone was staring at her. Eliza had no idea what had been said. She'd just zoned out on them.

"It's over ten thousand acres," Daniel said, voice impatient. "You really going to stand there while we comb over everything? It's not necessary, Eliza. You don't need to be there."

Yes, she did. "My father owns it. I will be there."

Daniel jerked his head, and she took that for agreement and relief started to fill her—

"Limited capacity only," Daniel barked. "You come out, you get one hour there, and if you don't remember anything else, you leave the professionals to do the job, understand?" His expression remained tense. "This could be nothing, Eliza. But if word leaks to the press that you're out there while we're searching, we both know this will turn into some sort of media frenzy. We need to keep things low-key."

"Low-key is my middle name," Memphis assured him. "Eliza and I can certainly handle that."

"I don't think there is a damn low-key thing about you," Camila returned with a shake of her head. "Do you even know what it means to be subtle?"

"When it suits me, I can be incredibly subtle." This time, his hand reached out and curled around Eliza's. "Get the paperwork moving. Eliza and I will be on the property—initially—for an hour. If nothing stirs in her memory, we will be leaving because there are other leads that we intend to pursue."

Why did his touch always make her feel so much warmer? Safer?

"Other leads?" Daniel's eyebrows flew up. "Like what?"

"You'll find out soon enough."

"No. No, I will find out fucking *now*. I am the lead detective here. If you've got something else to share about this case, you tell me. You don't leave me in the dark, not ever." His head turned toward Eliza. "Haven't I always helped you? Haven't I always been there when you needed me?"

Yes.

"You know that you can count on me, Eliza."

She opened her mouth to reply—

Memphis tightened his hold on her hand. "That is so sweet. Thanks, Daniel. Makes me feel warm and tingly inside. Good to know that you have our backs. So, if our other leads pan out, we will tell you all about the developments, just like we came straight to you with the sunflower field. Now, how about we all get moving? Daylight is burning."

Memphis's voice had been completely civil, but his jaw was locked tight. His hold seemed a little too firm around her. He wasn't hurting her. She didn't think he would ever physically hurt her, but there was no give, no way to escape him. They left the detectives. Got in the new rental, another SUV. Black, sleek.

He shut her door and hurried around to the driver's side. Without another word, he cranked the vehicle and got them out of there.

She could feel the tension in the air. But, more than that, she could have sworn Memphis was angry at her. "Did I do something wrong?" Her index finger tapped against her thigh.

"What the hell makes you ask that?"

Yes, definitely angry. "I thought you didn't go for bullshit."

"I don't." Snapped.

Her head turned to study him. If he clenched that powerful jaw of his any tighter... "You were bullshitting Daniel. You didn't feel warm and tingly."

"That was sarcasm, not bullshit. As soon as Tony finds the other vics out in those fields, the Feds will step in and your buddy Daniel will be getting a backseat to the action. He's a temporary problem for us."

She sucked in a sharp breath.

"Fuck." He braked. They were at the edge of her father's estate. His head swiveled toward her. "That was one time when I should have used tact, wasn't it?"

Her finger tapped faster against her thigh. "You think they're all dead. All of those other women..."

"You and I both know it is exceedingly unlikely that they would still be alive after all this time. Does it sometimes happen that a victim has been kept—alive—and prisoner for this many years? Yes, we've both seen the news stories before. But that is *rare*. And Elijah believes this perp only takes a new vic when the last one is gone. He's not a collector. That's not his MO."

Pain twisted her heart. "If I could have remembered things sooner, I could have stopped him. I could have helped those women."

"I'll tell you again—and I want you to *believe* what I say. This shit isn't on you. You didn't hurt those women. You didn't take them. You were a victim, too. Don't play the blame game. Hell, I won't let you do that to yourself."

"You can't control everything. You can't make me feel something." He couldn't magically turn on or off her emotions. She couldn't do that, either. Though she had certainly tried over the years.

He glanced away. "Tell me something I don't fucking know."

"*I* want to know why you're angry at me."

"I'm not."

"Bullshit," she called. Just to say it. Just to see—

His head whipped toward her. "You don't want to go down this road with me right now."

"You have no idea what I want." No one did. No one really knew her. She didn't even really know herself—

"After last night, I have a pretty fucking good idea." He leaned close. His hand lifted and curled under her chin. "You want me, princess. You want me to drive into you as hard and deep as I can, and when I'm in you, you won't care if the world burns around us because you're finally free with me. You can claw and scream and come as much as you want, and you know I will never let you down. I will be there because I don't care if things get scary or intense or dark. I will be there."

The rush of her breathing sounded too loud in the car.

"But you think I don't *care* about you," he growled. "You think I'm just fucking you for the hell of it?"

"I didn't say that."

Someone honked behind them. Eliza twisted to look back. The detectives were behind them. Daniel waved with his hand to motion them forward.

"He's a problem." A flat statement from Memphis. "I don't trust him. Either he's insanely inept or he's deliberately screwed up your case."

Just that fast, her attention swung back to Memphis.

He'd settled back against his seat. He drove forward. Appeared unruffled. As if he just hadn't been talking about them and wild sex and Daniel screwing up the investigation—

"Can't decide which yet, but I'm working it out." He didn't look at her as he drove.

Her breath heaved in and out.

"Don't trust him," Memphis ordered. "Actually, don't trust anyone but me." A pause. "For the record, I would walk through fire before I let you get hurt. I don't plan for so much as a bruise to touch your skin. And I'm not just fucking you for the hell of it, either."

Then why are you fucking me?

"Say it, baby," Memphis urged her as he drove. "You know how I love it when you talk dirty."

"Why are you fucking me?"

He sent her a lazy grin. "Because I'm obsessed with you. You get me hotter than anyone else ever has. If I had my way, I'd be inside of you right now."

CHAPTER FOURTEEN

During the day, the ground on the old fields appeared cracked and dust dry. The wind blew the dirt in little swirls, and the old barn door sagged to the right. No music played from the wind chime because it was already gone. The crime scene team had bagged that item first. Then they'd carefully brought out pieces of broken wood—the bar that had been in stall number three. Other bars, too, in case they contained evidence.

And nothing seemed familiar.

Eliza kept her arms loosely at her sides as she watched the hum of activity. She wasn't getting in the way, she was staying back just as she'd been ordered by the cops, but she was watching. Watching everything as closely as she could.

It doesn't feel the same.

During the day, the place looked so different from the flashes in her memories. Old. Abandoned.

At night, it had been terrifying. The long shadows. The moonlight...

"Eliza, you need to go home."

At the masculine voice, Eliza couldn't help but tense. Her head turned to the left, and she caught the worried stare of Holden Gerard, the head of her father's legal team. She hadn't been surprised to see him arrive at the property. After all, she knew her father would want him personally overseeing everything.

Especially if this scene might be turning into a legal nightmare for Prescott.

"The cops are doing their jobs. You don't have to watch, and it can't be good for you to...to be in this place, not when you think it was..." But Holden trailed off. Cleared his throat. Seemed a little lost.

So she finished for him, saying, "When I think it was the place I was held?" Holden had come on board at the Robinson Corporation just two years before, so he hadn't been there for all the big drama. But he'd certainly gotten filled in on her life fast enough. Gossip traveled ever so quickly, and *bad* stories traveled at the speed of light.

He edged closer to her. He'd rolled up the crisp, white sleeves of his shirt and loosened the top of his collar. The Texas heat slickened the sides of his thick, brown hair, and his amber eyes gleamed with concern. "The mind can play tricks on you," he said. "I am sure you *want* this to be the location—"

"I want the nightmare over." That was what she'd always wanted. To put the past behind her.

The cops brought out more chunks of wood—they'd been bagged and were loaded into a black van.

Her head turned as she surveyed the scene and looked for Memphis. He'd slipped away moments before, saying he needed to meet Tony.

His friend had been due to arrive at any moment. Dr. Antonia Rossi. The woman who searched for the dead.

Eliza's hands pressed to the sides of her jeans.

"I have to stay here, Eliza," Holden said. "But you don't."

"I *want* to be here." Then she saw Memphis. Striding toward her, but he wasn't alone. A woman kept perfect pace with him. Her long, black hair was twined into a loose braid that draped over one shoulder. She wore khakis and a red shirt. No-nonsense boots were strapped onto her feet. And a dog—a beautiful German shepherd—stayed at her side. The dog loped easily, not the least bit distracted by all the commotion at the scene.

Memphis swept his gaze to Holden, frowned slightly, then locked his stare on Eliza. There had been a different intensity about Memphis ever since they had left her father's house. Eliza couldn't quite figure it out but...something had changed.

I'm obsessed with you. You get me hotter than anyone else ever has. If I had my way, I'd be inside of you right now.

"Eliza..." Memphis's voice was a rich rumble, dark and so deep. "I want you to meet Tony. If there are bodies here, she'll find them. Count on it."

The woman didn't smile. Her gaze was solemn. But she extended her hand. "I've followed your story."

That was all. Not that she was sorry it had happened. None of the awkward comments that so many people made.

Eliza shook Tony's hand. "Thank you for coming out here."

"It's what I do." Tony released her grip. Assessed the scene with a critical eye. "I have a few assistants who will be showing up soon. We've gotten the legal all clear to help the locals. I'll do my survey visually first over the land, see if I can detect any ground variations. From there, we will consider using ground penetrating radar."

The wind blew up the dirt again. In her mind, Eliza heard the echo of the wind chime. But it was just an echo. A memory. The chime was gone. Yet she still looked toward the barn, as if expecting it to be there. "Why would he bring them all here? That doesn't make sense to me. He took them in different places. Wouldn't it be risky to transport them all back here?"

"I don't profile the bastards," Tony replied, voice grim. "I leave that to folks like Elijah—and Memphis." She patted his arm. "Memphis might try to act like he doesn't understand them because he doesn't have a wall full of degrees, but I personally have never seen anyone more in tune with the monsters out there." Tony reached down and gave her dog a quick rub along the back of her head.

The dog remained calm and relaxed.

But Memphis tensed, and when Eliza glanced over at him, she caught a flash of—

"Excuse me," Holden cut in to say. "You think there are *dead bodies* on this property?" His strangled voice came out sounding utterly horrified.

"Who's he?" Tony asked Memphis as she tilted her head.

"Holden Gerard," Holden announced before Eliza could make the introductions. He offered his hand to Tony. "I'm Prescott Robinson's chief legal counsel."

"Oh." She shook his hand. "So you're out here to make sure the nightmare is contained as much as possible." She released him. "Good luck with that."

He offered his hand to Memphis.

Memphis stared at the extended hand, then took it in a brief, strong shake. "Memphis Camden." He released the other man's hand.

"The new head of Eliza's security." Holden nodded. His stare swept over Memphis's tense body. He cleared his throat. "Glad you're on board."

Memphis's expression turned hooded. "Yep, that's me. The head of security."

"If there is anything I can do to assist, just say the word," Holden continued easily. He offered Memphis a smile. "Eliza is a friend, and I want to do anything I can to help her."

"I'll keep that in mind," Memphis assured him. His tone wasn't the friendliest. But then again, it rarely was. Part of his charm, Eliza realized. Or rather, his not-charm.

He just always gave off a badass vibe.

"Since you are in charge of her security, perhaps you can convince Eliza that it's time to leave the scene?" Holden inquired. "The cops said she had an hour here, and that time is nearly up."

Memphis just shrugged. His gaze came back to her. Seemed to warm a little. "You remember anything else, Eliza?"

No, she hadn't. She hadn't remembered—

Engines. Her head snapped to the right as she heard the growl of engines approaching. Her hand lifted to shield against the sun as she saw the line of vehicles coming toward them. Various sizes. Several vans. There was something written on the side of the front van—

"Someone tipped off the reporters," Tony murmured. "This will be my cue to take a backseat. The limelight has never been for me."

She was right. That *was* a news logo on the side of the first van. Even from the distance, Eliza could see the big letters for the station.

"Don't worry, this is my forte." Holden straightened his shoulders. Adjusted his shirt a little. "I'll handle them. One of the reasons Prescott wanted me out here." He sent Eliza a smile. "I can say 'no comment' in a thousand different ways."

She didn't smile back. She'd wanted to stay beneath the press's radar longer. Their arrival was far too soon.

Someone tipped off the reporters. Tony's words. But who had done that?

Memphis's fingers brushed over Eliza's shoulder. "We need to go."

But all of her wanted to stay. If the other women were buried here...

"Ten thousand acres," Memphis said, as if reading her mind. "It's going to take a very long time to search. And if anything is discovered..."

"I'll call," Tony interjected instantly. "I've got clearance to be here. They need me and my team. Nothing is going to happen without me being aware. I'm your eyes and ears." She dipped her head toward Eliza. "You can count on me."

The line of vehicles seemed to be approaching faster.

"You need to be gone before they get here," Holden urged Eliza. "Otherwise, they will be splashing your face all over the media."

Once more, Memphis's fingers smoothed over her arm. "There are other ways for us to work on this case. Other leads to follow."

Her head moved in a jerky nod. So many flashes had come to her before. She'd been so sure that by coming out there again—something else would happen.

But it hadn't. Nothing new came to her.

Nothing.

And her hour was nearly up, Holden was right on that point. She inclined her head toward Tony. "I appreciate your help. Thank you for assisting in the search."

A shrug of one shoulder. "It's what I do." Tony turned away. Her dog stared up at Eliza, then followed obediently with Tony.

"Don't worry about the press," Holden assured her. "I can handle them in my sleep." Sympathy softened his gaze. "You've been through enough. I've got this."

"Thank you." The cars were almost on them. Several cops in uniform were already rushing out to block the surprise visitors. But they couldn't be a surprise to everyone. Someone had sent the reporters out to this remote location.

Who?

"Time to go," Memphis declared, and then they were almost running back to the rental vehicle. He got her inside, jumped into the driver's seat, and had them heading away from the scene even as the other vehicles were arriving.

She was very, very grateful for the security the vehicle provided. "It's a good thing this SUV came with such darkly tinted windows. Otherwise, they would have seen..." Her words trailed off as an unsettling thought hit her.

No, had to be wrong. Ridiculous.

Memphis didn't race away. He took his time. Drove like it was no big deal. She realized he was taking note of all the news crews. And there was the faintest curl to his lips...

"*You* tipped off the press," Eliza realized.

"Why would you say that?"

He hadn't denied the act. Disbelief flooded through her. "Why? They've made my life hell. Why would you do—"

He pulled off the road. Jerked to face her. "I would not do *anything* to hurt you."

She looked back. Could still see the reporters and their vehicles. "This story is going to be all over the news tonight, and you *want* this to happen. You want them running with this development!"

"Yeah, I do want the story to spread. Because attention will make the bastard nervous. I think it will make him sloppy. When he's sloppy, I have the advantage."

Her breath heaved. "You should have warned me—"

"*I* didn't tip them off! Like I said, I wouldn't do anything to hurt you."

Her mouth hung open. She snapped it closed.

"You believe me?" Memphis pushed.

"You haven't lied to me before."

His fingers drummed on the steering wheel. "Right. I haven't lied before." An exhale. "I made a mental note of the reporters—the first van was the most important one. The one I'll be targeting later. I will find out who tipped them off, and I'll deal with the person." His stare lingered on her face. "You have to trust me for this to work. You can see shit that makes you doubt me, you can see stuff that makes you hesitate, but in the end...*you can't stop trusting me.* I am in this with you one hundred percent. Whatever I do—it's because it's the right thing for the case. Keep that in mind, would you? Even if you get pissed and want to tell me to go to hell?"

The case. Right. This wasn't about her. This wasn't about them. It was about the case. Finding the monster. Stopping him. "What's the next step?"

"You're walking back through that night. The night you vanished."

"H-how?"

"We'll start at the bar where you were last seen. We'll go from there."

She swallowed. "The bar isn't open any longer. It shut down years ago." She knew because she was pretty sure her father had made the place close. "It's just a shuttered building now."

"Yeah." He pulled the vehicle back onto the road. "And what we just left only a dry-as-dust field, but you still remembered something when I took you there yesterday. So we're gonna try visiting that bar, shuttered or not."

Yes, they would try.

Her gaze slid toward the window.

"I'm not a fucking monster," he growled.

Her attention flew back to him.

"I don't want you to be scared of me. I don't want you to think I'm like them." Gritted. Seemingly torn from Memphis. "I might fight dirty. I might play hard and rough. I might be able to figure out what they would do too easily, but I am not *them*. Don't be afraid of me."

"I'm not." On this, she was adamant. "I feel safer with you than I ever have with anyone else."

His fingers tightened around the wheel. "Dammit, princess, when you say shit like that, how am I ever supposed to let you go?"

***

Once, it had been the most popular spot in town. People had stood in line for hours so that they could get inside the bar. Bouncers had kept the crowds at bay, and the bands with their eyes on stardom had played inside all night long.

Now, the building on the edge of the block sat with boards covering its first-floor windows and a giant, *No Trespassing* sign had been nailed to the front doors. A big chain, sealed by an equally big lock, secured those doors.

On the second level, she could see the cracks in the windows up there. Holes. A heavy darkness seeping from the inside.

Clouds had rolled in as they grew closer to town. The dark sky surrounded the top of the building. So foreboding. Like a warning telling her to stay away...

Lightning flashed in the distance.

"We'll go around back," Memphis told her. "Don't worry, I can get us inside."

She peered toward the alley on the side of the building. Long. Twisting. Her stomach clenched at the sight of it.

"This way, Eliza," Memphis directed.

She followed him into the alley. A siren wailed from a nearby street. This part of the city hadn't flourished like so many other areas. In fact, many of the other businesses were closed, just like this one. The buildings had been boarded up. Forgotten.

Old boxes littered the ground of the alley. Some ragged clothing. A stained sofa had even been tossed back there. It looked as if the alley had become a dumping ground.

"The bar's back door isn't secured like the front one. Come on."

Like she was going to be left behind. The alley sent shivers over her, and it was too easy to imagine...

Stopping. Putting a hand on the brick wall. My head is spinning...Why won't it stop spinning?

"Eliza?"

Her head whipped up. She'd—she'd put her hand on the brick wall. Was that a memory or—

"I can help you." A voice in her head. Soothing. Rumbling.

"I can help you." From Memphis.

She staggered back a step.

Memphis frowned at her. "You okay?"

No. "Yes."

"I said I can help you get inside. Just come this way with me."

"Come with me." A whisper that was again—only in her head. Eliza took another step back from Memphis. Was she hearing voices? "I don't want to be like her."

"What? Baby, let's get inside."

"Seeing things that aren't there. Hearing things. I don't want to ever be like her." Her lips pressed together. "Don't let me be like that?" A plea.

Memphis hurried toward her. "I don't know what you're talking about. You aren't imagining—"

"I was here, and I was sick, and I think someone said they could help me." She swallowed. "But is it real? Or is it me trying to make a memory so we can catch him? Or..." Worst of all... "Is it just me imagining everything?"

His left hand closed over her shoulder. "You are one of the strongest people I've ever met. I don't think you are imagining anything. We started the memories coming out at that old barn. Maybe they're coming faster because it's like a dam in your head. You start with a trickle, then you end with a flood once that dam gets broken."

She wasn't sure about that. And she didn't like to feel broken.

"Tell me about the voice," he said.

"It's a whisper."

She heard a rustle behind her. Jerked and looked back.

"Just a rat, baby. Just a rat. Come on." He took her around the building, and, sure enough, there was another door in the back. One not secured with a big chain. In fact, it looked as if someone had kicked in the door. It hung drunkenly by its hinges.

"Not the first ones to use this door," she said.

He wasn't looking at her. "Nope." He pushed it open. Went in first. She noticed that he pulled out his gun. She'd seen him take it from the glove box, and now he kept it at the ready as they went into that old building.

Silence. Thick air. Stale.

It shouldn't have been like that. Flashing lights should have filled the space. The pounding rhythm of music. Voices and laughter and so many bodies as they danced.

They crept through an old kitchen. Some broken bottles littered the floor.

"Watch out for the glass," Memphis advised her.

It crunched beneath his feet.

Then he was shouldering open a swinging door. Taking them into the main part of the place.

The long bar counter waited to the right. It was so dim in there that she had to strain to see. Some light trickled in from windows on the second story. Broken windows, but with the approaching storm, the light that came through wasn't very strong.

She took out her phone. Turned on the flashlight. Swept it around the scene.

Dust. Cobwebs. Overturned chairs. Trash. A big, bulky blanket.

A blanket?

"Someone has probably been taking shelter here," Memphis noted. "Stay on guard."

Like she needed to be told that. But Eliza still pulled in a gulping breath, and her light slid to the floor. Dust covered, too, except...

Except for the footprints she could see in the dust. Dark, like they'd been stained with mud. Memphis was right. Someone *had* been taking shelter there. The footprints were large, and they headed—

Wait, not toward the blanket that had been tossed in the far corner, but toward the long, gleaming bar top. She found herself walking toward that bar, too. "I danced on that bar," she heard herself say. That night felt a million miles away. The person she'd been that night—*a million miles away.* "Bethany and I had shots to celebrate, and when the band played this one song..." She could not pull it up in her mind. Just remembered the pounding, fast beat. The laughter in the air. "About five girls jumped up onto the bar, and Bethany and I were with them. We got up there, and then..."

Then the room spun. She put her hand out to the bar. For a moment, everything seemed to spin around her. "Too hot. It was all too hot, and I needed to get down." She'd wanted to go home. So she'd grabbed her phone and—

"What happened after you got down, Eliza?" Memphis asked. He'd shadowed her steps.

She frowned as her light swept behind the bar. "Is something back there?" Back where the liquor used to be stacked on the shelves. Squinting, she leaned forward more. Yes, something was definitely back there, she could just see—

Her light hit the object.

A sunflower. A wilted sunflower that sagged forward in the middle of those old shelves. She whipped back. Slammed her elbow into Memphis—

"Come with me. I can help you." And, once more, a whisper filled her mind. A whisper from the past that seemed horribly real.

Eliza screamed.

"What the fuck?" Memphis snarled at the same moment. "That fucking sunflower wasn't here before!"

Before? Before—when?

He leapt over the bar. She backed away. Kept backing up and her light swept over the entire scene.

"He's been here since I searched," Memphis snapped. "Sonofabitch."

"You searched?" What was happening? Her light kept hitting every dark corner. A rat's bright eyes stared at her before he ran away. "You searched in this bar? You've been here before?"

"Eliza..."

But, yes, Memphis must have been there before. How else would he have known about the back door? And why hadn't she questioned him about it before? She should have thought to ask how he knew with such certainty that there would be a way to get inside the closed building. But she hadn't. She'd just followed him blindly. Trusted him, completely.

Something fell upstairs. Shattered. Glass breaking? Her head whipped up.

And then she heard a snarl from behind her. Low, rumbling...

Her breath hitched as she spun around. The light in her hand shook—because her fingers were shaking—as it darted over the dim interior. Went toward that crumpled blanket. Only something was moving under the blanket. That something was a whole lot bigger than the rat she'd just seen.

Memphis eased in front of her. "Eliza..."

Something—*someone*—jumped from beneath the blanket. "*Get out!*" The figure lurched forward. He had a broken, jagged bottle gripped in his hand. "*Get out of my p-place!*"

CHAPTER FIFTEEN

Memphis reached back with his left hand and curled his fingers around Eliza's hip. He pulled her closer to him because he was damn well going to shield her body. Then he told the figure lurching unsteadily toward him, "Calm down. We're not here to hurt you."

Eliza's light kept shining on the man who did *not* stop or appear to calm down.

Yeah, not like Memphis had thought the fellow was going to immediately listen. *Of course, this situation is turning into a clusterfuck.*

"Get out!" A bellow from the man as he swung his bottle wildly in the air. *"Get out, get out, get out!"* Spittle flew from his mouth. His grip on the bottle didn't waver. As he came closer, the scent of booze wafted off him.

The guy didn't even seem to see the gun in Memphis's hand. Maybe he *didn't* see it.

"You came back," he ranted. "Came back and I t-told you to stay away!"

"You don't know me," Memphis replied. Yeah, like reason was going to work here. *Nope.*

"Brought your flower for the pretty girl—*I see you, pretty girl!"* A scream. "I see you and he sees you and he's going to take you and you shouldn't be in my place!"

And in the silence that followed those shrieks, Memphis clearly heard the pad of rushing footsteps up above them. Just as he had clearly heard the sound of glass breaking moments before. *Upstairs.* Battle-ready tension and adrenaline flooded through him. "Who else is in your place?" he asked calmly.

"You're here!" Another scream. "You're here again! I told you to stay away, but you brought the flower and you think you get the pretty girl." He craned to see Eliza. "You're going to disappear. He's gonna make you disappear...A magician. He's a magician." More spittle. The broken bottle whirled in a circle as he made an arc motion in the air. "Tricks. He showed me his tricks. Boom. Abra...abra..." He frowned.

Okay. This scene was seriously fucked up. Memphis didn't look back at Eliza because he didn't want to risk taking his gaze off the man before him. If he did that, the guy might charge him. "Eliza, I want you to go out the back door. Get to our car. Lock the doors and wait inside the vehicle for me." A slow exhale. "Take the keys from my front pocket and *go.*" The first priority was getting her out of there.

"But—" Eliza began and he knew she was going to argue. With a man brandishing a broken bottle at them and who the hell knew what waiting upstairs—she was going to argue.

"We fucking talked about this," he growled. The guy was weaving in front of him. And he kept trying to look at Eliza. *Keep your fucking eyes off her*. "In dangerous situations, you don't ask questions. You just follow orders. *Go*."

"Dammit, Memphis!"

Dammit, Eliza, just go! This wasn't the time to argue. "Someone is upstairs," he told her. Could be a buddy of the man facing off with him or it could be the prick who'd left the sunflower. Either way, Eliza needed to get out of there. *"Go."*

Her hand snaked in front of him. Dipped in his pocket and took the keys. Then she rushed away.

The tension didn't leave his shoulders. "Who are you?" Memphis asked the man before him.

Eliza had taken the light with her, but Memphis could see the guy clearly enough...his shadowy form. The bottle in his hand.

The man's chest puffed out. "I'm his assistant. He told me that's what I was. Because I'm important."

"Good for you." Memphis's gaze darted up. "He waiting up there?"

"He doesn't like you," he revealed in a whisper.

"Tell me about it." *No, tell me about him.*

"I don't like you, either," the man added, but his words singsonged together like one long exclamation. And— *"Get out of my place!"* He jumped forward and thrust out the bottle like it was a sword.

Hell. Memphis swung up his arm and blocked the attack. The bottle went flying from the SOB's hand and shattered on the floor.

The sound was far too like what he'd heard moments before. From upstairs.

The bastard before him—small, skinny, and wearing oversized clothes that wanted to swallow him—tried to slam his head into Memphis's face.

Memphis jerked back to avoid the blow and then he drove his fist into the guy—

Smoke.

He looked up. The squirming SOB before him used that moment to kick his shin. Fuck that. Did he not care that Memphis held a gun? At all?

More smoke. The crackle of flames.

Shit. *Shit.*

When his attacker came at him again, Memphis didn't hold back. He drove a hard blow straight into the guy's gut. The smaller man fell onto the floor, grunting. Gagging.

"When you said he showed you his tricks," Memphis rasped, "just what did you mean?"

The jerk laughed. "*Boom.* End of the show. Finale!" And he ran—ran up the curving stairs on the right.

Ran up...toward the growing smoke and the crackle of fire.

Fucking hell. Memphis chased after him.

***

Eliza hit the button to unlock the SUV, and she jumped into the passenger seat. Leaving Memphis behind felt *wrong*. Yes, dammit, she'd agreed to follow his orders in dangerous situations, but that had been *then*. And now—now she just wanted to go back and help him and—

Ring. Ring. Ring.

She jumped. Jerked. Slammed her elbow into the passenger side door. Her phone was ringing in her bag, and Eliza yanked it out.

Bethany's smiling face appeared on the screen.

She tossed the phone onto the dash.

Ring. Ring. Ring.

Eliza turned and peered through the passenger window. She also made sure to get her taser at the ready. Eliza yanked it out of her bag. She could help Memphis. She could—

Ring. Ring. Ring.

Bethany was calling again. Eliza grabbed the phone, swiped her fingers over the screen. "Bethany, this is just not a good—"

"You've been ghosting me!" Bethany accused. "Listen, that is not cool. Not what friends do to friends. And I've got big news. Like, the kind of news that changes your life—"

She squinted and stared up at the building. Something was happening upstairs. Behind the broken glass up there. Eliza could swear that she saw— "Fire?"

"Yes, this news is totally fire. It's that huge. And you're going to be excited for me, I know it. Eliza, I think I've found—"

That was definitely *fire* on the second floor. "I have to go. The building is on fire."

"What? *Eliza? Eliza!*"

Eliza tossed aside the phone and shoved open the door. She caught the scent of smoke in the air, seeming to drift from the building, and terror filled her.

Memphis was in there. "*Memphis!*"

Grabbing her bag, she took off running for the alley. She had to get to him. She should *never* have left him behind. She should—

A hard hand flew out from the darkness. An arm locked around her waist, and Eliza was hauled up against a strong, powerful body.

"That's not happening," a growling voice told her. "Better think again."

She screamed. Elbowed him as hard as she could. He didn't let go. If anything, his hold just tightened.

No, no, no. Memphis was in the building, it was burning, and he needed her. She was not going to abandon him.

"Gonna need you to calm down," the growling voice said again. "Taking you out of here—"

He wasn't taking her *anywhere.* Her hand dove into her bag, then flew up. She shoved her taser back against his shoulder.

"Fuck." He let her go as his body jolted. He stumbled back. Swore and shuddered.

She fell forward and slammed down onto the dirt and the grime and the cement buried beneath all that crap. The right knee of her jeans ripped. She felt the scrape on her skin, and the taser slid out of her hand—

He kicked it away. Sent it hurtling into the darkness of the alley. She spun over, prepared to kick and fight him because this was not happening again. Her worst nightmare. Her terror come to life.

Not again. Not ever again.

A guttural scream tore from her as the hulking shadow came at her.

"Get the fuck away from her!" Memphis roared. "Can't you see that you're scaring her, dumbass?"

Her heart stopped, then began to race in what felt like a triple-time rhythm. Her whole chest shook as her breath sawed in and out, in and out.

The shadow eased back.

"Dammit, man!" Memphis voice was even closer. "Tact. Have some of it."

"She *tased* me!"

"You probably deserved it," Memphis huffed. "Look, take this SOB, would you?"

Her head swung around. She could just make out Memphis. He had something slung over his shoulders.

Someone, not something.

The shadow rushed by her and grabbed the *someone* from Memphis.

"Take him away from the building, but don't let him out of your sight," Memphis ordered. Then he crouched in front of Eliza. "Princess?"

"I was coming to help you." Her voice came out stilted.

"That wasn't part of the deal." He reached for her hand. "You were supposed to follow orders, remember?" *His* voice was oddly gentle, but she had the odd thought of...

The calm before the storm.

"The building is on fire," she said.

He pulled her up—and straight into his arms. "Yeah, that's why you're supposed to run *away* from it. You don't run to the flames. That's a basic survival tip for you."

She couldn't stop shaking. Weird, because she wasn't the one who'd been tased. "You were inside. I was running to you."

His hold tightened. "Promise me you won't do that shit again."

It wasn't a promise she could make.

He took her out of the alley even as the scent of smoke and the crackle of flames deepened. He carried her across the street—to where he'd parked the SUV earlier. And the hulking figure was there, a man who now stood under a streetlamp. Big, with thick hair and hard, fierce features. Tattoos on his hands. Dark swirls.

Another guy was on the ground at his feet. Seemingly out cold. "What did you do?" Eliza asked.

The stranger with the tats winced. "Seriously? This was your boyfriend's doing, not mine. And thanks for the tase, by the way. Total highlight of my week."

He didn't seem to be suffering any ill effects. In fact, he barely seemed phased at all.

"Pro tip," he told her. "Turn up your wattage. And be prepared in case you use it on someone who's been tased a few times before. I got a pretty good tolerance."

"Stop bragging," Memphis snapped. He lowered Eliza to her feet.

When he stepped back, she grabbed tightly to him. "What happened to the guy on the ground?"

"Had to knock his ass out. He wouldn't stop fighting me, and the fire was growing." He pulled out his phone. "Saint, keep an eye on him. Got to get the cops here."

Saint? "You know each other?" Of course, they did. Her attacker had referred to Memphis as her *boyfriend* and that sure wasn't random. "Are you a partner of Memphis's?" Eliza asked, uh, Saint.

"Hell, no. I'm one of his collars. He hunted me down, dragged me out of the dark, and slapped cuffs on my wrists. Then he sent me to jail for murder."

Eliza took a step back. Where was her taser?

"*Saint,*" Memphis snapped. "Not now." He swore. "No, dammit, I was not talking to you!" he said into the phone. "I'm on the scene of a blaze, and we need fire trucks here, ASAP! Yes, yes, someone was in the freaking building when I got out. The person who set the fire and I—"

"*Eliza!*"

She whirled even as both Memphis and Saint surged to get in front of her. She squinted and tried to make out who was rushing toward her—

"Alec?" Eliza managed. Yes, yes, that was Alec racing toward her. What was he doing there?

He grabbed for her.

Saint shoved him back. "Oh, I do not think so. I didn't get tased just so you could—"

"He's my bodyguard," Eliza blurted. But, no, he wasn't. Memphis had taken over her security detail. So why was Alec there?

"Get the fire trucks here," Memphis barked.

He was still on the phone. Alec and Saint were glaring, and the man on the cement was out cold.

"You said she'd be safe with you!" Alec snarled. "This isn't safe! The building is on fire!"

"Yeah, and the bastard who set the fire is close by," Memphis snapped right back as he shoved his phone into his pocket. "He's right the fuck here so instead of screaming at me, how about you do something useful and help me search?" His head swiveled toward Saint. "Did you see anyone come out before me?"

"Again, I was *tased* by your lady. Hard to focus when you've got volts running through your body. You never mentioned that she'd be so aggressive." He moved to the right. "I can go search the nearby buildings—"

Alec's hand curled around Eliza's wrist. "You're coming with me."

"What?" Why would she go anywhere with him?

"*The hell she is,*" Memphis growled at the same instant.

"It isn't safe!" Alec's grip tightened on her as he raged at Memphis. "It's not safe for her to be anywhere near you! Don't you see that? The building is on fire! She was inside—I saw her go in with you! You put her in danger, *again*. Her father pays me to protect her, and that's just what I am going to do." He started to drag her away.

She wasn't in the mood to be dragged. Eliza dug in her heels. "I'm not going with you."

"You don't have a choice," he gritted back. "And your father will be firing that bastard because otherwise, Memphis will get you killed—"

She twisted her wrist. Tugged and yanked and—

"Want me to knock him out?" Saint asked curiously. "Or would you like that treat for yourself? I can get the taser for you, if you prefer that method."

"Get your damn hand off her, now." Lethal. Low. A savage warning from Memphis.

Alec froze. He looked over at Memphis. "I'm trying to do what's right. You want to use her. I want her safe."

"Hand. Off."

She realized that Memphis had clenched his hands into fists. Eliza knew this scene was about to get even worse. And, frankly, how was that possible? A fire was raging, an unconscious man was at their feet, and now—

"No!" She jerked hard once more on Alec's grip. This time, he released her wrist. "We are not fighting in the streets. Alec, you are *not* telling me what to do. And we are—"

An explosion. The shattering of glass from the upstairs windows of the old bar. Not a boom but more of a body-shaking thunder, and she automatically whirled to see red and gold flames shooting out of the upstairs windows even as shards of glass erupted into the air.

"Eliza!" Memphis yelled her name.

The glass shards flew out like knives.

Memphis grabbed her and curled his body around hers. They hit the pavement about three feet away. His body surrounded her, covered her, protected her.

And the building burned.

CHAPTER SIXTEEN

"A hospital was completely unnecessary," Eliza muttered as she tugged at the bandage on her right hand. The skin had gotten ripped away when she hit the pavement—she wasn't really sure if that injury had occurred when Memphis had tackled her or when she'd fallen in the alley. Either way, it was a ridiculously small injury in her mind, and it certainly hadn't warranted a trip to the ER.

"It was necessary," Memphis retorted from his position near the exam room door. He'd stood watch from that position the entire time she was evaluated by the doctor, even as Memphis had refused his own medical treatment.

Like that was fair.

The fire trucks had quickly arrived at the scene, followed by wailing cop cars. Even before the blaze had been extinguished, she'd been shoved into an ambulance and whisked away.

Memphis had ridden with her. She had no idea what had happened to Saint or Alec or even the man that Memphis had hauled out of the fire.

"I want to go home," Eliza said as she swung her legs to the side of the exam table. The doctor had left moments ago—a bubbly blonde who'd assured Eliza that she was fine.

Something I knew all along.

"There's gonna be some problems with that," Memphis said.

How did that not surprise her? She jumped off the table. "Want to elaborate?"

He crossed his arms over his chest. Maintained his position near the door. "Reporters are outside." A pause. "A whole lot of them. They've smelled the blood in the water, and they want their story."

Her lips pressed together. *You knew this would happen.* "They were at the old sunflower field—"

"Some of them, yes, but word has spread because of the fire. Someone snapped pics of us outside as the building blazed. You're on every major gossip site again, baby, and you're not gonna be able to just slip away from this."

She rubbed her chilled arms. "There are about a dozen different exits at this hospital. They can't be camped at all the doors. They can't—"

The door flew open. Her jaw almost hit the floor when she saw her father—with Alec crowding at his back. Both wore thunderous expressions.

"What are you doing here?" Eliza asked, truly confused.

"You're in the *hospital!*" Her father threw back. "Where the hell else would I be?"

"I—"

"You were almost killed!" He barreled closer. His gaze seemed too bright. And the hands that reached for her trembled. "Alec told me everything, and I thank Christ he was there."

"Oh, yeah," Memphis drawled. "Let's give him a round of applause." He clapped his hands. "The man was a real lifesaver the way he stood there and did nothing."

Alec whirled toward him. "You put her in danger—again!"

Her father's gaze swept over Eliza. "Where are you hurt? Why isn't the doctor in here with you? You need a private room. You need twenty-four-hour observation. You need—"

"I need you to let me go," she told him quietly. "Because I'm fine."

His jaw hardened. "I saw the clips online. You were right in front of that fire. Eliza, Alec told me you were *in* the building before it erupted."

"I—" Okay. Fine. "Yes. But I got out before the fire started. When the man with the broken bottle charged at us, Memphis told me to—"

Her father's face whitened. "Someone came at you with a broken bottle?"

That had probably sounded worse than she intended. Her gaze cut to Memphis as she sought help. And just what clips was her father talking about? She didn't remember anyone filming the fire scene.

Memphis shrugged. "True story, I'm afraid. The guy living inside the bar did charge at us. Don't worry. I dealt with him. As we speak, the cops are continuing to question him and get him checked out for—"

"I was *there* when the cops interviewed him at the scene," Alec burst out. "Know what he said?"

Memphis rolled his eyes. "How the hell could I know? I was with Eliza in the back of an ambulance."

"He said that *you* had been in his place before! The man swears that you came in and he saw you there before!"

A shrug. "Okay."

"Eliza..." Her father's low voice pulled her attention from Memphis. "Where are you hurt?"

Her scrapes weren't even worth mentioning. "I'm not, Dad. I'm okay. When the windows exploded, Memphis covered me with his body."

Wrong thing to say. Her father's eyes doubled in size. "The windows exploded—"

"Glass rained down," Memphis explained easily. "Didn't want her cut, so I covered her. Hmmm. Does anyone think I should get a round of applause for that?"

Her father squeezed his eyes shut. "*Jesus.*"

"You see what I was saying?" Alec chimed in. "He has no regard for her safety."

Uh, sure he did. "He protected me." How could Alec miss that?

"He put you at *risk,*" Alec corrected. "You never should have been at that scene in the first place. You never should have been exposed to that kind of danger. And now the reporters have the story. They will pull up every sordid detail from before. It's going to happen all over again, Eliza. All over again."

It's been happening all over again for years.

Her father's eyes opened. He dropped his hold on her and stepped back. "This was a mistake."

"Yes, I didn't need to be in the hospital at all. I shouldn't have gotten into the ambulance. We need to get out of here, and I was telling Memphis that there were at least a dozen exits so I am sure we can get away without having to talk to the press—"

Her father turned away from her. Pointed at Memphis. "You're fired."

Memphis smiled at him. "You and Eliza. I can see the resemblance now. Didn't see it at first. Now, I do." He nodded. "You both like to fire people who don't work for you. What an interesting family trait."

"You think this is a joke?" Prescott demanded as his hands went to his hips.

"He thinks everything is a joke!" Alec exploded. "Have you *listened* to the man talk?"

Memphis didn't bother looking at Alec. His attention remained on Prescott. "I think you've forgotten that I don't work for you. Never did. Never will. You can't buy me. You also *can't* fire me."

He had a point. Eliza started to mention that to her—

"I can keep you away from my daughter. I can, and I will," her father said flatly. "I can also get any judge I want in this town to issue a restraining order against you. I can say that you're a threat to her—"

"Not sure that's how those restraining orders work," Memphis murmured as he scratched his chin.

"It's how they work when you're Prescott Robinson," her father stated with a pompous thrust of his chest. "Son, you go up against me, and you will lose every single time. I can guarantee it."

The faint amusement that had gleamed in Memphis green gaze vanished. "I think you have me confused with someone else." He pointed toward a smirking Alec. "Maybe with him. Weird. Cause we don't look a damn thing alike."

Eliza swallowed. The antiseptic scent in that room stung her nose.

Memphis's hand fell back to his side as he sized up Prescott. "You think I'm someone who gives a shit about who *you* are. Newsflash, I don't care about your money or whatever power you *think* you possess." He took a step forward. "And there is only one thing that will ever keep me away from Eliza."

Her breath came faster.

"What's that?" Prescott glared at him.

But Memphis was looking at her. "Eliza," he said softly.

Her lips parted.

"If she tells me that she doesn't want me in her life, then I'll step back." His gaze did not leave her face. "I'll still keep working the case, I'll still keep eyes on her, and I won't give up until this bastard is locked away—or dead. But I won't get close to her. If she doesn't want me close, then *she* can be the one to tell me to fuck off."

"Eliza." Her father waved toward Memphis. "Tell this psycho to fuck off. We don't need him. He's putting you at risk, and I will not allow you to be around someone like—"

She walked toward Memphis. "Memphis and I aren't done."

Prescott's voice shook with rage and fear as he declared, "Yes, you are."

She looked back at her father, and very clearly, very deliberately said, "We are not done."

A curse burst from Alec. "Dammit, Eliza! Can't you see what he's doing? He was *in that building* before! The guy who lived there said he saw Memphis come in and search the place!"

She glanced at Memphis.

He inclined his head. "I did go in before. I believe in being thorough, so I scouted the scene. By the way, the blanket and the guy *under* the blanket were not there during my first visit."

"He did more than scout the scene!" Alec huffed. "He *left* that freaking sunflower for you. Yes, I heard all about that. The guy Memphis *assaulted* told the cops he'd left it. He told the cops that Memphis had set that whole place to blow, he told—"

"Yeah..." A drawl from Memphis. "Before I had to knock him out so I could save his ass, the same fellow told me that he was Superman, that he could fly, that fire wouldn't hurt him..." An exhale. "Don't think you can believe everything that man had to say. His speech was slurred, he smelled like a brewery, and I'm pretty sure he'd gotten access to some strong drugs recently. Not the most reliable of witnesses."

Alec advanced on Eliza. "I heard Memphis tell the cops that a sunflower had been left inside, but I think *he* put it there because Memphis wanted to get a reaction out of you. He took you to that place deliberately. He is playing with your emotions because he just wants to catch the perp! He is hurting you, and he will keep hurting you. Keep putting you in danger!"

Memphis stiffened. "I didn't expect the fire."

Her head turned toward him. Found his intense gaze sweeping over her.

"Not really our perp's MO, is it?" Memphis continued. "But maybe we made him nervous. Maybe we scared him. Maybe he just wanted me out of the way, and he was waiting in there to take a shot at me. If that's the case, we have a big fucking problem. He knows we were making progress, and he's trying to stop that progress. Stop *us*."

"You have a lot of big fucking problems!" Alec charged.

Memphis ignored him and kept speaking to Eliza. "Only a few people know that you had flashes out at that old field. People in your inner circle. I thought he was close to you, and this sure seems to prove that point."

She was afraid it did.

"What are you saying?" her father asked.

The door opened. The doctor poked her head inside. "How is the patient—"

"Five more minutes," Memphis said. "Just need five more."

The doctor blinked. "You are, uh, telling me to get out?"

"No," Prescott clarified. "I am. I want five minutes with my daughter. I donated a damn wing to this hospital, so five minutes hardly seems a lot to ask in return."

The doctor ducked out.

Prescott advanced on Memphis. "Just who the hell do you think in my daughter's *inner circle* is to blame for this mess?"

"Well, you have to understand, I'm not just talking about the fire." His hands shoved into the pockets of his jeans. "I'm talking about Eliza's original abduction. I'm talking about all the disappearances since that time."

"You're talking *crazy*," Alec chimed in. "That's what you're doing!"

Eliza didn't think he was crazy at all. Goose bumps covered her arms.

"Do you think I'm crazy, Eliza?" Memphis asked her softly.

She shook her head.

"It was the field that sealed the deal. The field and the damn barn—the place where Eliza was held, a place that just happened to be bought by the Robinson Corporation. I mean, come on, like that didn't scream suspicious?"

"What the hell are you saying?" A disbelieving snarl from Prescott. "You think *I* had something to do with my own daughter's disappearance?"

"I think...that you've been hiding something."

Her father looked away. "Bullshit."

OhmyGod.

His gaze flew back to Memphis. "You're just trying to stir up trouble—"

"I do like stirring up trouble. One of my favorite pastimes. Just like dragging monsters out of the dark. We all need to do things that bring us joy." One eyebrow lifted. "Tell me, exactly where is Benedict tonight? You know Benedict, right? Your son? Eliza's loving and devoted brother?"

"Benedict is out of town." A fast reply. Too fast?

"Um. Is he." Not a question.

Eliza's head shook in a hard, negative movement. Surely Memphis wasn't suggesting—

"Eliza's inner circle..." Memphis pursed his lips. "It would involve you, Prescott. Your wife. Your son. Your lackey over there." A nod toward a glaring Alec. "And, of course, your chief legal counsel. He was out at the property today. I'm curious—did he stay at the field when we left or did he cut out for other business?"

Her father's lips pressed into a thin line.

"He left," Memphis revealed. "That was a trick question. Well, not a trick really. I already knew the answer because a friend informed me about his disappearance. Seems odd, doesn't it? If his job was to stay on scene and supervise."

"The weather turned bad," her father gritted. "The search had to be delayed."

"Is that what happened? That why Detective Jones also had to rush from the property so suddenly? All of these people—close to Eliza. Close and suspicious as hell. But sure, go ahead and tell her to leave *me*. Tell her to step away from the one person who actually wants the truth. Because that doesn't scream stupid or dangerous to me. Not at all."

And she could see it. Beneath his careful veneer. Beneath the cool mask. The taunting smile. Eliza wondered why she hadn't noticed it sooner.

Memphis was coldly, furiously angry. A deep rage burned just beneath his surface. But it wasn't a hot fire. She'd expected hellfire but instead, his fury was frozen. And all the more lethal for that...

"Eliza." Her father cleared his throat. "This has gotten out of hand. It was a mistake to allow this—this person into our lives when he clearly has his own agenda. I think it would be better if you came home with me. I'll get you on the family jet, and you can get out of the country for a while. Until all of this blows over. You can go to Spain. You know how much you love to visit Madrid."

She took a step back as she understood what was happening. "You're afraid."

"Eliza—"

"You *have* been keeping something from me." The guilt she'd caught a moment ago had been impossible to miss. "What is it? What happened?"

Sweat dotted her father's brow. "You're imagining things. There is—"

"I am *not* imagining anything." Just like that, *her* temper exploded. Only it wasn't cold and banked, not like Memphis's. Her rage was white-hot, blazing from the inside. Pulsing out and fueling her with a stunning energy that she hadn't felt in so very long. "You want me out of town because you're afraid."

"You could have been killed tonight—"

"No. You're afraid...because the anniversary is coming. Because it's so close and everything is going to hell around us." Because the truth was coming back—coming out. "What do you think will happen?"

Prescott looked at his watch. “We need to get out of here. And you were right about the other exits, let’s try to leave by the employee—”

“*What do you think will happen?*” Eliza pushed.

“I think he’ll take you!” Her father’s eyes widened in horror. He looked at Alec—

“He hasn’t come for me before,” Eliza said. She locked her knees. “Why would he come after me now? Why would you think that he would come—”

“Because he made fucking contact, didn’t he, Prescott?” Memphis asked in his icy voice. “You got contact from him, and you didn’t tell anyone.”

Her father looked at Alec—

Memphis spun to face the other man. “What do you know?”

Alec’s face twisted with his anger. “This is none of your—”

Memphis grabbed him. Shoved him back against the nearest wall.

“See this, Eliza?” Alec didn’t fight back against Memphis’s hold. “Do you see this savage behavior? Do you see how he resorts to violence? You don’t need him. He can’t protect you, he can’t—”

“You’re a liar.” Memphis released him. “You didn’t get contact. You made it up, you told Prescott that you did so he’d let you get your job watching her again. But you got *nothing*. Nothing but some sick-ass obsession with Eliza and her family, and that shit is about to end.”

Alec licked his lips. “Eliza, you see what he is—”

Her temples throbbed. The room seemed too small. Too hot. "I want to go home."

"I'll take you," Alec offered at once. "Your father and I have a car around—"

"How did he contact you?" Eliza asked him. Memphis thought Alec had made everything up, but she wanted to hear more.

Alec hesitated, then said, "He left a photo at your father's gate."

"And he wasn't caught on security footage? You didn't see his face?" She knew there was a ton of security at her father's place.

"No."

"I want to see the photo," Eliza said. Why would they have kept it from her?

"It's...surveillance of you. He's obviously been watching you, and he means to take you again!" Alec's gaze blazed. "You are in danger."

"Yeah, I want to see the fucking photo, too." Memphis's deep voice filled every corner of the room. "Though why you didn't immediately turn it over to the cops—*if* the thing is legit—I don't know. I still smell bullshit, and I freaking *hate* bullshit." Memphis marched to the door. Yanked it open. Frowned at the doctor who jerked back. "Eavesdrop much?" Memphis wanted to know.

Her face flushed. "I wanted to check on my patient."

"Sure." Memphis sighed and swung his gaze back to Eliza. "Your call, sweetheart. Always will be. You can go back with them...or you can get the hell out of here with me."

Easy choice. She headed for the open door.

"Eliza..." Her father's voice followed her. "Don't do this."

Her head turned so she could look back at him. "What are you keeping from me?"

"I just want to protect my children! That's all I have ever wanted."

Oh, God. Her hand went to her stomach. "Where is Benedict?"

His face whitened.

"We're out of here," Memphis stated. "Come on, princess."

"I'm not a fucking princess." She strode past him. Marched into the hallway. Saw all the stares from the staff members. Caught the rush of whispers. Gossip.

The press would be outside. Waiting.

She could sneak out one of the exits...she could run and hide...

Isn't that what I've been doing for years? Hiding who she really was? Pretending? Playing everything so safely when all along...if Memphis was right, all along, the threat—the real danger had been right beside her every moment.

She turned and made her way to the waiting elevator. Memphis stepped on right behind her. The doors slid closed.

"Want to clue me in on the game plan?" he asked.

"Why? You've been keeping secrets from me." He'd been to that building before. That old bar, he'd known just how to get inside.

"I *didn't* leave the sunflower inside. I wouldn't play mind games with you like that. *He* did. He's messing with you."

"You're right. He is." An exhale. "So I think it's time that I messed with him, too."

"Eliza..."

The doors opened. The main floor. She didn't hesitate but walked straight out. Straight past the reception area. Straight past the watchful gazes of the security guards as they waited in uniform near the doors. Beyond those glass doors, reporters waited. She could see them, standing back just the right amount...

Hungry. Eager for a story. They smelled blood. Just like sharks.

So she'd chum the waters for them a bit more.

The doors automatically opened for her, and Eliza strode into the night. She didn't try to avoid the reporters. Instead, she went straight to them.

They hurled questions at her. Filmed every instant.

She picked one woman—locked on her. "Seven years ago, I was abducted."

More questions. More filming.

"The authorities were never able to apprehend the man who took me. My memories of that time were very distorted. Rough. I couldn't give them a clear description of what had happened to me."

"Eliza..." Memphis's fingers brushed over the base of her back. There was a warning edge to his low voice.

She was way past the point of heeding anyone's warnings. She'd listened to warnings for years. She'd stayed quiet for years. The result?

Six other women who hadn't come home. And, if Memphis was right, another woman would soon go missing. Someone else who would vanish on the anniversary of Eliza's abduction and never be seen again.

There can't be anyone else. She couldn't carry another woman's pain. "A lot has changed in the time since my abduction." Eliza stared straight ahead. She kept her voice clear and cool. "My memories have crystalized—"

"Does this have anything to do with the search the police are conducting outside of Houston?" A shout from the back of the crowd. "We heard they were using dogs to hunt for bodies."

She swallowed. "I remembered where I was taken. I remembered how I got away."

More shouts. But there were indistinct, sounding more like a rumble to her ears.

Her chin lifted a little more. "And I remember the person who took me."

The shouts grew louder.

"What does he look like?" A yell that rose above all the others. "Who is he?"

"The police will be releasing that information soon. This man isn't just tied to me. He's taken other women. He took them and didn't care about their pain." She stared straight ahead. Her eyes felt grainy. "I care."

She paid no attention to the questions that erupted. Just kept looking forward. She stared into that camera because when he saw this footage, she wanted the perp to think she was staring straight at him. "I remember you. I'll now make sure that you never forget me. But then again, you never could, could you? How about you take those sunflowers and you shove them up your—"

A *roar* from the reporters.

"Okay, that's good. You got his attention." Memphis pulled her behind him. "That's all for now! The authorities will be releasing more information tomorrow morning!"

"Who are you?" Someone wanted to know.

"I'm her boyfriend. I'm also the one telling you all—clear a fucking path." He spread out his hands. "Because we are coming through."

And he led her through the reporters. She ignored their never-ending questions. Ignored it when someone reached out to touch her. Memphis curled one hand around hers, and he pulled her forward through the throng.

She caught sight of Saint. Standing by a black Mercedes. He opened the rear door.

She slid inside. Memphis followed behind. A few minutes later, Saint was getting them the hell out of there.

"So..." Memphis drew out the word. "You understand how a partnership works, yes?"

Eliza looked back. The reporters were still filming them.

"You *tell* your partner when you have some crazy plan in mind." His voice was mild enough, but she could feel the beat of rage beneath his surface. "Like say when you intend to go in front of a camera and taunt a killer. When you want to wrap yourself up with a bow and become a present for the fucker." Not so mild. The rage had broken through his control.

Her head whipped toward him. "I didn't use a bow."

"Sure as hell seemed like it." He leaned toward her. "You want him to come after you. If he thinks you remember, you believe he'll come."

Yes. "I can't let him take anyone else."

"Baby..." His fingers lifted. Brushed along her jaw. "Tell me when you came up with this plan."

"You won't like the answer."

"Tell me anyway."

In the front seat, Saint remained dead silent.

A low sigh escaped from her. "I came up with this plan...the minute you told me that he'd taken six other women. When I realized what he would do on the anniversary, I knew I couldn't let that happen. He can't take anyone else."

His touch remained feather-light on her skin. "So you think you'll get him to take *you* instead?"

She couldn't let fear control her. *Wouldn't*.

His mouth moved toward her ear, and Memphis whispered, "Over my dead body. He will never fucking take you from me."

CHAPTER SEVENTEEN

Eliza slipped out of the vehicle and rushed toward her building. Memphis lunged after her—

Saint grabbed him by the arm. "I think you should calm down."

He gaped at the guy. "You were *there!* You saw what she did. Eliza basically *begged* the bastard to come for her! If he thinks she remembers, he will do everything he can to stop her from talking!"

Saint peered toward her building. The security guard at the front had just opened the door for Eliza. "You had to know this was going to happen. The only reason she was safe all this time was because she didn't remember. You knew that. You also had to know that by coming here, by taking her to all those scenes and trying to stir up the memories, you'd be putting her in danger."

"*Watch it.*" He liked Saint, but that goodwill would only go so far. "And let go of my arm. I need to be with Eliza."

"She's right inside the building. Staring at us through the glass. You have eyes on her."

He wanted his hands on her. He needed to be able to touch her. If he wasn't close enough to touch her...

What if he takes her from me?

"You knew that if her memories came back, she'd be a target. Don't try to fool me, man. I know how you operate. You came to this town thinking that you'd use her to get the perp."

Everyone seemed to think he was using Eliza. Everyone...including Eliza.

"But she just stepped up the process with the reporters. She took control. She said she knew him—"

"She's *lying.*" Saint should get that. "She doesn't remember shit about him, and because I think he drugged her, Eliza probably never will. He could come straight up to her—could smile and offer her his hand—and she wouldn't know it." His fear. "He's close to her. He's always been close and now—"

"You like her."

Like her? *Like her?* He didn't take his gaze off Eliza as Memphis snarled, "Stop being an asshole."

"You like her, and you're worried about her, and you need to calm down. Because I have never seen you this on edge. Normally, you're calm. You're relaxed. You don't *care.*"

He needed to get to Eliza. He needed—

"Correction, you care only about a chosen few. The ones who slip past your guard. Like me, the brother you never wanted but still decided to save."

His gaze whipped to Saint. "You're a fucking annoyance most days."

"You cleared my name. Without you, I'd be rotting in a prison, serving time for murders I didn't commit."

"You were innocent. I just—dammit, I just...I got some friends to help me prove it."

"You and your Ice Breakers. You got Delilah and you got Tony, and you got to the truth. You helped me when you did not need to do it..."

"I'm going to Eliza." He jerked free.

"You didn't intend to be her hero, did you?"

He stalked to the building. "I'm not a hero."

"You can't use a person when you're in love with her."

He spun around. "I need you watching Eliza's back."

"I like her, too. Despite the fact that she tased me. Or maybe even because of it. I appreciate a woman who can fight hard and dirty." His gaze drifted to Eliza's building. "Honestly, you're lucky you saw her first. But I figure you deserve a little happiness, so that's why I'm giving you my warning...use care with her. I get that you're scared—"

"You don't get a fucking thing."

"But you have to get your control."

It was far too late for that.

Saint inclined his head. "I'll be close." He headed back for the car.

Memphis whirled and rushed for Eliza. The security guard hurried out of his way because they'd already had more than a few talks. Memphis had wanted the security beefed up in that place, and he'd given orders left and right. With Eliza's big reveal to the press, even more precautions would need to be taken.

For now, he wanted to get Eliza inside her penthouse. The princess needed to be secured in her tower.

He snagged her wrist as soon as he got near her side, and it finally became a little easier to breathe. When he touched her, when he had her at his side, she seemed safe.

I have to keep her safe.

They walked onto the elevator. He jabbed the button for the top floor. The doors slid closed.

"You seem...mad."

That prim little voice. That extra bit of care she had...

He swung toward her. "Mad doesn't even come close." And he couldn't hold on any longer. Saint thought that Memphis could still have control? Oh, hell, no. He was way past that point. He dragged Eliza closer, and his mouth took hers.

Fierce.

Desperate.

Consuming.

His tongue thrust past her parted lips, and he drank in her sweet taste. He drank *her* in. Took and took. His hands flew over her body as he urged her closer. Her curves pressed against him, her precious warmth. Her scent wrapped around him, and all he wanted to do was sink into her. To seal her to him. If he could bind Eliza completely to him, then maybe...just maybe...

I never have to lose her.

He pushed her back, kept his body flush with hers, and caged her against the wall of the elevator. He couldn't stop kissing her. Was freaking addicted to her mouth. Her lips. Her tongue. The way she gave that little moan in the back of her throat that told him she was as hungry and aroused as he was.

And to think she'd once told him that she couldn't let go, that she couldn't get lost in a lover...

Baby, you will be lost in me.

As lost as he was in her.

The elevator dinged. He heard the doors start to open. Hating it, Memphis lifted his head. Her lips were red, slightly swollen, so absolutely tempting.

Get her in the penthouse. Get her safe.

He took a step back.

"So...you're mad...and horny?" Eliza walked past him with ballerina grace. Spine straight. Steps sliding and poised.

His eyes narrowed at her word choice. "Yep, pretty much covers it." Actually, it didn't. Because Saint had been right. He was afraid.

Can't let anything happen to her.

And he was such a sonofabitch. Because originally...

I thought I could use her.

The part that burned the most was that Memphis realized...Eliza had known that truth all along. She'd known and she'd still let him get close to her. She'd known, and she'd still trusted him.

She'd known, and she was still willing to rush back into a fire in order to try and save me.

Might as well just go ahead and call it...he was done. Owned. Wrapped up completely in her. For him, there would never be anyone else.

Eliza held his heart.

She paused just outside of the elevator doors. "You think you're going to fuck me?"

Dammit. The way she said *fuck* in that prim voice...

Eliza smiled at him.

She knows what she is doing to me. She's trying to push me to the edge.

Trying to push him because she was afraid, too. The fear lingered in the darkness of her eyes. She wanted to fuck him. Wanted the insane avalanche of release that came when they were together because she was running on adrenaline and fear and need. Just like he was.

He bounded out of the elevator after her. "I don't think it..." Automatically, he searched the hallway. Urged her inside her place. When the door shut behind them, when he set the locks, he turned and put his shoulders against the wooden door. "I know it."

The curtains were drawn. No one could see in. He'd made sure on the second night at her place that there were no cameras or recording devices inside. A quick but thorough check he hadn't even told her about—he'd done it while she was in the shower. That long, never-ending shower of hers.

She shifted from foot to foot in front of him. Her only sign of nerves. He should probably try talking. Explaining some shit to her...

Eliza pulled off her shirt. Tossed it aside. Kicked away her sandals. Shoved down her jeans. Stood before him in a black bra and panties.

Talking was *off* the table.

He glanced toward the darkened hallway. Judged the distance to her bedroom.

Too far.

He started to reach for her.

Eliza shook her head. Then she eliminated the space between them. Caught the hands that he'd been extending and pushed them back against the door. She rose onto her tiptoes and pushed her lips against his. Hot, open-mouthed kisses. Delicate licks of her tongue. Darts inside his mouth that had his head jerking toward her when she would pull back.

Her hands freed his. Dropped to his waistband. Fumbled then jerked open his belt. Hauled open the snap and pulled down the zipper.

His teeth ground together. He knew what she was going to do—*Baby, I will go insane.*

She pushed down his jeans. Shoved the boxers with them. Stared at his cock as it bobbed toward her. A bead of moisture slid from the top.

Eliza eased to her knees before him. Sucked in a breath. "I may not be very good at this."

His hands fisted. "Trust me, you'll be perfect."

She leaned forward. Parted her lips. Took him inside.

Better than perfect. Each tentative, careful lick of her tongue sent pleasure blazing through his body. His teeth had clenched, his fists couldn't get tighter, and he was in hell and heaven combined as she took him in a little more. As she sucked a little deeper. As her tongue swirled over the head of his—

"Done." His hands flew out and locked around her shoulders. He pushed her back.

Eliza blinked. "I didn't…was it wrong?"

"Couldn't get more right." Growled. "Getting in you, *now*."

She rose to her feet.

He ditched his shoes, the jeans, the boxers—grabbed for the condom that he'd put in his wallet, because, yes, he'd wanted to be ready to have sex with her again *anytime*. He sheathed his dick in that condom in about two seconds flat, then he reached for her.

He tried to be careful with her panties. They were sexy as fuck, and he would have liked to see them on her again but…

They ripped beneath his greedy fingers. Then he was touching her. Stroking her clit. Feeling her slick heat and knowing that nothing on this earth could stop him from having her. *Nothing*.

He pushed one finger into her. A second. *So tight*.

She gripped his shoulders and rocked against him. Rode his hand. So sexy…

He pulled his fingers back. Clamped them around her hips and lifted her up. "Legs around me." A guttural order.

Her silken legs curled around his hips. His cock pushed at her core. He stared into her eyes, watching her as his dick thrust deep into her.

Her eyes widened. Her breath hitched, and her lips parted. Her head tipped back, a soft sigh escaped and—

She clamped so tightly around him.

He lifted her up, then plunged her back down. Again and again.

Her hands curled around his shoulders as she rode him. He had *never, ever* seen anything more beautiful. He stumbled a few feet with her in his arms. Made it to the dining room table. Sat her on the edge. Drove into her even faster and harder.

One of her hands flew back and slammed into the top of the table.

One of his hands slid between them. Went to work on her clit. Strummed it over and over, just the way he knew that she liked. The way that would make her come for him. Scream for him.

"Memphis!" She was almost there. He could hear it in her voice. Almost...

He slammed deep. Squeezed her clit.

She bucked against him and cried out in pleasure, a yell of fierce release.

His hips pistoned against her. Her inner muscles squeezed him so hard. And he just let go. Erupted into her. A shuddering, mind-blowing, body-bucking release that had pleasure pouring through every cell he had. His shout of release seemed to echo around them.

His hands slapped down on either side of her body. Her sex kept squeezing him, little aftershocks of release that drew out his own pleasure. Nothing—no one—would ever match Eliza.

She'd gone and ruined him for everyone else.

Fuck that lie. You knew she ruined you for everyone else the minute she poured that beer on you. The minute she'd stopped being a pawn in his masterplan. The minute she'd become everything. The minute that had changed his life.

So maybe it was time to share some secrets with her. Secrets that she might not like, but that she deserved to hear anyway.

Her lashes lifted. She met his gaze. Gave him a tremulous smile.

Screw it all. "Eliza, I love you."

Her smile stretched. Lit her eyes. Her nose did that adorable crinkle—

"But, princess, I have been using you."

And her smile vanished.

CHAPTER EIGHTEEN

He slowly withdrew from her. A careful glide.

"I don't think that's tactful," Eliza said as a shiver worked over her body. "Not...gentlemanly." She tried to push the haze of lust from her mind. "You shouldn't tell a woman you love her one moment..." And make said woman feel wonderfully, deliriously happy. "Only to follow up by saying you are using her."

He walked away. Ditched the condom.

She started to jump off the table—

Memphis whirled. "Stay there."

Stay...mostly naked on the dining room table? Uh, no. She didn't think so.

"And I never said I was a gentleman," he added. "That's not a word I've ever used to describe myself." He turned away.

She jumped off the dining room table. Her knees felt a little jiggly, but they didn't fall. Her sex did send a pulsing aftershock through her. She paused a moment and sucked in a breath at that lick of pleasure.

Then Memphis was back in front of her. Someone had sure moved fast. He gently pushed a warm cloth between her legs. Tenderly, he—

He was always taking care of her. Did he even realize that?

She swiped the cloth from him. "I've got this." She hurried away. Went to her bathroom and realized she was giving him a major view of her ass as he trailed after her. Not like she was going to waste energy on worrying about that issue. Not at this point. Eliza tossed away the cloth before rushing into her closet. She dressed in jeans and a t-shirt, toed into her flats, then marched out to confront him—

And she found Memphis sitting on her bed. He'd pulled on jeans. Ditched his shirt. Seemed to be waiting on her.

She took two steps toward him, then stopped.

"Tell me I'm an asshole," he said.

She could do that. "Okay. You're an asshole."

A nod. "Selfish and manipulative. Dangerous and destructive. I do not belong anywhere near—"

Oh, for goodness' sake. She took three more steps. Those steps brought her to the edge of the bed. Right next to his spread legs. "Did you mean it?" Because this was important. Extremely, crucially important to her. And she needed some clarity.

Somewhere in the penthouse, a phone began to ring. An unusual ringtone. Had to be his phone.

But he didn't move. "Mean that I'm an asshole? Yes, but I think you knew that from day one. That I'm selfish? Always have been. Always looked out for number one. That I'm manipulative? Goes with the territory. So does being dangerous and having a—"

"Not that stuff." She waved those points away. Stared down at him with determination. "I was asking, did you mean that you love me? Or was that just like...sex talk? Heat-of-the-moment talk."

His brows lifted, only to immediately sink down low in a glower. "I don't do heat-of-the-moment talk."

Her heartbeat surged. "So you meant it. You want me to believe that you love me."

His eyes narrowed.

"Is this part of your plan? You think I'll go along with things, be easier to manage, if I believe that you love me?"

He...laughed. A deep, rough rumble. The sound boomed around her, and it was so oddly warm and rich. She leaned forward a little more, as if drawn to the sound, but she caught herself. Straightened.

The phone had stopped ringing.

"Sweetheart, there is nothing manageable about you. Any fool who tried to manage you would be in for a rude awakening. You do whatever the hell you want, and you just push aside anyone who argues with you by dismissing them with that cool grace of yours. If I'd been *managing* you, you never would have gone in front of the cameras tonight." His laughter had faded completely. "You sure as shit wouldn't have tried to run back *toward* the fire."

"But...you wanted to use me." She wet her lips. "I knew that from the beginning."

"I knew you were the key." No hesitation. "I thought that you could draw him out. And I thought that, yes, dammit, once you told me that he was still keeping track with the sunflowers, that he might come for you. You were the key and you were in danger, and I wanted to be as close to you as possible."

"To use me..."

"I was using you and falling in love with you at the same time. That's pretty much just what a sonofabitch like me would do."

"Stop," she whispered. It *hurt*. "You don't have to say that stuff." *You don't need to say you love me.*

A phone began to ring again.

His brow furrowed. "Say what? I'm sorry. Yeah, I do need to say that shit. Because I am sorry. Sorry that I didn't sweep you away from this place the moment we met. I think your dad might be onto something. I think getting you out of the country is a good plan. You'll be safe. We can put a decoy in your penthouse. We can use a trained agent from the FBI—Elijah knows plenty of folks. We can—"

"Stop saying that you love me! I *knew* you were using me. Everyone knew it. Hell, even Kathleen tried to tell me that! And she *hates* me."

The furrow of his brow grew heavier. "Why would she hate you?"

"Because I tried to stop my dad from marrying her years ago. Because I found out that she'd cheated on him when they first got together, and I was going to tell him and then—"

He shot to his feet. "Then what?"

"Then I was taken and...and everything went out of control. I stumbled into their engagement party all blood-covered and confused and...I...I had to get help for a while. Therapy. I tried to put my life back together, and Kathleen was actually..." Now it was her turn to laugh. Though her laughter sounded brittle while his had been rich. "Kathleen was very kind to me. She even referred me to the therapist I used. She had gone to Dr. Kendall before. Kathleen said she wanted us to start over. That she had changed. That she loved my father."

"Fucking *hell.*"

He rushed around her. Bounded to the door.

Eliza's jaw dropped. "This is important!" And he was running away?

He swung back to her. "Yes, baby. It is. I needed to know this information back at the beginning. Would have helped a whole lot."

It would have helped to know that she'd had a fight with her would-be stepmom? Talk about irrelevant. But he slipped through the doorway. She raced after him.

His phone had stopped ringing, but he was reaching for it. She reached for him. Grabbed his arm. "*Stop it.*"

A muscle flexed along his jaw. "I've been texting my team updates all along." His head turned toward her. "Every time you gave me a new piece of information, I passed it along. When I learned about the sunflowers, when we got side-swiped on that old highway, when we were nearly set on *fire* at the bar—"

"*You* were nearly set on fire," she corrected him. "I was outside. Safe and sound."

His lips tightened. "I had them start digging into the people around you. When you wouldn't give me a list of your exes—"

"I don't have many! I haven't been involved with anyone in ages, I told you that!"

"I got them to look."

So he'd been ripping into her life without telling her. That was another of his big reveals? "One day, you'll have to tell me every secret you have." A huff of breath. *Focus.* "What have your people been doing, exactly?"

"I made a list of suspects—those closest to you. I wanted to get their financial info torn apart. I wanted to know exactly where they all were when the other women vanished. My friend Delilah is a top-notch reporter. I put her in charge of tearing into their lives."

"Since her sister vanished, I'm sure she's very motivated." Eliza swallowed. She didn't let him go.

"She won't ever give up."

Would Benedict have given up on her? Hell. She didn't even know where Benedict was. Her father had said he was out of town…*Why do I think he was lying?* "Who are the people that you have her investigating?"

"Your detective buddy Daniel. He was involved in the case from the very start. Your bodyguard who likes to stay way too close to you, Alec. Your brother."

Her fingers squeezed him. "My brother?"

"First, he threatens me, then he seems to vanish. Is he even in town any longer, Eliza? Or did he cut and run?"

"I—" She let him go. "Benedict wouldn't do this to me. He wouldn't hurt anyone. Benedict is gentle. He's always been gentle."

"Is he?"

"Yes!" A huff. *He is my brother. He wouldn't hurt me. I can count on him. I can...*A memory buzzed and drifted through her mind. Gone too fast to hold. Eliza shook her head. "If Benedict is standing back, it's just because he always does what our father wants. I'm sure Dad told him to stand back. I'm sure Dad told him—"

"Your father is protecting him from something, Eliza. There are secrets between them. You saw that at the hospital, didn't you?"

Yes. "Who else? Who else are you investigating?"

"Your father's lawyer sprang to the top of my list, too. Holden Gerard. Seemed awfully chummy with you at the scene—"

"You have some insane idea that every man in my life is sexually attracted to me. *Not* the case. Men don't look at me and get obsessed. That doesn't happen." If it did, she would have gone out on way more dates.

"It did to me. Stands to reason that it could to others, too."

Her hand jerked back. *It did to me.* "You lied to me."

"No, no, baby, I didn't. I just didn't tell you—"

"You said no bullshit. I respected the no-bullshit rule, but it was just a line. You didn't mean it." *He doesn't love you. Didn't want you from the first. Doesn't want—*

"What in the hell are you talking about?" Memphis rasped.

"You didn't get obsessed with me the first moment you saw me."

His eyes changed. Went hard. Flashed with green fire. Desire. Barely banked. Need. Possession. "Sure, I did. You walked out of that bar door, and I ran after you as if my life depended on it. I knew you were going to change my world, and there was no way I would ever let you go. If that doesn't sound like obsession, then tell me what does."

Her heartbeat seemed to echo in her ears. "Holden is gay. At the scene, he was busy checking you out, not me. You and your super-observant self should have noticed that."

His phone began to ring again.

"Not every man is interested in falling at my feet." She looked over at his phone. "Must be awfully important. We should answer." Her gaze returned to him.

"I'm interested," he growled.

Her eyebrows climbed.

"But how the fuck do you feel, my princess? How do you feel about me? Because I've told you exactly what you mean to me, but you haven't said anything about how you *feel*."

My was definitely possessive. Definitely rough. Definitely on edge. And *princess* didn't feel mocking. It felt like an endearment. Like a tender caress.

He grabbed for the phone. Swiped his fingers over the screen then turned on the speaker so that she could hear. "Memphis."

"Is it true?" A woman's voice. Desperate. Shaking. "Did Eliza remember him? Does she know who took Layla? OhmyGod, Memphis, this is huge! This is the break we needed, this is—"

What have I done? "I'm sorry," Eliza choked out as the world seemed to narrow around her. *I didn't think about the families!* Oh, no. Oh, *no*. "I-I don't remember him, but he's going to come for me, and we'll stop him, and we'll—"

Memphis took her hand. Squeezed her fingers. "It's okay." Soft. Careful. "We are going to get him."

I gave her false hope. I shouldn't have done that. I didn't think—

"Eliza?" The woman's voice was hesitant. The woman—she had to be Delilah.

"Y-yes."

"You said that on the news...you lied so he'd come for you?"

She held Memphis's stare. "Yes." *I'm so sorry about your sister. I wish I could have stopped him. I wish I could have—*

"You have to be careful," Delilah told her. "Do whatever Memphis says. Do not leave his side. You are in serious danger. I believed what you said—you looked so certain, so convincing—and I'm not fooled easily. *Please* be careful. Don't let down your guard, not even for a moment."

Delilah was worried about her?

"I want to find your sister," Eliza heard herself say.

"*Don't* find her by disappearing!" Delilah's voice cracked. "Don't do that. If you get hurt, if you die, that doesn't bring anyone back. Stick to

Memphis. I would trust him with my life any day of the week. He can keep you safe. *Trust him.*"

She'd trusted him from the start. Known that he was using her, and still gone along with his plan. She'd opened herself up completely to him. Not just her body, but offered him everything. And he'd...

Said that he loved her.

A man who professed to have zero tolerance for bullshit.

Does he love me?

And how did she feel about him?

"Kathleen Robinson," Memphis said flatly.

Eliza jerked at the mention of her stepmother's name.

"Add her to your deep dive, Delilah."

"The stepmother?" Delilah asked.

"She and Eliza had trouble right before Eliza vanished. The kind of trouble that could have stopped her wedding to a billionaire. If you ask me, that's one hell of a motive. Dig deep on her."

"Already at it." In the background, Eliza thought she heard the tapping of fingers on a keyboard. "And it helps to have my husband's resources at my beck and call..."

Her doorbell rang. Eliza pulled away from Memphis. At this hour...a visitor wasn't going to be a good thing. After pulling in a bracing breath, Delilah started for the door.

"Oh, found out something interesting about the brother." Delilah's voice stopped her.

Eliza looked back.

"Turns out, on the night of her abduction, he was in a jail cell. Got busted for drunk and disorderly conduct, but those charges magically vanished. You won't find them on any official record anywhere. Guessing her father pulled some strings, but hey, at least it's an alibi for him."

The doorbell chimed once more.

"I'm working on the others. Some stuff looks good on the surface, but not so sure it will hold up," she added.

"Someone's here," Memphis told her. "Got to go, Delilah."

"Is Saint with you?" Delilah rushed to ask. "Tell me he is. You need backup there, and Elijah said you told him to stay put—which he *hates* by the way, so you might see him showing up and—"

"Saint is here. He has my six."

"Good." Real relief.

The chime came again, only this time, it was followed by a fierce pounding on the door.

Memphis shoved his phone into his pocket.

Eliza reached the door first. She put her eye to the peephole to see who was causing all the late-night drama— "Daniel." Of *course,* he would stop by. He'd probably seen the news, too, and he'd want to know about the man she supposedly remembered.

He'd be pissed when he found out she was lying.

She started to open the door.

Memphis shoved his hand against the wood. "Nope, baby, we need to plan first."

Her head turned. He was right beside her. Mere inches separated them. "Look," she began, her voice a whisper because his had been, "I get that you have Daniel on your suspect list, but he's a cop. He didn't even *start* working my case until much later. He was one of the few people who believed me. He—"

"So far, Delilah has discovered that he doesn't have an alibi for two of the disappearances. He was on vacation. So-called fishing trips, so, yes, I do find that suspicious. I find him suspicious. Know who is good at not leaving incriminating evidence behind? *Cops.*"

More pounding. "Eliza!"

"If you're a woman alone at night...a woman who is uncertain, maybe drunk, quite possibly drugged...guess who you *would* allow to give you a ride home because you thought he was *safe?*"

"A cop," she replied as her body chilled.

"Damn straight. See why he's on my suspect list? And it's not just because he eye-fucks you too much, though that shit will be stopping. We need to handle this scene with care. Follow my lead. Remember, you were supposed to do that in dangerous situations?"

Her lips thinned. "You would go back to that."

"Yes, you forgot that rule at the hospital, didn't you? You also forgot it at the bar. You came *back* inside, baby."

"*Open the door!*" Daniel blasted.

Memphis winced. "For such a fancy building, the walls and doors truly aren't thick enough. I will be complaining to the owner, count on it." His eyes glinted. "Follow my lead."

"I went back inside because I was scared."

"When you're scared, you're supposed to stay away from danger."

A shake of her head. "I was scared you'd be hurt. I was afraid because I didn't want anything happening to you."

His eyes widened. "Princess, just what are you saying?"

"I'm saying..." *I don't know what I'm saying.* "If you're in danger, I'm not following any of your rules. I'll rush to save you anytime you need me."

"Fuck. That is beautiful." He pressed his lips to hers. Hard and fast and possessive. Then he wrenched open the door. "Detective!" Memphis boomed. "What an unpleasant surprise."

***

"Is it true?" Kathleen demanded the minute Prescott walked through the front door. She'd been waiting at the base of the stairs, a black robe wrapped around her body, full makeup on her face, and her hair carefully styled around her shoulders.

She always looked perfect. Pristine. He swore she even slept in her makeup because when he'd open his eyes in the mornings, she'd already have it in place.

There was no need for the makeup. He'd always thought she was lovely just as she was.

"Does Eliza remember what happened that night?" Kathleen's hands twisted in front of her.

Odd, she wasn't normally one to make nervous movements. Everything she did was careful. Almost practiced. As if she was afraid to put one foot out of order.

Benedict and Eliza's mother hadn't been so restrained. She'd been a brilliant, passionate burst of life. With her, everything had seemed to swirl by him at one hundred miles an hour. She'd lit up every room she entered. She'd had everyone laughing at her jokes, pushing to get closer to her undeniable beauty, admiring her wit...

She'd been such a brilliant light. One that had burned too brightly. Too hard. Because sometimes, she hadn't wanted to be the life of the party. Sometimes, she had just cried and cried, and he hadn't been able to comfort her no matter how hard he tried.

"Prescott." Kathleen crept toward him. Her slippered feet made no sound. "What did she tell you? And did you fire that annoying bounty hunter? He's trouble. He's feeding Eliza lies and—"

"He doesn't work for me." He turned away. Headed into his study. Went toward the small bar that waited. A bar stocked with the most expensive whiskey money could buy. "He never did." He reached for a decanter, then stopped. *Where is Benedict?* "Have you seen my son?"

"Why would I see Benedict? Is he supposed to be here?"

Benedict didn't come around often. Neither did Eliza. Eliza...she'd been so much like her mother when she was younger. Everyone she met had been drawn to her. *Like a moth to a flame.* And then, her flame had died. It had withered overnight.

I didn't even realize she'd been taken. I thought she was angry. That she'd gone out of town to spite me. That she was refusing to celebrate the engagement. God, he hadn't even looked for her that weekend. His precious girl...

When she came back to him, she'd been different. Fractured. Afraid. "I should have done more."

Kathleen curled her arms around him. Hugged him from behind. "What are you talking about?"

Whenever she hugged him, it always felt forced.

"I paid the press to stop talking about her."

"It was for the best. Those terrible stories were going to haunt her forever. And when everyone started saying it was all fake..."

He pulled away. Turned to face her. "Why did they start saying that?"

Her eyes widened. "I don't know. Gossip can be such a terrible thing. Especially for someone like Eliza. Someone born with a silver spoon dangling in her mouth. The privileged daughter who—"

"Her life has been far from perfect." He didn't think anyone had a perfect life. *There is no perfect life.* "Her mother committed suicide. Eliza found the body. She held her and she cried, and then she comforted *me*. She comforted me and her brother, and when she was sixteen, she started volunteering with a local charity to help prevent teen suicides." Because Eliza was good. *Far better than I will ever be.* "She never wanted a dime of my money. She got into college on her own. Went to a local school on a full academic ride. She worked her ass off for her grades. Then she was taken…" *Someone took my beautiful daughter. Someone tried to break her.* "She got the fuck away." Grim. Proud. "She got away, and she came back to me, and I never should have stopped hunting for the bastard. I should have destroyed everyone who called her a liar. I should have—"

"You were protecting her! We agreed that the best thing we could do was quiet the rumors. We needed the story to vanish. There were no leads. You gave her guards. You hired the best people to protect her. I sent her to my therapist! We did everything right." Anger stiffened her jaw. "Stop blaming yourself! Stop it! You are a good man."

A good man? Doubtful. Not even on his best days. And even a good man could still be a piss-poor father. After her mother had died, he'd had a string of affairs. One after the other. And he'd put distance between himself and his Eliza… "She just looks so much like her mother. Sometimes, it was hard to see…" *Her*. But it shouldn't have been. He should have treasured every moment with his precious Eliza.

Eliza worried that she would end up like her mother. That admission had been shocking to him because, deep down, he had always understood the truth…*Sweet girl, you are stronger than me. Stronger than anyone else in this family. Nothing will destroy you.*

"Hard to see what?" Kathleen asked.

He blinked. Focused on his wife. She wanted to have a baby. Wanted a tie to bind them. Would he make the same mistakes with another child?

"Prescott, you never told me…does Eliza remember what happened that night?"

He'd seen the footage of her talking to the press at the hospital. Pulled it up on his phone while his driver brought him and Alec back to the estate. "Why would she lie about that?"

She sucked in a breath.

"And, no, Memphis isn't leaving her side. I don't think anything on this earth could take him from her." A truth he had seen staring back at him from Memphis's eyes. "I believe that man would gladly kill to keep her safe."

She gasped and backed away. "Prescott, are you actually telling me that you would condone murder?"

He hadn't said that. But when it came to the bastard who had taken Eliza... "Someone has to pay for what was done. I think Memphis will do whatever it takes to get justice for her."

She covered her mouth. Stared at him in horror.

"Where the hell is my son?" he groused. Because Benedict *wasn't* out of town. He'd sent a note telling Benedict to meet him.

It was time for the truth to come out.

Someone will pay.

CHAPTER NINETEEN

"Eliza will be coming down to the station tomorrow—with her lawyer present—in order to issue a formal statement." Memphis made sure to block the entrance to her penthouse. "It's late now. Eliza has been through a truly exhausting ordeal this evening—I mean, did you *hear* about the fire?"

Daniel's eyes were angry slits. "You know I heard."

"Um. Well, then you can attest to the fact that it was quite dramatic. Eliza had to go to the hospital, and her doctor strictly ordered for her to receive rest tonight."

"Rest." Daniel's narrowed gaze raked him. "That why you're missing a shirt? Because you're helping her to rest?"

"Before your knock at the door, we were on our way to bed. Where people *rest*." He put his hands on the doorframe. "Good night, Detective." No way was he about to let this guy grill Eliza. All Memphis had to do was buy her a little more time.

Time for the Ice Breakers to dig a bit deeper.

"I talked to Clyde Burk," Daniel threw out.

"Wonderful for you." Memphis lifted his eyebrows. "And who might Clyde Burk be?"

"The man who was temporarily residing at the old Lasso bar. He told me that you'd been there before."

"Um. I have been made aware that the poor man has been giving interesting statements."

"He said you planted the sunflower." Daniel craned his neck, obviously attempting to see Eliza. "Did you hear that, Eliza?"

"Memphis didn't leave the sunflower." Low, but certain.

"How do you know?" A muscle flexed in Daniel's jaw. "The man is playing psychological games with you! He's taunting you, pushing you to the edge because he doesn't care—"

Nope. Done. "Stopping you right there because I am sick to death of people saying I don't care about Eliza. I do not care about many things in this world. A great many..." True enough. "But Eliza is something much different to me." She *was* his world. "I don't play games with her. I didn't plant the sunflower. I didn't set the building on fire. Someone else was upstairs, but he got away while I was hauling Clyde to safety." Talk about not being grateful. Jeez, could Clyde not help a man out? "Someone else set the fire. The same someone who left the sunflower in there for us to find."

"*Why* do that?" Daniel demanded. Once more, he craned to see Eliza.

Memphis just shifted slightly to block his view. "Because he was sending a message. He knows what we're doing, and he's prepared to fight back with lethal force. He's running scared."

Daniel swallowed.

"He should be scared," Memphis added. "Because pretty soon, everyone will know what he's done. There will be no shadows for him to hide inside any longer."

"She...you don't remember him, do you, Eliza? You were just saying that for publicity."

Memphis laughed. "Eliza does nothing for publicity, and you should know that." He paused. "But then again, you didn't really believe her when she said that she remembered that sunflower field, did you?" He waited just a moment before pushing a wee bit more. "Got a text from my friend Tony a few minutes ago. When the search was delayed because of the bad weather that rolled in, Tony just got herself access to more aerial photos. She thinks that she's found an area of ground variations in those photos that seem very, very promising."

Daniel backed up. "I-I wasn't informed..."

Yeah, because it hadn't happened. Memphis was lying his ass off to see what reaction he could get. "Maybe you should go check in at the station," Memphis advised. "Bet your commanding officer has some updates for you."

Daniel hesitated.

"Don't worry. We'll be at the station bright and early tomorrow." Memphis kept blocking the doorway.

Daniel spun away. Marched for the elevator. He stabbed the button. Waited impatiently for the doors to open.

Memphis never took his gaze off the cop. *Where is your partner tonight? Does she know you came here?*

The doors opened. Daniel rushed inside, then turned to face the front.

"Oh, Detective?" Memphis called.

Daniel looked at him. Glared.

"Gone on any good fishing trips lately?"

Shock and fear flashed on Daniel's face, right before the doors closed.

Memphis backed inside. Nearly stumbled right into Eliza as she frowned at him. Even frowning, she was absolutely gorgeous.

"What was that about?" Eliza wanted to know.

He locked the door. Triple checked the locks. "He wanted to see how much you knew."

"I know nothing."

"But he doesn't get that. And when I asked about his fishing trips, I saw fear on his face." He hurried past her and grabbed his phone. He fired off a quick text to Saint. *Detective coming down. Trail him. Make sure he doesn't see you.*

And Saint texted back...*Done.*

"Is that Tony? Has she really found the bodies?"

Now he winced. "I do apologize. That lie wasn't meant for you. I was trying to get a reaction from the cop."

Her lips pressed together. She blinked a few times, then said, "Because you don't trust him?"

"Not at all."

"If you're not texting Tony, then who are you contacting?" Eliza tilted her head, and a little line appeared between her eyebrows.

Baby, you still haven't told me how you feel. And he got it—a lot of shit was going down. He could hold back. Maybe. "Saint."

Her hands pushed against her thighs, and her index finger began to tap. "Did you really toss him in jail for murder?"

"Murders. Plural." He stalked to her window. Opened the curtain. Stared out at the city. Stared *over* at the tall complex right across the street. He kept coming back to that place... "Saint was the lead suspect in a series of murders. He ran from the law—guy thought he could catch the real killer...He was eighteen. Total dumbass."

"And you chased him down?"

"At the time, I'd recently discovered that he was my half-brother. I'd tossed my dad in jail, and thought, sure, I'll do the same to him." No, that hadn't been exactly what he thought. "I thought I had tainted blood. That my father's side of the family was just screwed, and that if I wasn't careful, I'd be screwed, too. I tracked him to prove to myself that I was better. That I wasn't like them." He kept staring straight ahead. The top two floors across the street were dark.

Can you see me? If someone was in that darkness, watching...

He raised his middle finger. Kept it in front of his body so Eliza wouldn't realize what he was doing.

But...hell. No one was there. He'd gotten records for the place. The top five floors weren't even finished yet. Under construction to be the next deluxe set of condos.

I still want to get over there. Walk around. Make sure it's empty. Because no one should have been in that old bar, either...

"Saint is not in jail." Eliza's voice was closer.

"No. Because he managed to convince me that his crazy ass actually was innocent. I got this reporter I knew at the time—Delilah—to help me do some digging. We were able to find solid alibis for the kid. Able to find DNA proof that someone else had done the killings. And he went free." *Saint*. Not his real name. A nickname that he'd gotten while in the system. Because he kept protesting his innocence so much, and no one had believed him. They'd mocked him. Called him Saint.

And because his brother had grown into one major badass over the years, he'd owned the name. Turned it into something that a whole lot of people feared.

He'd also gone into the family business. Bounty hunting. And cold-case breaking.

"You saved him." Her hand brushed against his shoulder.

"Nah. I was the one to toss him in jail. I just helped to get him back out." He turned toward her. "Don't make the mistake of thinking that I'm some kind of hero."

"Liar." But the way she said it...

Like it was a caress.

"Why do you call me princess?" she asked him. "You know I don't like it."

About that..."I'm an asshole."

Her gaze held his.

"We should move away from the window." His body was blocking hers but still...tension snaked through him.

I don't want her vulnerable. I have to protect her.

"Why do you call me princess?" Eliza repeated.

Apparently, his being an asshole wasn't explanation enough. He got that. So he'd delve deeper for her. "Because you're something precious. I knew it the first time I saw you. I wanted to put the world at your feet. Wanted to give you a world to rule. Wanted to give you..." Jeez, now he sounded all sappy and shit. Saint would laugh his head off at him. But... "Everything." He still did want to give her everything. Memphis knew he'd always want that.

Eliza stared up at him. Didn't speak. He turned and yanked the curtains closed. There. Now no one could see them.

"Remember when we were at your dad's place and I told everyone that I wanted you to get so wrapped up in me that you'd run away from everyone else? That you'd escape with me?" He glanced back at her.

Eliza nodded.

"I meant it. See, Eliza, when it comes to you, I knew what I wanted from the beginning." And what he wanted? "It was you." *It will always be you.*

She smiled at him. Beautiful. Full. Real. A smile that lit her eyes, crinkled her nose, and showed him her absolute joy. "Good," Eliza told him. "Because guess what I want? It's you. I love you, Memphis—"

Glass shattered. The curtain flew up and hit him. Something stung his side.

More glass broke.

Eliza screamed.

He pushed her back and felt the second hit. Shoved her hard even as he thought—*so sorry, baby, so sorry*—but she was in danger. His shoulder burned. Blood had flown across the carpet, hit the wall. His blood. Because he'd been shot at least twice. Bullets were coming through the window. And as high up as they were, the angle they were at...

Came from across the street. The building...the building...

"Get...covered..." He dropped to the floor. Blood pumped out of him too fast. Too hard. Shit. He shouldn't be losing this much..."Get...back..."

Eliza didn't get back. She rushed to him. Put her hands on him to try and stop the blood flow. Horror twisted her beautiful face.

The only sound he'd heard had been the breaking glass. *Across the street. Came from across the street.*

Daniel wouldn't have been able to get over there so quickly, would he? If he had, Saint would have seen him... "S-Saint..."

"You're bleeding too much! Oh, God! Memphis, what do I do?"

"G-get..." *Out.* Because he was afraid that the bastard's first goal had been achieved. The goal he'd had back at the bar. *Get me out of the way.*

"I'll get help," Eliza promised. She darted away. Grabbed his phone. He heard her talking to the nine-one-one dispatcher…

He tried to move toward her.

His body felt numb. Too weak. He needed his gun. He couldn't push to his feet, so Memphis started crawling…

"What are you doing?" Eliza rushed back to him. "Dammit, stay still! Help is coming!" Her hands flew out and pushed him down. She pushed against his wounds. One on his shoulder. One on his side. "God, there is so much blood."

He could feel her shaking. Or maybe he was the one shaking. "G-gun…" He needed his gun. Because he was very afraid that whoever had shot him would be bursting through the door any moment. That the person would be coming to take Eliza.

To make her disappear.

"You don't need your gun!"

The fuck he didn't. "G-gun…" It was close. He could see it.

"I'm supposed to apply pressure. I took a first aid class not too long ago. I'm supposed to help you. I'm supposed to—"

Pounding at the door. Hard, heavy bangs. Powerful.

And then…

The door flew in. It had been kicked in. It bounced against the wall. Memphis craned up to see Daniel standing in the doorway, with his weapon drawn and aimed right at—

Eliza. Me. Oh, hell, no. The bastard would not get her. Memphis surged over, using all his strength, and he grabbed for the gun he could see so close by.

"What happened?" Daniel swept his gaze around the scene. "I was downstairs when I got the report about this building—"

Memphis curled his fingers around his gun. He lifted it up even as pain pulsed through him. "St-stay...the fuck away fr-from her..."

Daniel frowned at him. "Lower that weapon!"

"St-stay..."

Saint burst in behind the detective. "What the—*Memphis!*" He shoved the cop out of his way.

Dizziness flooded through him. Saint was there. Saint would... "Take care...Eliza..."

Darkness swam in front of his vision.

Saint caught his hand. Wrenched the gun from his grip. Pushed him back. Saint and Eliza both started poking at him. Only Memphis couldn't quite feel their touches.

They'd both turned their backs on Daniel. A dangerous move.

"It wasn't him," Saint growled.

Wait, had Memphis been talking? Maybe he had. Maybe he'd told Saint not to turn his back...

"I watched him. He was in the lobby. Got some alert on his phone and came tearing back up here. It wasn't him."

"The shots came from across the street," Eliza said.

"You're sure?" Daniel's urgent voice.

Only it seemed like his voice was distorted. Drifting in and out.

"They burst through the window," Eliza said. "He was hit at least twice. God, where is the ambulance?"

Memphis wanted to tell her not to worry. He'd been shot before. He'd be fine. She needed to focus on herself. Because this...this was just another attempt to get her away from him.

That couldn't happen. He couldn't be taken from Eliza. Eliza couldn't be taken from him.

Memphis tried to reach for her hand.

And he passed out.

***

A blaze of lights flashed outside of her building. Eliza rushed after the EMTs who were pushing the gurney—the gurney that held an unconscious and blood-soaked Memphis.

This can't be happening. It can't be happening. They'd been talking. She'd just told him that she loved him—

And his blood was all over her hands. His blood had pumped through her fingertips as she fought to save him.

The EMTs carefully loaded him into the back of the nearby ambulance. She raced to get in that ambulance with him—

"You're not leaving." Daniel manacled his hand around her wrist. "No, hell, no, Eliza."

She yanked as hard as she could. "Memphis needs me!"

"He needs a freaking doctor, that's what he needs! You aren't going with him. Dammit, I'm taking you into protective custody."

Memphis was inside the ambulance. His hand fell down, and she could see blood—

Pain burned through her. "I want to be with him!"

Saint burst to her side. "What in the hell is happening here?" He glared at the detective. "Get your fucking hand *off* her!"

"I'm a detective, you don't tell me—"

Saint went toe-to-toe with him. "Hands off Memphis's lady. Now. If she wants to go with him, she's going. She's—"

"She's the reason your friend is in that ambulance," Daniel gritted back at him. "Haven't you figured that out? Eliza told the perp that she knew who he was, so he took those shots. He did it so she would never have the chance to tell *me* and the other cops what she'd remembered. He was trying to silence her, but instead, your friend got hit. Memphis was caught in the crossfire. Those bullets were meant for her. Not him. Another attempt could come on her life. She is *not* going into that hospital where I can't control the environment."

The ambulance's siren wailed. It was going to leave—

Memphis would be alone. Someone had to stay with him. Someone had to watch over him.

"She's in protective custody. Want to fight me on this? I'll arrest your ass," Daniel threatened.

Saint looked more than ready to—

"Get in the ambulance with Memphis!" Eliza cried.

His head whipped toward her. "What?"

"You're family. His brother—"

"He told you?"

"You can go with him. You can make any medical decisions that need to be done—and you do it and you make sure they keep him alive!" She glared at him. "Don't you let me down, Saint. Take care of him! Protect him!"

"He won't like it—he'll want me to stay with you—"

"The ambulance is *leaving!* Go!"

Swearing, he whirled and ran to the ambulance. He jumped in the back.

Her shoulders sagged. *Memphis isn't alone. Saint will watch him. It's okay.*

"They're brothers?"

She didn't look at Daniel. She watched the lights from the ambulance fade as it raced away.

"Eliza, Memphis is in good hands. The doctors will take care of him." Daniel's voice was stilted. "And I'm sorry, but you have to come with me."

He led her toward a patrol car.

Wait, a patrol car?

"Get in the back," he ordered.

He wasn't serious.

"You'll be safe in the back. I'll have a uniform keep an eye on you. I need to talk to Camila, let her know what's happening. I'll only be gone a few moments, then I'll come back and take you to a safe house."

This was not happening.

"I don't trust you not to run," he told her flatly. "So I have to keep you secured."

Her heart raced too fast. She looked around, wanting help—

A uniformed officer rushed toward them. Eliza opened her mouth.

"Put her in the back of your patrol car, Officer Bishop. She is not to leave until I return, understand? She's in protective custody."

"Is this even how protective custody works?" Eliza demanded. "You can't just lock me up! My lawyers will—"

"They can rip me a new one, later." Daniel wasn't concerned. "But you'll still be alive, and maybe instead of being pissed, you and your lawyers will realize that you should be grateful to me."

Moments later, she was in the back of the patrol car. Officer Bishop stood on the other side of the door. Dozens of cops were swarming the area. Everything seemed crazy and...

The blood had dried on her fingertips.

Memphis. There had been shock on his face after the first bullet hit him. Shock and rage and...fear. But she didn't think he'd been afraid for himself.

For me. He'd wanted her to get his gun. To protect herself.

She didn't have any weapons. Didn't have her bag or a taser or even a phone. She was trapped in the back of a patrol car. Memphis could be dying, and she wasn't with him.

Fuck. This.

Some of the cold—the numbing shock—that she'd experienced as the ambulance fled began to melt away. She turned toward the door. Banged on the window to get Officer Bishop's attention—

But as she watched, he ran away, pulling out his radio and motioning toward a group of reporters who'd just arrived. Even in the dark, she could see their cameras. Even in the—

A knock sounded nearby. Knuckles tapping at the window on the other side of the car. Eliza jerked around. She squinted and slid across the backseat to get toward that window.

Knuckles tapped again.

And—

"Eliza?" Bethany asked her, voice shocked. "Why are you in the back of a patrol car?"

Bethany. Relief had her head spinning. "Open the door!" she cried.

"What?" Bethany's face pressed closer to the glass. "Can't quite hear you."

She slammed her hand onto the glass of the window. "Open the door!" Because she couldn't open it from the inside. Bethany had to know that—

"Oh." Bethany looked down. Then back up. "You haven't like...killed anyone or anything, have you?"

"*Open the door!*"

Bethany grabbed the handle. Opened the door. As it swung open, she said, "Is it supposed to just open like that? I mean, don't cops lock it or—"

Eliza sprang out of the car and grabbed her.

"OhmyGod!" Bethany shuddered. "There is blood on your hands. I specifically *asked* if you had killed anyone."

"I didn't! Someone shot Memphis!"

"Memphis? Who is—"

Eliza crouched and looked back. Officer Bishop would return to the car or Daniel could come bounding up at any moment. Memphis hadn't trusted Daniel. Saint had said that Daniel hadn't fired those shots, but Eliza didn't know what to believe or who to trust.

No. I do know who to trust. I always knew. Memphis. "I have to get to the hospital. Please, Bethany, take me to the hospital."

"Okay, okay...my car is just around the corner. Come on."

They pretty much raced to her red Benz. Bethany hit the key fob, the lights flashed, and the doors unlocked. Eliza dove inside. Bethany took the driver seat and slammed her door. She cranked the engine and glanced into her rearview mirror. "Are the cops going to follow us?"

"Not if you move fast, they won't!"

Bethany shoved her foot down on the gas pedal, and they flew away from the curb. "My God, Eliza!" she breathed. "What is happening? I texted you like a dozen times in the last few hours, and you just ignored me. Then I see that segment online about you remembering what happened all those years ago..."

Eliza glanced back. No sign of the cops. "Remember the guy from the bar the other night, the one you dared me to—"

"The bodyguard?" Bethany cut in.

"No, he's not a bodyguard. He's...he's Memphis. He's been helping me to track the perp who took me."

"And...you remember?" Careful. Cautious. She kept driving fast.

"Which hospital is the closest?" Eliza tried to figure things out. "I think it's Providence. We need to turn at the next right."

"Who took you, Eliza?"

"Memphis was shot tonight. Right in front of me. I-I can't stop shaking. I love him, Bethany. I love him and—" And they had driven straight. Not taken the next right. "You missed the turn. It's okay. Just take the next—"

"You don't remember a damn thing, do you?"

Her head whipped toward Bethany. "Why are you slowing down?" They were *stopping*.

Bethany sighed. She reached into her bag. The bag that rested between the two front seats in the small console area. "Because I need to do this." Her hand moved in a lightning-fast blur. She jabbed Eliza.

Eliza blinked. Stared down. Bethany had a syringe in her hand. "What..."

"Yes. That's good." She shoved the syringe back into her bag. "You'll be out in less than a minute. Bet you're already feeling it, aren't you?" And once again, she shoved her foot down onto the gas. Shot them forward.

Shot them forward even as Eliza tried to grab for the door handle. But her fingers felt all uncoordinated. Stiff and hard.

"Oh, Eliza. You shouldn't have lied. If you hadn't lied, then we could have just kept going as we had been..."

Bethany just injected me. Bethany is...

"It was me, sweet friend. I'm the one who took you away all those years ago, and I'm the one who will make sure that this time, you vanish for good."

She couldn't touch the door. Couldn't...

Couldn't feel anything at all.

CHAPTER TWENTY

"He's dead."

Eliza squinted. Groaned. Every muscle in her body hurt. As if she'd been beaten. But...

Her eyes flew open. She could smell hay. Dirt. Her breath came fast and hard, and she shuddered as—

"Yes, I know the news is tough. But the bullet wounds were fatal," Bethany said as she stood just a few feet away.

Eliza was on the ground. Sprawled in the dirty hay. And her hands—both of them—were cuffed to a thick, metal bar.

"Made some improvements," Bethany said.

OhmyGod, no.

"You can't break that bar. Made of steel, and it's cemented into the ground." A lantern sat by Bethany's feet. "You're going to drift in and out for a while because of the drugs. That's normal. Don't worry. But I wanted to go ahead and tell you about, ah, Memphis, I believe his name was? I wanted to tell you about him because you seemed quite worried earlier."

Memphis.

"He died in the ambulance. I saw the report on the news. He's gone." She crouched. Smiled. "Don't worry. Soon, you will be, too."

No, no, no. Memphis could not be dead. But Eliza felt tears streak down her cheeks. "Wh-why?" Her voice came out all distorted.

"Why will you be dead? Because I'm going to kill you, of course. Just like I killed all the others."

Eliza shook her head. Dizziness nearly knocked her out.

"Do you know what a fucking Mary Jane is, Eliza?"

She could barely hear the words.

"You're a Mary Jane. Every guy always falls at your feet, don't they? You walk in, you look all delicate and sexy, and they want you. I *hate* Mary Janes. No one could see me when you were beside me. The fucking other night—when we were at the bar—it happened *again*. The first time in *years*. You had been like a ghost, so I didn't mind you as much—you were barely there at all. But then you started your shit again the other night."

"I..." *Didn't do anything...*

"When you are next to me, they don't see me." She glared. "Now, they won't see you."

This wasn't happening...it *wasn't*.

"Didn't even intend for all this. Want to know the truth?"

What she wanted...*Memphis*. To get away. To get to him. But he was...

Dead? *No, no. Memphis can't be dead. He can't.*

"I was paid to take you all those years ago," Bethany revealed with a laugh. "Just a prank, you know but..." Laughter. "I liked it..."

Her head throbbed. Nausea rose, and Eliza thought she might vomit. She swallowed. Choked. But managed, "The other...women?"

"All just like you. Men flocked to them. They lit up fucking rooms. That first bitch—Amelia..."

*It's true. It's true. She knows them...*Eliza gagged.

"She looked just like me. We were at the same bar, but she was the one getting all the free drinks. She was the one getting all the attention. I was so over that shit. It just wasn't going to happen again. It *wasn't*. I went there to get away, it was the stupid anniversary, and I didn't want to think about you—then she was there. Stealing the light just like you always did."

Eliza shook her head. "No, no, I n-never meant..."

"She asked for a ride. Can you believe that? Just got in the car with me. I realized how easy it was. I knew just what to do..."

"Y-you...killed them all."

"Um. And I'm going to kill you. But not yet." She rose. Brushed hay off her jeans. "Got to go act all worried first. Get my face on TV. Get my alibi. I'll be back though, don't you worry." She advanced on Eliza. "I want to be able to enjoy our time together. After all, it's not every day that you say goodbye to your very best friend in the whole world."

Something was in her hand.

"I learned from my mistakes," Bethany said.

She jabbed Eliza again with a syringe. Cold seemed to pour through her veins.

"I don't *think* that will kill you, but, it will sure as hell stop you from getting away." Then she turned and picked up the lantern. Moved toward what looked like an old, wooden ladder. Climbed up. "Oh, you might have broken a few bones when I shoved you down here. I should apologize for that."

What?

"But I won't." She climbed up the ladder. Took the light with her.

Eliza shivered. All she knew was the dark.

Memphis. He couldn't be dead.

***

"*Eliza!*" Memphis roared.

"Restrain him!" A female voice. *Not* Eliza. "Restrain him now before the stitches tear again—"

"*Get...Eliza...*"

Someone grabbed his right arm. Then his left. Shoved him back as he yelled his fury and fear. He needed Eliza. He had to see Eliza. Where was—

"*Eliza!*"

"Sedate him. Now."

***

"Hey."

Memphis groaned. His eyes fluttered open.

"Hey, are you with me again? And are you gonna stay in control?"

Saint's voice. It was Saint leaning toward him with a worried expression on his face and with his hair sticking up in about a dozen different directions.

Memphis squinted at him. "What are you..." Damn, his throat felt funny. Dry and achy. He—

Jerked. Tried to bolt upright.

Machines beeped and buzzed.

"You need to stay calm, Memphis."

That *wasn't* Saint talking. It was a feminine voice. Careful. Sad. His gaze jerked to the left. His friend Delilah stood there, with her husband Archer right behind her. "It's hard, I know," Delilah continued, and her eyes held heavy shadows beneath them. "But we have to take care of you first before..."

Before what?

But Delilah stopped talking. Archer put his hand on her shoulder and squeezed. What was going on?

"Where..." He needed some water for his throat. "Eliza?" She should be in there. He wanted to see her.

"I'm sorry." From Saint. "She...wanted me to get in the ambulance with you. There were cops everywhere, so I thought she'd be fine."

The machines beeped faster. He pushed up.

Delilah rushed toward the bed. "Don't tear your stitches!"

Someone else had told him that shit. He could vaguely remember the scene. Like he cared about his stitches. He only cared about Eliza. "Where is..." His voice was getting stronger. A good sign. "Eliza?"

Saint looked at Delilah—

"Where," Memphis snapped.

Saint's remorseful gaze swung back to him. "I don't know."

The door opened. Elijah Cross strode in. *Elijah?* He should have been in Florida. It looked like he hadn't slept in days. Stubble covered his jaw. Shadows like Delilah's lined his eyes and...

"How long was I out?" Memphis rasped.

Elijah positioned himself at the foot of the bed. "Too long."

That wasn't a real answer. They weren't giving him real answers, and Eliza was not there. "I want Eliza." After he saw her, he could figure out his next move.

Silence. Thick and heavy. As if they were all trying to decide which one would say—

"Eliza is missing," Delilah told him. "She disappeared while you were on the way to the hospital."

Memphis shook his head. "No." That couldn't be right.

"And..." Delilah's voice held pain. Heartbreak. "You've been here for two days."

Impossible. He would have known—

"They had to sedate you because every time you woke up, you tried to fight them and find Eliza. You tore open your stitches—"

He swung his feet to the side of the bed. Lunged up.

Would have fallen right on his face if Saint hadn't grabbed him.

"I'm so sorry," Saint whispered in his ear.

Memphis just shook his head. *"No."* Two days. Two days? "Get me the fuck...out of here."

***

"You need to be in the hospital!" Saint snapped at him. "Look, I get that you want to find her—"

"You don't get a fucking thing." He slammed the car door. Took a minute to brace himself because, dammit, he was weak. Too weak. His shoulder ached like a bitch, while his side burned. But there was no way he was sitting on the sidelines. Forty-eight hours had passed.

Darkness surrounded them as he glared up at the entrance to Prescott Robinson's home.

"Their lawyers shut us out," Delilah said as she came to stand beside Memphis. She and Archer had followed in their rental while Saint, Elijah, and Memphis had been in the lead car. "We've been involved with the locals in the hunt, but there aren't any solid leads for us."

There were about to be. He looked at Elijah. "We still think it's someone close to her."

"Intimately close."

"Then we're going inside."

Saint braced him as he walked, and though he hated it, Memphis needed the support. Elijah was on his left, Saint on his right, and they went up those steps with Delilah and Archer at their backs.

One of the front doors swung open. Alec blocked their path. "You should never have gotten past the guards at the gates—"

"Yeah, I'll tell you what I told them," Memphis growled. "Get out of our way or I will destroy you."

Alec raked him with a glance. "So much for keeping her safe. You know that you killed —"

He lunged for him. But Saint beat him to the punch. Literally. Saint swung out a powerful fist and drove it straight into Alec's jaw. The guard fell back onto his ass, dazed.

"Didn't want you tearing stitches," Saint said.

Memphis marched into the entranceway even as Kathleen rushed toward the guard. She crouched next to him as her hands fluttered in the air around him. Horrified, she looked back at Memphis. "What are you doing?" she cried. "You can't just—"

He pointed at her. "We'll start our questions with you."

"Help!" Kathleen screamed.

Really?

Help came running. Help in the forms of Benedict and Prescott Robinson. Eliza's brother's eyes were red-rimmed. His face haggard. He looked like a man on the very edge.

"Change of plans," Memphis decided. His hand swung toward Benedict. "We start with you." He marched toward him. Didn't even need Saint's help. "Why the hell do you feel so guilty?" He could *see* the guilt on Benedict's face. It infuriated him. "What did you do?"

"Don't say a word," Kathleen called out. "We need the police. Prescott, call Detective Jones—"

Prescott didn't move. He seemed to have aged twenty years. "I've hired every PI in a hundred-mile radius." His breath shuddered. "No one can find her. My baby just disappeared. One minute, she was in the back of a patrol car—"

"Why the hell was she there?" Memphis thundered.

"Cops were taking her into protective custody," Elijah told him.

"Then she was gone," Prescott finished. "No one saw her. No one knows anything. Her phone was still in the house. Just a dozen texts on it from Bethany. All before Eliza vanished. Her friend is devastated. I saw a news story where Bethany was nearly hysterical..."

"*I'm* calling the cops if you won't." Kathleen jumped to her feet and rushed across the foyer.

"Don't call anyone." Prescott's voice firmed. He stared at Memphis. Looked at the people behind him. "I don't know them."

"They're with me." The whole crew had his back.

"You...trust them?"

"With my life."

Prescott's lower lip trembled. "I trusted you with my daughter's life."

Memphis took the hit straight to his heart.

Saint jumped in front of him. "He was fucking *shot!* Two bullet wounds and enough blood loss to scare even the devil. It's not his fault that she was taken, you sonofabitch! It's *mine*. He had me in town to watch her, and I screwed up. The only thing he's ever asked me to do and I—"

Memphis touched his brother on the shoulder. "The one we blame is the one who took her." Growled.

Saint jerked his head, but Memphis knew his brother wasn't believing those words. He should.

"You know me," Archer spoke up to say. "We've done business together for years."

"I know you were suspected of murdering that young woman...your ex-fiancée..."

"Archer didn't do it," Delilah snapped. "We found the real killer. Proved his innocence. You must watch the news like everyone else. I'm sure you saw the story."

"*Yes, I need Detective Jones, please.*" Kathleen's frantic voice. "Get him out to the Robinson—

"Put the phone down, Kathleen," Prescott ordered.

Memphis glanced at her. Alec hovered by her side. Alec's hands fisted and released. Fisted. And—

"It's my fault," Benedict burst out.

The weak link. Memphis focused on him. "*Why?*"

Benedict's breath sawed out. "She called me. A-all those years ago. Called me and wanted a ride because she wasn't feeling well...She wanted my help. All she ever did was help *me*. Got my ass out of messes over and over...Lizzie just wanted a ride home." He rocked forward. Back. "She wasn't feeling good. Said everything kept spinning. She needed me. The only time. *Ever*. Lizzie was with Bethany, but Bethany didn't want to leave...Lizzie just wanted to come home."

Memphis's heart hurt far more than the bullet wounds. *I will bring you home, sweetheart.* "But you were drinking, too. You got pulled over by a cop and tossed in jail—"

"Wasn't drinking." He swallowed. "I was high. Bethany could always get a hookup, and she'd given me stuff earlier in the day. When Lizzie called, I wanted to go to her, but I crashed my car after driving half a block. Then I couldn't remember any damn thing until Dad got me out of that cell the next day. And by then..." His shoulders hunched. "Jesus. *Jesus*. My sister was gone! It took me *days* to even remember that I was supposed to get her, I was so messed up, my memory trashed..."

Like Eliza's had been.

Benedict's guilt-ridden face lifted toward Memphis. "I wanted to be better. I haven't used since then, I swear it, and when I met with you at your hotel...and you—you said you'd find out what happened, I *wanted* you to hunt down the bastard. But I knew you'd also figure out what I'd done, and I was so ashamed. She *needed me...*"

"She needs you now," Memphis blasted. "She needs you, and she needs me, and we're not going to start weeping in fucking corners. Eliza is still alive. She's out there, and we are going to bring her back." He nodded. "Or maybe she'll bring herself back, just like she did last time. Maybe she will walk right through the doors any minute..."

Please, baby, please come back through the doors.

He even looked toward them. But—

Ding.

His eyes jerked toward Delilah. She had her phone out, and her face darkened as she read whatever news had been sent to her.

Not Eliza. Please, God, just not—

"We found the payout," Delilah said. She motioned toward a watchful Elijah. "He called some of his forensic accounting buddies to help us out. Took some untangling, but we found the original payment that was sent in order to make Eliza disappear years ago."

"Make her disappear?" Benedict rubbed a hand over his face and swiped away the tears on his cheeks. "What are you talking about?"

Prescott took a halting step toward Delilah. "Are you saying...someone *paid* to make my daughter vanish?"

Delilah nodded. "That's exactly what I'm saying."

"This is absurd!" Kathleen cried. She still gripped the phone in her hand. Had she hung up? Memphis didn't know. But...

He knew guilt when he saw it. Panic. Fear. "It was you."

Her mouth dropped open. Then snapped closed. Her frantic gaze flew around until it finally landed on Prescott. "Throw these people out! They don't know what they are talking about! They don't know—"

"You had an affair," Memphis said flatly. "Eliza caught you. She was going to tell her dad. Stop him from marrying you. You paid for her to vanish. That way, you could have your big engagement. You could have everything that you wanted."

"No! No, that is not what happened! Not at all!" Kathleen's voice was nearly a screech. She bounded toward Prescott and grabbed his arms. "It wasn't—"

"Ten thousand dollars," Delilah announced. "That was the amount of money that disappeared. It was hard to track because you pretended it was part of the catering fee for your engagement party, but it wasn't. Elijah's forensic accountants *talked* to the caterer. Got the receipts from their end. You gave that money to someone else."

Even Alec was starting to glare at her.

Prescott stared at Kathleen as if he'd never seen her before. "Why?"

"I...it's not what you think!" She tightened her grip on him. "I just...I was going to get incriminating photos of her! Stuff I could use to stop her from telling you about the one time—*only once*—that I messed up. I loved you, and I wanted to be with you. She was just supposed to get really drunk or high and then...then she was going to—"

"Who did you pay?" Memphis cut through her words because time was *wasting*.

She gasped. Turned her head toward him. Blinked.

"Who?" But his mind was spinning. Bits and pieces. Things all coming together. Too late. Too slow...

Eliza had been with Bethany seven years ago.

Bethany had given Benedict drugs.

Bethany had stayed close with Eliza, stayed right by her side all of these years even as other friends had turned away.

He'd once told Eliza that the female victims would have felt comfortable getting into the car with a police officer. They would have felt comfortable with Bethany, too. He'd seen the tall redhead with Eliza the night that he'd first crossed paths with his princess. The night she'd poured a beer on him.

Because Bethany had dared her...

"Bethany," he whispered.

Kathleen's head moved in a jerk. A jerk that was a yes...

"She's a real estate agent," Delilah told him. "I did a brief background check on her, too, when you started getting me to look at those close to Eliza. Bethany would have access to a ton of properties..."

"She makes acquisitions recommendations at Robinson Corporation," Prescott said, sounding dazed. "She..."

"She was probably the one who recommended the corporation buy the damn sunflower field," Saint snapped.

"Get the cops, get the Feds," Memphis thundered.

Elijah already had his phone out. "On it."

"We need an APB for Bethany. We need to look at every property she's recently visited, we need to search every—"

"I've already looked at every sunflower field within a five-hour radius," her father confessed. "Sent team after team..."

"She's been on the news." Benedict had gone white as his skin bleached of all color. "She was crying for my sister. She was at my door...less than two hours after Eliza's disappearance. She was *crying* and saying how sorry she was for me."

Two hours. "That gives us a search guideline." Two hours. "*Every bit of property she's visited,*" he growled again. "We need to look for something close but isolated. Something that would allow her to keep Eliza prisoner. She wouldn't make the same mistakes this time. She'd have Eliza locked down tight."

He thought of the profile they'd made on the perp. Someone in Eliza's inner circle.

Bethany.

Someone obsessed with her.

Bethany.

Someone who wanted to hurt her.

Bethany.

Someone well connected. Someone who could travel easily, without attracting undue attention.

Bethany.

Someone who could easily lure the victims.

Bethany.

Fuck, fuck, fuck. Eliza had been afraid her abductor could be standing beside her, and she'd been right.

Kathleen shook her head. Again and again. "I never...this isn't...This isn't what I wanted!"

Prescott jerked his hands from her. "Get the hell out of my house."

"Prescott!"

Memphis spun away from them. Stormed for the door. Eliza. He had to get—

Alec stepped in his path.

Healing bullet wounds or not, I will end—

"Let me help?" Alec asked.

CHAPTER TWENTY-ONE

"Eliza!"

She jerked. Her lips were parched, broken open in slits. Her left ankle was broken, too. Maybe her ribs. In the long hours that she'd spent in the dark, Eliza had realized that Bethany hadn't lied.

The bitch really had thrown her down.

But that bellowing shout...that wasn't Bethany...

"H-here!" Eliza tried to call, but her voice was too weak. She'd been left alone for so long. She was weak and tired. And she'd screamed at the beginning. Screamed and screamed.

No one had heard her.

Did Amelia scream, too? Did Layla scream?

"Eliza!" A man's roar.

She kicked out with her foot. The one that wasn't freaking broken. Hit the wooden ladder. Made a little thudding sound. She did it again. Again.

And there was a wrenching, groaning creak as a door was opened. Not really a door. More like...

She squinted because a flashlight was being shone down on her.

Like a trapdoor in the floor. A trapdoor...

She knew the smells around her. She was in a barn. But not handcuffed in a stall.

A hidden trapdoor in the floor.

She was in the ground. *I'm in a grave. I've been left in a grave.*

"It's all right," he told her as he rushed down the ladder. "You're going to be okay."

Eliza flinched away from the light. Her wrists were raw and bloody. She'd fought and fought to get out, but the pole had truly been cemented in the ground, and she couldn't break free.

"I've got water for you," he said. "Here, take it."

He was a familiar voice behind the light. When he put a water bottle to her lips, she drank greedily, almost choking because—

"Where is she?" he asked softly.

I know that voice. Eliza strained to see. He'd put the flashlight down. "D-Daniel?"

"Where is Bethany?"

"I..." Talking was so hard. She wanted more water, but he'd taken the bottle away. "D-don't know..."

"What did she tell you?"

Eliza shook her head.

"Did she mention the others?"

"She...k-killed..."

"It's okay. I know. I know what she did. I'm not going to let her do that to you." His hand brushed against her cheek. "You should have just stayed in the patrol car. I was trying to keep you safe."

Daniel had found her. That must mean he'd brought lots of cops with him. But...why weren't the others rushing in to save the day? She wanted out of that hole. *Get me out of this grave.*

"She disappeared from her house about an hour ago, so I knew she'd be coming back to you. I had to get here first." He looked up. "Did you hear that?"

She hadn't heard anything.

"It was a car," he said. He sprang up. Pulled the trapdoor closed again.

Why? "Wh—"

He turned off the flashlight. "It's okay." Low. Soothing. "I'm going to get her when she comes inside. I'll stop her, and she'll never hurt you again."

"Cuffs..." Eliza rasped. "Off...*please*..."

"I'll get them off. But you have to be quiet. Don't make a sound. We don't want her to know I'm here."

She could barely think. Barely focus but...this didn't feel right.

OhmyGod, Eliza! Like anything feels right. He's a cop, and he's here to help you. He's here to...

"Did she mention me?" Daniel asked her.

Eliza stopped breathing. "N-no..."

"Good, good." He stroked her arm.

She refused to flinch away, but she wanted to so badly. So very badly.

"I'm going to take care of her," he promised. "Then we'll never have to worry about Bethany getting between us again."

I'm not worried about her getting between us. I'm worried about her killing me.

And now...now...

I'm worried about you, too. Because Daniel was crouching behind her. She heard him pull out his gun, and he was staring straight up at the darkness.

He had also made no move to get the cuffs off her.

***

Splitting up had been the best course of action. They'd gotten a list of potential properties to search, places that Bethany had visited or listed in the last six months. Places that were completely vacant and private enough to be used as holding spots for Eliza.

She is still alive. She has to still be alive.

Memphis wouldn't consider any other option. His Eliza was alive.

The locations they had were also close enough that Bethany could have dumped Eliza then gone right back to act as the grieving and shocked friend.

Archer and Delilah had taken some of the places. Elijah and Alec had been another team. And that left...

"The ranch is about five miles away," Saint told him, speaking in the comm unit that connected them. They were flying in a chopper—Archer and Prescott had gotten them all choppers, and they had raced away to search. "We'll be there in just a few minutes."

Not fast enough. The last three stops had been fruitless. He needed to find Eliza.

"She's still alive," Saint said.

Memphis moved his head in a nod. He wouldn't believe anything else. He *couldn't*.

But...

But Bethany Bancroft was missing. Her neighbor had told a patrol officer that she left about an hour ago and...

And the detective, Daniel Jones, had also gone off the radar. Camila had told them that he'd wanted to follow up on some hunches, but when they'd all tried reaching out to him, he hadn't answered his phone.

"There it is," Saint announced.

The dark ranch waited. The chopper began to descend. Memphis's heart seemed to pound in time with the whir of the helicopter's blades.

***

Steps creaked overhead. Dirt rained down on Eliza. She couldn't see the dirt, but she could feel it. Her breathing seemed too loud.

So did Daniel's.

The steps grew closer. Then the groaning, creaking sounded as the trapdoor was opened.

"I don't make the same mistakes," Bethany called out. "One of the changes I made...I set up a camera so that I would know if you tried to get away. Or if someone tried to help you."

"Fuck," Daniel whispered.

"I know he's down there with you, Eliza. But what *you* don't know...it's that Daniel helped *me*."

Her body stiffened.

"He helped me the night you disappeared seven years ago." Bethany didn't climb down the ladder. She stayed up top, and her voice drifted to them. "He was my supplier back in those days. Let me tell you, cops have access to the best stuff. We met at a party, he gave me the hookup, and then...well, let's just say business got going for us. It was booming back then. There were always people in our group looking to have a good time. I helped your brother out on plenty of occasions."

Eliza's hands twisted against the cuffs.

"Your stepmother hates you, do you know that? She hates you so much that she paid me ten thousand dollars to set up an incriminating scene that involved you. You were supposed to look like one crazy party girl. I dosed you, I got you out of the bar, and then...dammit, then *you* got away. Daniel had come out to check up on you, to make sure you were contained, and you got *away*."

Eliza remembered running out into the night. The moonlight hitting the sunflowers. A man's roar.

"She's lying," Daniel breathed into her ear.

Eliza shivered.

"He chased after you, but you hid in the woods. Really pissed him off. I think he would have killed you if he found you that night."

"Lie," Daniel breathed again. "I would never hurt you."

But Eliza didn't believe him.

From up above, Bethany kept talking. "You climbed into the back of some delivery truck—which I find fucking hilarious, by the way—and you escaped. He saw the truck leaving—it had been parked at a gas station—and by the time Daniel could catch up to it again, you were already out of the vehicle. Then the next thing we know, you're at your dad's house. And you don't remember *anything*."

She didn't cry. She couldn't cry.

"That's when Daniel started getting close to you. He did it at first as a test, to see if you remembered him. But I told him, 'Dumbass, if she doesn't remember me, she doesn't remember *you*.' Am I right?"

Yes, Bethany had been right.

"Do you know why he's here now?"

"To save you," Daniel breathed.

Eliza shivered.

Bethany's laugh drifted to her as more dirt rained down. "He thought he would kill me and that you would never know what he'd really done. I think he fell in love with you. You and that Mary Jane bullshit. He probably thinks he is going to get a happy ending with you. Be your big hero. But I had my camera, and I saw him, and now you know the truth. There won't be any pretending he's the hero. You won't be grateful to him. You won't ever love him."

Daniel's hand gripped Eliza's shoulder. Painfully.

"He used to follow you all the time. Take pictures of you. I found one of the photos at his place, and I left it for your dad to see."

"Bitch," Daniel whispered.

How can I get out of this? If she could get Daniel's gun...Eliza's fingers stretched in the cuffs. Daniel was behind her, and she touched his waistband.

Then she realized...he'd brought his right hand in front of her. And his right hand held a gun. "Tell her to come down here," he ordered.

Like Bethany was going to do what Eliza said. If that was the case...*Um, I would have just said let me go and she would have!*

"Tell her!" The fingers of his left hand brutally squeezed her shoulder.

"Come down here!" Eliza yelled.

Bethany laughed.

***

"Not here, dammit!" Saint spun away from the ranch. "Let's get back in the air. Next spot—"

"Why was he at the bar?"

"What?"

"The first night that I met Eliza, she was at a bar with Bethany. And right outside the place, Eliza stumbled into Daniel. He'd been heading for that same bar." A pause as dark suspicion rolled through Memphis. "Why was he at the bar?"

"Uh, to get a drink? Listen, we know our perp, it's—"

"Eliza remembered a man screaming her name when she escaped. A man. Not a woman."

"She was drugged. She—"

Memphis pulled out his phone. "I will always believe Eliza." He dialed fast, knowing that he was going to be breaking the law and not giving a shit. One of his contacts answered on the second ring. "Detective Daniel Jones," Memphis said. "I want you to find his location. He should have his cell phone with him, but he's not answering."

A woman queried, "Uh, Memphis? That you?"

"Our debt will be settled when I have the info. Just get this for me."

"You want me to do a search on a *cop?*"

"I want you to do the search on the cop right the hell *now.* I want you to tell me exactly where he is. I don't care what kind of tech you use or what laws you break, I need this info."

He held his breath. He waited. If she couldn't get this for him...

"I'm a fucking CIA agent, I can get anything," she snapped back.

Not just an agent. A hacker extraordinaire.

And...

"He's not far from you," she told him just a moment later.

She had Memphis's location, too? Already? And why was that not really surprising? But the fact that *Daniel* was close...

"Looks like he's at an old dairy farm, twenty miles away. I'll send you the coordinates."

The dairy farm had been next on their list. *Fucking hell.* "Thank you, Genie."

"Yes, well, this is the last wish I grant for you. Consider me *off* your debt list."

If this worked, if this sent him to Eliza... "Put me *on* your list. I'll come running when you need me."

And he took off for the chopper.

***

"I'm going after her," Daniel growled.

"No, please!" Her mind spun. "Uncuff me first. Daniel, *please*. Don't leave me in the dark like..."

Footsteps pounded overhead. Bethany was running. Shit.

"Here." He shoved a metal object into her hand. Bounded for the ladder.

He'd given her a key. Handcuff keys were mostly universal, so she twisted her wrist. Shoved the key into the hole. Heard the sweet precious *snick*. Yes! Yes—

Bam.

A gunshot. From overhead.

Eliza's head whipped up. Then she scrambled to her feet.

And promptly fell right back down when her broken ankle didn't hold her weight.

Sonofabitch. Her hands flew out, and she grabbed for that ladder.

Bam. Bam.

She had to get out of there. Had to get away.

She hauled herself up those steps.

***

"Did you hear that?" Saint demanded. They'd just touched down. Just rushed from the chopper, and the sound was distorted but...

Yeah, he'd heard it. "Gunfire."

"Maybe the cop found Bethany?" Saint had his own weapon out.

So did Memphis. "Maybe he always knew where Bethany was. Maybe he knew where Eliza was, too." But he'd waited, picked his moment…

Bam.

This time, the gunfire was unmistakable. Saint and Memphis ran toward the echoing blast. And as he ran, Memphis felt blood begin to soak the shoulder of his shirt.

The fucking stitches could tear. He wasn't slowing down. He *was* getting to Eliza.

***

Eliza hauled herself out of that hole in the ground. *A grave. It was like being trapped in a grave.* Her ears echoed with the thunder of the last gunshot, and she looked around.

A lantern was to the right. And near that lantern…

Bethany. Sprawled with her arms outstretched.

Eliza rose on unsteady legs. Hobbled slowly toward Bethany. She didn't see any sign of Daniel. Where was he?

The light from the lantern spilled onto Bethany and onto the growing, thick circle that spread from beneath her body. A circle of blood.

Eliza sucked in a hard breath.

"Don't feel bad for her. She would have killed you."

Daniel.

Eliza spun around. Nearly fell again when pain knifed through her ankle, but she managed to stay upright at the last moment.

Daniel waited in the shadows to the right. He still had his gun gripped in his hand.

"We'll call this in," he told her. "We'll say that I had to shoot her while I was saving you."

Eliza backed up a step. She'd only released one wrist from the cuffs so that she could get free, and the handcuffs dangled from her left hand and bounced against her thigh. As she backed up, her foot hit the lantern. It wobbled. The candlelight danced from behind the glass.

"I saved you and had to kill her. It's a simple story." He slid from the shadows. "And it's exactly what happened."

"H-how..."

"I shot her. But she shot at me first. She *did*. Forensics can check her weapon. They'll know."

Her heartbeat was so loud. It almost sounded like the beat of a helicopter. "H-how..." Eliza tried again. "D-did you know...I'd need water?"

"What?"

"H-how..."

He advanced on her. "It stood to reason that you were being held captive. Unlike Memphis, I didn't give up on you."

Memphis. "He's...not dead?"

"No, he's not. That what she told you?"

"Y-yes." *Memphis wasn't dead!*

"He's alive, but he's not hunting for you, Eliza. He didn't come for you. I did. I never gave up. I never would give up."

But she remembered what Memphis had once said about Daniel...

I don't trust him. Either he's insanely inept or he's deliberately screwed up your case.

"I brought water because it's been two days, Eliza. If you go three days without water, your organs will begin to shut down. I knew we were working against the clock, so I came prepared to help you. All I've ever wanted to do was help you."

He had his gun gripped in his right hand. The gun wasn't pointing at her. It was pointed down at the ground.

"Eliza, you don't need to be afraid of me. You don't need to be afraid of anything. It was Bethany. She was in the building across from yours. She'd go to that top floor and watch you. Hour after hour. She shot at Memphis. She kidnapped you. She took all of those other women—my God, I didn't even know she was doing all that."

I didn't even know she was doing all that.

The phrasing was off. Everything was off.

Eliza bent and picked up the lantern. It felt so heavy in her hands. Was that because it was heavy or because she was just weak? Her body swayed. *It's because I'm weak.*

"I didn't hurt those other women. When the first one was taken, I was right here in town with you. Remember?"

Her throat was so painfully dry. "F-first one?" But she knew who the woman had been...

"Amelia Lake," he supplied immediately. "Hell, she looked just like Bethany. No, correction, she was prettier than Bethany. That's why Bethany was taking those women. Do you believe that crap? Because she felt like they were in her limelight. They'd always gotten attention, and Bethany said she'd make everyone forget they ever lived. She took the bright lights, and she made them vanish. She was sick and twisted, and she had to be stopped."

Eliza remembered the first anniversary of her abduction. Bethany *had* been out of town that weekend. She'd said that she needed to go back to Alabama for a high school reunion.

Back to Alabama.

But...

But that same weekend, a sunflower had been delivered to Eliza's new place. Had Bethany arranged for that delivery or...

"I was with you that weekend," Daniel said. "I'm always with you on the anniversary."

Oh, no. Memphis had told her that there had been two occasions when Daniel wasn't in town for the anniversary. There had been two occasions when Eliza hadn't been in town, too, but the sunflowers had still shown up...

They showed up because he followed me. When I left, he would follow. "Why?"

"Why am I with you? Because I love you. I just killed for you. Doesn't that prove it?"

"*Eliza!*"

Her body jerked at the call. That voice—*Memphis's voice.* He was outside. He was coming for her.

"No!" A snap from Daniel as he lunged toward her. "He's not saving you. I saved you. I was right here. I found you, and I saved you, and I killed for—"

Bethany's hand flew out and grabbed his foot. "B-bastard..."

He slipped in her blood.

"Y-you…h-helped…" Bethany rasped.

He shot her. Aimed and shot and as she jerked, Eliza screamed. She also raised the lantern and slammed it into the side of Daniel's head as hard as she could. The glass shattered and chunks cut into his skin and the light sputtered out.

Daniel was yelling. She didn't care. Eliza turned and ran for the door. Only she couldn't move fast enough because of her ankle. She hobbled and twisted, but kept going for the door that gaped open a little bit…

She shoved it out of her way. Rushed into the night. Into the moonlight. She looked to the left and expected to see a field of sunflowers, but there was only tall grass. Tall grass swaying slightly. Her ankle burned.

"Eliza!"

He was chasing after her. Running after her, just as he had that night. And just as she had done back then…

Eliza looked back.

The moonlight hit his face.

I remember you.

Daniel lifted the gun in his hand.

"Down!" A shout from Memphis. "Down, Eliza!"

She dropped. Hit the ground hard, and gunfire blasted. Four fast retorts.

Her palms shoved into the dirt, and she rolled over. She looked back.

Daniel still stood just in front of the barn door. But the gun had dropped from his hand. He reached up to touch his chest, a chest that she could see darkening with his blood. Then he looked at her. Smiled. “Do you...hear the music?”

She didn’t.

“Our music...always play it...So loud...now...”

His knees buckled. He fell forward.

“Make sure he’s dead, Saint!” Memphis yelled.

Saint ran past her. She tried to push to her feet, but Memphis grabbed her. Locked his arms around her and pulled her up against him. *Memphis*. Alive. Real. Warm against her. He was there. He was safe. Her arms wrapped around him and...

Wet.

No, that wasn’t water. That was blood on his shirt.

She jerked back. “He shot you!”

“Didn’t get a chance. That’s from last time, baby. Fucking stitches.” He pulled her closer. Squeezed so hard. “I was so scared.”

She couldn’t stop shaking.

“Tell me you’re okay.” And it wasn’t an order from him. It was more of a plea. “Princess, I’m sorry I wasn’t here sooner. I’m sorry they took you. I’m sorry...”

She grabbed his face. Kissed him. Soft, because that was all she could manage with her parched lips. But the kiss stopped the apologies and the ramble of words because none of that mattered.

He mattered. Memphis was alive. She was alive.

They were okay. They were going to survive this night. This *nightmare*. They were going to make it, and no one would take away their future. "I love you," she whispered. "Please, take me home."

"Baby, you are my home."

Her eyes squeezed closed. *Memphis is alive.* When she'd been in that grave—*it will always be a grave to me*—she'd cried and she'd ached and she'd prayed because she'd been so afraid that Memphis was gone. That she would never see him or touch him or love him again.

But he was with her. He was strong and holding her so tightly.

"I will take you anywhere," he promised. "*Anywhere.*"

Right in that moment... "All I want is to get the hell away from here."

CHAPTER TWENTY-TWO

She stayed in the hospital for twenty-four hours. Stayed hooked up to IVs. Graduated to jello before she left. Was pampered and questioned and had Memphis at her side every moment—he even got his shoulder re-stitched while holding her hand.

The Feds took over the investigation. They searched Bethany's place. Found a diary that she'd kept for years.

Ever since Eliza's first disappearance.

Bethany detailed how she got the drugs to use on her victims—from Daniel. She talked about how she picked her prey. The women that she judged and hated and envied. Described how easy it was for her to lure them into her car.

And, in the end, she described where she'd put their bodies.

Elijah had revealed all of that to her and Memphis. Given updates in his quiet, calm voice. Delilah had been there, with her husband at her side. She'd cried. And Eliza had cried with her.

Delilah would finally be bringing her sister home, just...not how she'd wanted.

The Feds had searched Daniel's place, too. Found too many pictures and too much surveillance footage of Eliza. Found a wind chime just like the one that had been collected at the barn—that second chime had been on his patio.

They'd also found a receipt for a recent purchase of a dozen sunflowers. The flowers had been bought at a grocery store. The Feds believed Daniel was the one who'd put the flower at the old bar. He'd known that Eliza was retracing her steps with Memphis, and he'd left the flower for her. They also thought that he had tailed them to that location and started the fire because he'd been trying to eliminate Memphis. Turned out, Daniel knew the man who'd been found inside the place. He'd arrested Clyde Burk a few times in the past.

But the shooter? The one who had fired those bullets into Eliza's penthouse? The Feds found a rifle in the back of Bethany's car. Only her prints were on it. Eliza remembered that Bethany's father had been a military sniper. Bethany had often gone on hunting trips with him. She'd once mentioned how proud he was of her shooting abilities.

And the giant truck with the grille that had nearly run Eliza and Memphis off the road? Bethany had been driving it, too. The truck had belonged to her father, and when he died, it went to her. She'd kept it stashed at his old hunting camp.

Daniel was dead. So was Bethany.

But her diary gave them all the closure that so many families desperately wanted.

But it didn't give them their daughters back.

A soft knock sounded on her hospital door. Eliza had just finished dressing. She'd been more than ready to ditch this place.

Memphis frowned at the knock. The door swung open a moment later. Benedict stood there, He pulled at his collar. "Eliza...?"

She straightened. A special boot was on her foot, going half-way up her calf because of the broken ankle. She could get around fairly well, the hobbling was getting less lurchy.

Her gaze slid over Benedict. She'd been wondering when she'd see him. Memphis had told her all about Benedict's confession.

Her brother peered down at the floor. "I...I couldn't wait any longer. I know you hate me. I know you don't want to ever see me after this but..." He glanced at her. "I love you. I have always loved you, and I am so sorry—"

"Just come and hug me, Benny."

He flew across the room. Wrapped her up tight.

"Let her breathe," Memphis groused. "Hug her without suffocating her. She's still weak, man."

Benedict's grip eased, just a little. "I'm so sorry."

"Benedict, Bethany knew the drugs were going to take you on a bad ride." That confession had been in the diary, too. "It was part of her plan. You didn't do this to me."

"I want to be better." Whispered.

He had been better. For years. She'd seen him fight to end his addiction. "How about we keep being better together?"

His eyes swam with tears. "Please don't ever vanish again."

"She won't," Memphis promised. "Never, ever again."

Benedict slowly released her. "They're getting a divorce."

Her brow furrowed.

"Dad and Kathleen. Turns out, she's been having an affair with Alec, too. Guess that's why he moved into the guest house." He rolled back his shoulders. "She confessed and said...Kathleen admitted she was the one who first told the tabloids that you were making up the abduction. And she'd been tipping off reporters about what you were doing lately." A ragged exhale. "Dad, um, he's outside. He was afraid you wouldn't want to see him."

Memphis shook his head and strode to the door. He wrenched it open and poked his head into the hallway. "Get your fool ass in here," he snapped.

Her father slowly walked inside. Eliza put her hand to her chest when she saw his face. So many lines. So much pain. Her father didn't look the same, not at all.

"I did this to you," he said.

She shook her head.

"I brought Kathleen into our lives...I did this..." A swallow. "The police are reviewing charges, and I am making sure she is cut from our lives. And I-I know you will want to cut me from your life, too."

"This family." Memphis threw his hands into the air. "Dramatic." His hands fell back down. After a beat, he pointed at Prescott. "No."

"Excuse me?"

"Eliza needs her father. She loves you, even though I have told her at length that you can be a real bastard. She needs you to step it up and be a *good* father while your ass is still on this planet. And you..." He swung to Benedict. "You were a victim, too. One thing I have known from the first time I saw your loafer-wearing self at that country club—it's that Eliza loves you. I could see it in her eyes when she looked at you. And know what I see when you look at her?"

Benedict glanced at Eliza.

She gazed into his eyes.

"You love your sister," Memphis concluded. "So how about we all focus on healing? On moving forward? Martyr scenes are for bitches, and I'd much rather focus on an ending that gives my princess everything she wants."

Benedict hugged her again.

Then he stepped back. Her father lumbered toward her. His lower lip trembled as he slowly opened his arms. "I'm sorry," he rasped, and he wrapped her into his embrace.

"That's a start," Memphis said.

Her rich and powerful father began to cry.

***

It was the swankiest of swanky suites. Memphis stood on the top floor of the expensive hotel—behind bulletproof glass—and stared out at the city.

"Are you going to take my daughter away from us?" Prescott asked him.

Because, sure, Prescott had followed Memphis and Eliza to the hotel. Mostly because he *owned* the place.

"You once told me—told us all—that you were going to seduce her. Get Eliza to need only you. And then convince her to run away with you."

The bedroom door opened. Eliza stepped out. Moved slowly because of her ankle. She smiled at Memphis. Took his breath away. That smile of hers would always be killer.

"Eliza..." Memphis said, teasing her because he wanted her smile to stretch. Wanted to see her nose crinkle and her eyes light. "Will you run away with me?"

But, at the question, her smile vanished. "Yes."

Memphis blinked. "You...yes?"

She crossed to him with her slow, careful walk. Still looked like the most graceful thing in the world to him, broken ankle or not. "Yes."

"Eliza..." Her father's whisper.

"You can come to visit," she assured him. "Benny, too. As often as you like. But I want to go somewhere new." She gazed up at Memphis. "I want to start somewhere fresh, and I want to be with you."

He didn't care where they went, as long as he could be with Eliza. "Mountains? Countryside? City?" Or, he remembered her father once saying... "Madrid?"

Her hand rose and pressed to his cheek. "I like the beach. Know any good places? I want to be able to look out and just see waves crashing back at me. I don't want to feel closed in. Like I'm..."

Buried.

He knew what haunted her. She didn't need to tell him. His sweet Eliza's pain was his own. Memphis turned his head. Kissed her hand. "I think I know a spot you'll like. Ever hear of Pensacola Beach? Got some old military buddies down there. They say it's beautiful. White sandy shores for miles and miles." He looked over her shoulder and inclined his head toward her father. "I'm betting there will be a high-rise somewhere down there. You can go buy yourself a condo or a whole condo building."

"I'll do that," Prescott said at once.

Memphis knew the guy wasn't joking.

"For now, Eliza," her father spoke a bit gruffly, "I know you need to rest. I'll just...let you two get settled." Her father made his way to the door, but stopped before he reached for the door handle. He pulled in a breath and turned back around. "I have always admired your strength, Eliza."

Eliza glanced at him.

"I have always been proud of you. I have always loved you. You are the strongest person I know." He swallowed. "Your mother would be very proud of you, too. Ahem." He cleared his throat, twice, and eased out of the suite.

The door closed with a soft click.

"He's not a complete bastard," Memphis told her. "I see potential there."

"He likes you."

"That's why I see potential." But he really didn't want to talk about her father. What he wanted to talk about... "When I woke up in the hospital, and you weren't there...I nearly lost my mind."

"Not you, you—"

"I don't love easily. Never had the crushes and relationships that everyone else did. I just didn't get involved that deeply. I wasn't even sure I could." He wanted to explain, but Memphis feared he was screwing things up. "Then a beautiful princess poured a beer on me, and I knew right then and there that I was in love. Hell, I even told you so. Pretty sure I remember beer dripping off me as I said, 'I think I might be in love.'"

Her lashes fluttered. "You...you didn't mean that..."

"I don't bullshit, remember? I knew love when it hit me. Or when it was poured on me. The trick, though, was getting someone like you to fall for someone like me."

"Someone like you," she mused. "You mean someone strong and brave and smart?"

"And sexy," he added. "You forgot sexy."

She smiled at him. "Someone who makes me want to laugh when I feel like I've carried nothing but a weight of sadness and guilt for years? You thought it would be a trick to get me to fall for you?"

"Yeah, yeah, so I—"

Eliza curled her hands around his shoulders. “There was no trick. I knew exactly what I was getting with you.”

You didn’t know, baby. You didn’t know how hard I’d fight to make you mine.

“I love you, Memphis.”

No bullets tore through the windows to interrupt her confession this time, and he just drank in those precious words. “Love me enough to marry me?”

He heard her swift inhale. “What?”

“You’re my forever, sweetheart. The only thing I see when I think about my future.” Eliza. A house on the beach so she could see the pounding waves every single day. And, if she wanted...kids. Two daughters who looked just like her would be amazing.

“You’re mine, too,” she told him. “Yes.”

The word echoed through him. *Yes.* He would give her everything he had. Put the world at her feet. Protect her with his last breath. And love her?

He would love her *always.*

EPILOGUE

Her hands reached for the French doors, and her carefully manicured nails gleamed in the evening light. The silk of her dress fluttered around her feet even as her elegant train trailed behind her.

The doors opened, and the sweet music teased her ears. The harpist played with a smile on her face, and everyone in the massive hall turned toward Eliza.

A hand reached for her. Her father stepped up on her left side. Her brother on her right. Both wore dashing tuxedos, and she would have admired them...

But she was too busy admiring the man who waited for her up ahead.

Memphis smiled his rakish grin, and he winked at her as she began to walk toward him. All of his Ice Breaker friends were there, and a pregnant Delilah dabbed gently at the corner of her eye. They'd found out yesterday that Delilah would be having a little girl. She and Archer planned to name her Layla Marie.

Eliza didn't carry any flowers. She was quite over flowers, thank you very much. Memphis's eyes widened as she drew closer to him. And when they were just a few feet away...

"Fuck it," Memphis muttered.

She almost laughed.

He rushed toward her. Kissed her right then and there as the people seated nearby gasped.

"Couldn't wait," he said against her mouth. "You are so beautiful."

He took her hand. His fingers twined with hers.

A few moments later, they were married.

As everyone cheered and as her new husband stared at her as if she was the most precious thing in his life, Eliza knew...

She was safe.

***

"This is dangerous," Memphis warned her. His arms curled around her body. "Exceedingly, devastatingly dangerous."

Eliza laughed. "It's a dance, Memphis." She'd changed into a short, sleek dress. One that was bright and bold, and she was ready to dance the night away at her reception. Provided, of course, that her sexy groom would move what she had just discovered were two very stubborn left feet.

"Everyone is watching," he whispered.

She could feel their eyes. Their stares. "I don't care." And she didn't, not anymore. People could stare. People could gossip. They could do whatever they wanted. She was tired of pretending to be perfect. Tired of holding everything in. She wanted to be free, and she wanted to feel happy.

Her cast was long gone. She'd healed physically, and it was time to enjoy her life. "Relax," she told him. "And remember...if you follow my lead in *dangerous* situations like this one, things will be just fine."

He threw back his head and laughed...

And they started to dance.

THE END

A NOTE FROM THE AUTHOR

Thank you for reading FALLING FOR THE ICE QUEEN. I hope that you enjoyed Memphis's story!

From the first moment that Memphis appeared as a secondary character in FROZEN IN ICE, I knew that I wanted to give him a book of his own. He was such a fun, fiery character, and I loved his unpredictable nature. And, now, of course, there's the little matter of Memphis's brother Saint...

If you'd like to stay updated on my releases and sales, please join my newsletter list.

https://cynthiaeden.com/newsletter/

Again, thank you for reading FALLING FOR THE ICE QUEEN.

Best,
Cynthia Eden
cynthiaeden.com

ABOUT THE AUTHOR

Cynthia Eden is a *New York Times*, *USA Today*, *Digital Book World*, and *IndieReader* best-seller.

Cynthia writes sexy tales of contemporary romance, romantic suspense, and paranormal romance. Since she began writing full-time in 2005, Cynthia has written over one hundred novels and novellas.

Cynthia lives along the Alabama Gulf Coast. She loves romance novels, horror movies, and chocolate.

For More Information

- *cynthiaeden.com*
- *facebook.com/cynthiaedenfanpage*

HER OTHER WORKS

Ice Breaker Cold Case Romance

- Frozen In Ice (Book 1)

Phoenix Fury

- Hot Enough To Burn (Book 1)
- Slow Burn (Book 2)
- Burn It Down (Book 3)

Trouble For Hire

- No Escape From War (Book 1)
- Don't Play With Odin (Book 2)
- Jinx, You're It (Book 3)
- Remember Ramsey (Book 4)

Death and Moonlight Mystery

- Step Into My Web (Book 1)
- Save Me From The Dark (Book 2)

Wilde Ways

- Protecting Piper (Book 1)
- Guarding Gwen (Book 2)
- Before Ben (Book 3)
- The Heart You Break (Book 4)
- Fighting For Her (Book 5)
- Ghost Of A Chance (Book 6)

- Crossing The Line (Book 7)
- Counting On Cole (Book 8)
- Chase After Me (Book 9)
- Say I Do (Book 10)
- Roman Will Fall (Book 11)
- The One Who Got Away (Book 12)
- Pretend You Want Me (Book 13)
- Cross My Heart (Book 14)
- The Bodyguard Next Door (Book 15)

Dark Sins

- Don't Trust A Killer (Book 1)
- Don't Love A Liar (Book 2)

Lazarus Rising

- Never Let Go (Book One)
- Keep Me Close (Book Two)
- Stay With Me (Book Three)
- Run To Me (Book Four)
- Lie Close To Me (Book Five)
- Hold On Tight (Book Six)

Dark Obsession Series

- Watch Me (Book 1)
- Want Me (Book 2)
- Need Me (Book 3)
- Beware Of Me (Book 4)
- Only For Me (Books 1 to 4)

Mine Series

- Mine To Take (Book 1)
- Mine To Keep (Book 2)
- Mine To Hold (Book 3)
- Mine To Crave (Book 4)

- Mine To Have (Book 5)
- Mine To Protect (Book 6)
- Mine Box Set Volume 1 (Books 1-3)
- Mine Box Set Volume 2 (Books 4-6)

Bad Things

- The Devil In Disguise (Book 1)
- On The Prowl (Book 2)
- Undead Or Alive (Book 3)
- Broken Angel (Book 4)
- Heart Of Stone (Book 5)
- Tempted By Fate (Book 6)
- Wicked And Wild (Book 7)
- Saint Or Sinner (Book 8)
- Bad Things Volume One (Books 1 to 3)
- Bad Things Volume Two (Books 4 to 6)
- Bad Things Deluxe Box Set (Books 1 to 6)

Bite Series

- Forbidden Bite (Bite Book 1)
- Mating Bite (Bite Book 2)

Blood and Moonlight Series

- Bite The Dust (Book 1)
- Better Off Undead (Book 2)
- Bitter Blood (Book 3)
- Blood and Moonlight (The Complete Series)

Purgatory Series

- The Wolf Within (Book 1)
- Marked By The Vampire (Book 2)
- Charming The Beast (Book 3)

- Deal with the Devil (Book 4)
- The Beasts Inside (Books 1 to 4)

Bound Series

- Bound By Blood (Book 1)
- Bound In Darkness (Book 2)
- Bound In Sin (Book 3)
- Bound By The Night (Book 4)
- Bound in Death (Book 5)
- Forever Bound (Books 1 to 4)

Stand-Alone Romantic Suspense

- It's A Wonderful Werewolf
- Never Cry Werewolf
- Immortal Danger
- Deck The Halls
- Come Back To Me
- Put A Spell On Me
- Never Gonna Happen
- One Hot Holiday
- Slay All Day
- Midnight Bite
- Secret Admirer
- Christmas With A Spy
- Femme Fatale
- Until Death
- Sinful Secrets
- First Taste of Darkness
- A Vampire's Christmas Carol

Made in United States
Orlando, FL
29 January 2023

29201190R00192